## "ALL HANDS, RIG FOR SILENCE!"

Admiral Jack Boxer turned to Clemens. "Unless that Russkie starts hammering us with radar, we'll just sit quiet and hope they pass us by."

Boxer looked around the room. His men were well trained for this. All eyes were glued to their instruments. All Boxer could hear was the sound of their breathing.

And then it came. A single ping reverberated through the sub. A series of four more followed. And then the Soviet sub was hammering the *Manta* with its sonar, blasting a staccato message through the hull.

"They know we're here, Skipper," Clemens said.

Boxer keyed his MC. "FTO, load and arm one and two. EO, all ahead two-thirds." He grinned at Clemens. "Well, as long as they know we're here, Clem, let's give them something to worry about!"

## ACTION ADVENTURE

**SILENT WARRIORS** (1675, $3.95)
by Richard P. Henrick

*The Red Star*, Russia's newest, most technologically advanced submarine, outclasses anything in the U.S. fleet. But when the captain opens his sealed orders 24 hours early, he's staggered to read that he's to spearhead a massive nuclear first strike against the Americans!

**THE PHOENIX ODYSSEY** (1789, $3.95)
by Richard P. Henrick

All communications to the USS *Phoenix* suddenly and mysteriously vanish. Even the urgent message from the president cancelling the War Alert is not received. In six short hours the *Phoenix* will unleash its nuclear arsenal against the Russian mainland.

**COUNTERFORCE** (2013, $3.95)
Richard P. Henrick

In the silent deep, the chase is on to save a world from destruction. A single Russian Sub moves on a silent and sinister course for American shores. The men aboard the U.S.S. *Triton* must search for and destroy the Soviet killer Sub as an unsuspecting world races for the apocalypse.

**EAGLE DOWN** (1644, $3.75)
by William Mason

To western eyes, the Russian Bear appears to be in hibernation — but half a world away, a plot is unfolding that will unleash its awesome, deadly power. When the Russian Bear rises up, God help the Eagle.

**DAGGER** (1399, $3.50)
by William Mason

The President needs his help, but the CIA wants him dead. And for Dagger — war hero, survival expert, ladies man and mercenary extraordinaire — it will be a game played for keeps.

*Available wherever paperbacks are sold, or order direct from the Publisher. Send cover price plus 50¢ per copy for mailing and handling to Zebra Books, Dept. 2737, 475 Park Avenue South, New York, N.Y. 10016. Residents of New York, New Jersey and Pennsylvania must include sales tax. DO NOT SEND CASH.*

# #12 WARMONGER

BY IRVING A. GREENFIELD

**ZEBRA BOOKS**
**KENSINGTON PUBLISHING CORP.**

ZEBRA BOOKS

are published by

Kensington Publishing Corp.
475 Park Avenue South
New York, NY 10016

First printing: August, 1989

Printed in the United States of America

*The writer wishes to express his thanks
to Michael Bergman
for his technical and editorial suggestions.*

# Chapter 1

"Torp in the water, Skipper. Bearing zero one five . . . range three five zero zero . . . speed six five and closing."

Boxer ordered, "Fire one and two. Helmsman, hard right rudder. Come to zero nine five. Whitey, bring us up to one zero zero."

The *Manta* veered hard right and surged ahead at flank speed. Chief White blew some forward ballast and the sub rose sharply at the bows. Boxer hung onto the COMMCOMP console handrail. The inclinometer read forty-five degrees.

The *Alfa's* fish kept coming, pinging hard at them. "Damn!" Boxer cursed to himself. "That *Alfa* skipper is good."

The Soviet hunter-killer sub held its ground, guiding her remaining wire-guided torpedo from the sonar image that the fleeing American sub was producing. The *Manta's* cavitation sounds seemed to scream their position to the enemy.

Boxer maneuvered hard left and dived, trying to dislodge the enemy fish from his tail, but the torpedo was too fast, and it had happened all too quickly. His exec, Clemens, was wide-eyed watching the blip closing in on the UWIS screen.

"Prepare to take a hit," Boxer said into the MC. His voice was tinged with anxiety. As the blip closed in, he looked at his exec. "Brace yourself, Clem."

At that moment, Boxer tried one last desperate maneuver, jinking his sub upward. The torpedo exploded against the sensitive shaft plates, contorting the propeller and bending the shaft at an odd angle. The shaft housing was the *Manta's* most vulnerable area, and the *Alfa* had exploited it.

The *Manta* spiraled downward, the diving officer trying desperately to keep her under control. There followed a loud popping sound, from the stern, and the sea began forcing its way in. Boxer shouted, "Damage control, get the pumps going aft!"

The Manta touched bottom with a crash, bouncing once before settling on its keel. They were under two thousand feet of ocean. Already there were screeching and popping noises heard throughout the boat.

"DCO, report on damages and injuries." Boxer was pissed with himself for getting bushwhacked by the Soviet sub. It should never have happened. He began to sweat.

DCO fed data into his console, giving Boxer the picture he needed on his main computer screen. The stern was in bad shape. He'd have to suggest major changes there if he ever got out of this one alive.

A second torpedo exploded against the top of the sail. The ten feet or so that protruded when the tower was retracted into its well to streamline the hull made it very vulnerable as was any area where there was a flange or seal, rather than a weld.

The *Manta* shook mightily with the hit. It shuddered against the sea bottom when the explosion gouged a chunk out of the outer hull, and caved the topmost part of the sail in on itself. Bodies were thrown to the deck and into bulkheads. Priceless electronics modules were smashed beyond repair as sailors careened off them. An acrid smell soon permeated the sub.

Boxer pulled himself up. He was bleeding profusely from a head wound. He wiped the blood away with his sleeve and tried to regain control of the situation. Half his crew appeared to be dead or injured. "Oh, my God," he muttered before slipping back to the deck.

"Jack, wake up. Wake up, please."

"Wha . . . ?"

"You were having a bad dream, darling. A nightmare."

Boxer's body shuddered for a few seconds. He and the bedsheets beneath him were drenched in sweat. "My men . . . too many men lost. Some were no more than boys."

Ona pressed a damp washcloth to his forehead, gently caressing his bare chest with her other hand. "It's no good to keep blaming yourself for what's in the past, darling. It's eating you up inside."

Boxer looked up at the beautiful native Hawaiian woman at his bedside. She was naked. Her long black hair spilled over her shoulders, softly caressing her full pear-shaped breasts. His hand went to the firm flesh of her narrow waist. "But it was my fault that they died."

Ona shook her head. "There were great risks involved. You did more than anyone else could have, under the circumstances. And it all worked out in the end."

"Maybe so, but at far too great a price." Boxer glanced at the alarm clock on the bedside table. 0530. "I have a meeting with Admiral Willis this morning, and you know how he likes to get started early.

She stretched provocatively, giving him an eyeful of her incredible body. "I'll start the coffee while you're in the shower." She kissed his cheek. "You know," she said, "you're my favorite submarine skipper."

He scooped her up into his arms and hugged her to his chest. "And you're my favorite CIA agent. In fact, I can't think of any others I'd rather go to bed with." He ducked as she went for his head with a pillow. By the time he got out of the shower, the trepidations of the night before were already forgotten.


Boxer hopped out of the Jeep, followed closely by his

9

executive officer, Captain Mark Clemens. Together they strode briskly across the quad and past the saluting MPs guarding the entrance to CINCPACFLT headquarters at Pearl Harbor. Boxer had been summoned to a meeting by Admiral Willis, and he had no intention of keeping the old man waiting.

A marine corporal escorted them to a meeting room within Willis's office suite, knocked on the door, and left them standing there at the doorway. They were greeted by the admiral's aide, Captain Ted Lewis, who motioned them into comfortable leather chairs. Willis was seated behind a polished teak table along a side wall in the richly paneled room.

Boxer snapped to attention and saluted crisply a second ahead of Clemens. Admial Willis returned the salute and got right to the point. "Jack, Clem ... I've got something I want you to see. The CNO sent it down for me to have a look at. I'd be willing to bet you may find yourself involved in this, once we get the *Manta* out of drydock."

As he spoke, Captain Lewis worked the controls that soon had a movie screen emerging from the ceiling to fill the entire wall in front of the room. The lights dimmed. A ceiling-mounted projector whirred as the film leader played out, followed by an aerial view of the earth, seemingly from atop the northern ice cap. "This was taken by Starlab III," Willis said.

Boxer nodded. The Starlab III satellite orbited over a good part of the Soviet Union and its East European hegemony before continuing south.

The action slowed considerably while satellite cameras zoomed in on the Soviet island groups that dotted the Arctic. "Okay, hold it right there, Ted," Willis ordered. A mountain peak rose above the ice at the southernmost edge of the glacier. Below that the sea was packed with ice floes that had recently calved off from the constantly changing ice shelf. "Notice anything strange?" the admiral asked Boxer.

"I take it we're looking at the leading edge of the permanent ice field. If memory serves, Starlab III orbits over the northwest Soviet Union, including the island chains we call North Land and Franz Josef Land, as well as the big island of Novaya Zemlya."

"Your memory's doing all right for itself, Jack. And your pronunciation's pretty good, too."

Boxer smiled. "I know a few Russian words, Admiral. My favorite's Stolichnaya."

Willis chuckled. "That hunk of land is Komsomolets Island, the northernmost big island in the North Land group. Off to the left there's a smaller island." Willis used an electronic light-emitting device to point out the area to Boxer. A circle of red light highlighted the location. "Notice how the zone between the two land masses is blue instead of white like the rest of the site?"

"Now that you mention it."

"Ted, overlay the infrared imaging footage. Jack, watch what happens to that blue area."

"Bright red. Holy shit. Sorry, sir. There must be a huge nuclear device up there to cause that."

"My sentiments exactly, Boxer. Cultrain's boys have it on good evidence that the Russkies have built a submarine bastion right there, a warm-water port within the polar ice cap. And it's powered by a nuclear power plant that dwarfs the old Chernobyl site. Just think of the ramifications."

Boxer was shaking his head. "The thought of it gives me shivers, Admiral. If this is really what they claim it is, it sure gives Ivan the edge. They can strike anywhere in the northern hemisphere with impunity and run back to their lair. It would be simple for them to set a mine field, and we wouldn't dare bomb the place. Can you imagine the damage the ice melt would cause?"

"Tidal waves, shore erosion. The sea would rise enough to submerge entire islands and coastal towns. Great Britain would become another Atlantis." Willis used the butt of his cigarette to light another. "The State Department is working on that right now. President Spooner has given them an ultimatum: close the place down, or face a boycott on wheat and food crops forever. Not to mention our Star Wars system. It wouldn't take much to change it from a defensive to an offensive weapon, you know."

"Where do I fit into this, Admiral Willis? It seems the boys from State have everything under control."

"The President wants a plan from you, Jack, on how to slip a submarine into that bastion and put the whole operation out of business, if need be . . . if diplomacy fails."

"The old carrot-and-stick."

"Exactly. You've got one month to work it out, while the *Manta* is being repaired."

The lights came back on, and the screen receded into the ceiling. Admiral Willis stood up and walked to the door. "That's it, men. Do it."

After Willis left the room, Boxer and Clemens looked at each other. What the old man had ordered was nothing less than a suicide mission for Boxer and his men. The hair on the back of Boxer's neck prickled as he got up out of the chair and followed Admiral Willis out.

# Chapter 2

It was snowing heavily on the Kremlin as twenty dour-faced Politburo members took their seats in the cream-colored meeting room. They sat in comfortable upholstered chairs facing a podium, and behind that a movie screen. Alongside the lectern was a display table covered with a light green tarp.

Party General Secretary Rimsky took his place at the podium and called the meeting to order. The dozen full members and the eight non-voting alternates settled down. "Comrades, we are convened to discuss the fate of our new submarine bastion in the Arctic, and the *October Revolution* Nuclear Power Plant on Severnaya Zemlya that makes its existence possible. The US is making demands that we shut down our operation, which, of course, is absurd. For us, it equates to them removing their forces from Manila.

"In addition, there have been some concerns voiced here about the security, and, indeed, the very safety of the nuclear reactor. I wish to open the discussion with the minister of energy. Comrade Druznyi."

No one spoke as Eduard Druznyi hoisted himself out of his seat onto his aluminum crutches and made his way slowly, painfully, one deliberate step at a time, to the podium. He rested his "sticks" against the side of the lectern and steadied himself by holding onto it for support. A barrel-chested man with massive arms and a large balding head, the seventy-year-old energy minister more than made up for the loss of his crippled legs with his brilliant mind. Some said he was the brightest of all the Politburo members.

Druznyi hyperventilated, gradually calming his hard breathing caused by the stress the short walk had caused him. Finally, he said, "Comrades, I am here to express my concern for the new power plant in North Land. As you know, the project was started by my predecessor, Comrade Rubkovsky, my immediate superior at the time."

As he spoke, the screen behind him became filled with a detailed map of the Soviet Union above the Arctic Circle. "It was Rubkovsky's dream to open up the northern islands to habitation, to expand the limits of our fishing and sea mammal hunting beyond a few summer months. His dream was to place nuclear power plants on these land masses to create self-contained communities with their own energy supplies. From this, all else could be made possible."

Druznyi's eyes studied the members of his nation's ruling body. All had given him their rapt attention. He pressed a switch on the podium, and red circles highlighted the map behind him, denoting sites on North Land, the New Siberian Island group, Novaya Zemlya Island, which was once thought of as a peninsula jutting off the mainland, and the many tiny islands that made up Franz Josef Land, the northernmost outposts of the Soviet Union. The minister of energy continued, "While I shared Comrade Rubkovsky's vision, I disagreed with him over some aspects of the structure of the reactor."

There were mutterings amongst the Politburo members. Rubkovsky had been very popular during the twenty-odd years prior to his untimely death. It seemed that his successor was turning over old bones.

"Yes, comrades, it is true. While my predecessor wanted to continue with the same technology that caused the Chernobyl disaster almost a decade ago, I was bent on adapting the American water-moderated systems. Considering the proximity to such vast resources of water in the Arctic, this method seemed the most logical choice, and was my recommendation for the prototype unit on North Land.

"However, for political reasons, this did not occur. Rubkovsky argued that to adapt an American system would have been admitting the inferiority of the Soviet-designed reactors. Most of you agreed, and so the new power plant was struck in the mold that the former minister of energy cast for it, albeit much larger and more powerful."

He flipped another switch, and the tarp was removed from the display table and lifted to the ceiling by an attached cable. A model of a nuclear plant was revealed. "This, comrades, is a scale model of the *October Revolution* plant on North Land. It is perched here on the coast of this island, Ostrov Komsomolets, and is powerful enough to produce electricity for the entire island group. I was here with Comrade Rubkovsky during the initial testing of the reactor when he suddenly died."

Furtive looks were exchanged by two men in the dimly lit room, the minister of defense and the minister of the interior.

Druznyi looked to the seat closest to the podium and asked the general secretary to remove the outer cover of the power plant mock-up, revealing a cutaway view of its innards. "The building is seventy meters high, and as you can see, comrades, it houses a pair of side-by-side reactors." Druznyi used a pencil-thin light beam to point out two large cylindrical columns within the massive confines of reinforced concrete housings. Straddling each reactor were dozens of pumps and turbines fed by miles of pipes.

"To harness a nuclear reaction, the neutrons released by the splitting atoms must be slowed to increase their chances of striking uranium nuclei. Therefore, a very important part of a reactor is the moderator which surrounds the nuclear fuel and maintains the reaction. The Americans use water as moderator in their plants. We seem intent on continuing the policy of using massive carbon blocks for this purpose."

Defense Minister Charkov stood up. "Comrade, I fear you are boring most of us to death with your little physics lesson. Please get to the point, or stand aside and let someone else have the floor."

Druznyi hated the thin younger man, who seemed to be going out of his way to annoy him. He felt a burning within his chest and reached into a pocket for a small medicine vial. He popped two nitroglycerine tablets under his tongue and waited a few moments for the wave of pain to subside. "The point, comrade, is safety. The American reactors must be shut down to replace spent fuel. Ours do not. And though you may have been too young to miss the implications of the Chernobyl disaster, they were not lost on me. Operator error during refueling was the direct cause of the catastrophe. And that brings up another point, that of security."

Charkov frowned and regained his seat. Druznyi continued. "If this reactor were to fall into inept hands, the damage would be insurmountable. The water level would rise as a result of the melted ice cap. Our entire Arctic coast would drown, along with North Land and our other island groups. Nuclear fallout would devastate the entire northern hemisphere, almost half of which is occupied by the Motherland. But more of this later. I want to get back on track.

"On our fact-finding trip to the reactor, I noted that the heat produced by the power plant had melted the surrounding sea ice, and realized that could lead to all sorts of possibilities. So I duly notified the general secretary, who realized the military potential of a warm-water port in the Arctic and made provisions to enlarge the plant." Druznyi took a sip of water. "Along with the ministry of defense, he came up with a plan to use the area as a submarine bastion. I am told that this would give our missile submarines enormous first-strike potential within a highly defensible position."

Charkov sneered. Even his egghead rival had to admit the enormous value of his plan.

The energy minister continued, "Fine. I could deal with the plant design as long as it would be properly maintained by experts taken from throughout the Motherland and housed on North Land. The Navy could coexist with the civilian inhabitants, and we would have the best of all possible worlds." He noticed that his reference to Voltaire was lost among his colleagues.

"However, comrades, when I learned that the plant would be run by convict labor under the jurisdiction of the military, I became appalled. There are too many ways that unskilled or hostile hands could sabotage the reactor. We could be facing a nuclear disaster unequaled in the lifetime of this planet."

"Those are the unfounded fears of old grandmothers, comrades." Charkov was on his feet again. "The reactor is of sound design. There hasn't been any more trouble since Chernobyl. I think we've all learned our lesson from that. Comrade Druznyi's apprehensions have no basis in fact."

"I agree." The stout interior minister was out of his seat. "Comrade Charkov is right. Besides, who would we get to live out their lives up there voluntarily? North Land makes Siberia seem like a vacation paradise."

That brought a smile from Charkov. "Comrade General Secretary, I call on you to end this nervous tirade by the energy minister and open up the discussion."

Druznyi grabbed his crutches and edged his way to the display. "You are a fool, Charkov. And an enemy of the state for putting the welfare of the entire project under the control of that miscreant Popov. If anything goes wrong with the project, I'll hold you personally responsible. I'll . . . I'll . . ." Druznyi was livid with rage. The burning in his chest returned. He reached in his pocket again for his pills. His hand shook so that the tiny vial spilled its contents to the floor. A crutch slipped away, and Druznyi crashed onto the display table. He looked up to see the face of his tormentor smiling benignly down at him.

The pounding in Druznyi's chest increased. His face turned scarlet and his tongue protruded from his lips as he made a last-ditch grab for Charkov's throat.

Charkov held the wrist, checking for a pulse, and placed a hand on Druznyi's forehead. As he felt the life slipping out of the minister of energy, he noted to the others, "Looks like our comrade has gone mad. A pity. He once had a fine mind. I fear his mania has killed him."

# Chapter 3

Boxer was looking forward to a few weeks of R&R in Hawaii before having to report back to the CNO for his next assignment. He was dreaming of having nothing to do with his time except to "hang loose," as the natives say, with Ona in this tropical paradise when the call came in from Admiral Willis's office. Boxer was to report to CINCPACFLT on the double.

He had the feeling that his layover on the island was soon to become something other than the vacation he'd been looking forward to. By now a familiar figure to the MPs guarding fleet headquarters, he was shown directly to the Admiral's quarters.

Captain Ted Lewis admitted him to the inner sanctum. He said, "The old man will be with you in a minute. He's got some kind of special assignment to keep you from getting bored here." Lewis was grinning broadly.

"I'll bet. Just when I was dreaming of hula dancers and luaus on the beach, a tropical drink in my hand, a beautiful wahine in each arm . . ."

Lewis laughed. "I think Admiral Willis has other plans for you. Sorry."

The intercom in Lewis's spartan office buzzed. "Have Boxer come right in," Willis ordered.

Lewis wished him "Good luck" as Boxer let himself into CINCPACFLT's private office.

"I've got a little job for you," Willis said without preamble. "I want you to test out some new features we kicked around after the *Manta* limped in following your last battle with the Russkies. May as well run them through their paces now, before we have to play the game for real again."

"Sure. As the Soviet submarine technology keeps improving, it's getting more and more difficult for me to keep ahead of them. Last time was almost my last time."

Willis got up from behind his desk and walked over to a huge TV console. He turned on the VCR beneath the set and popped in a tape. "Have a look at this. This is up-to-the-minute stuff. You'll do the first actual battle testing of what you're about to see here."

A nuclear hunter-killer sub came into view. "That's the *Newport*. She's a conventional nuke, but look what we've done to her."

The camera zoomed in on the surface of the *Newport*. "Notice the hull covering?"

Boxer nodded. "Looks like rubber anechoic tiles."

Willis said, "Even better." The view became magnified, and the rubber tiles seemed to be perforated with randomly punched gouges. "These are even more soundproof. I'm thinking of having the turtle-skin on the *Manta* replaced with these."

"But Admiral, they're bound to slow us down." Boxer was not happy with this so-called improvement. "Besides, the turtle-skin can stop the Russkie's killer darts. We've taken a weapon away from them."

"But it didn't do much good at stopping a torpedo from destroying your propeller shaft, did it? Sure, there'll be trade-offs, Jack. You'll lose about two knots, but if those tiles work as well as we think they will, they may save your sub—and your life."

Boxer's face reddened, but he held his tongue.

"Take a closer look at the stern," Willis continued.

Boxer didn't notice anything unusual.

"Watch this, Jack." A second propeller popped up above the original one, and seemed to rotate in synch. "That's activated from inside on demand. It doesn't do a lot to help propel the boat, Jack, but it won't hurt you much, either."

Boxer caught on immediately. "To the Russkies, I'd sound like one of their own *Alfas*, what with the twin cavitation sounds. Now *that* I really like. It could come in real handy in close quarters."

"Right. We've also got some new decoys and noisemakers to test, and something to help protect your tail. The *Manta* seems most vulnerable to a direct hit on the stern, so we developed the torpedo blaster for you."

Boxer looked at Willis, somewhat puzzled.

"The blaster is set right into the stern, surrounding the main prop. If a torp is chasing you, you can activate it from the COMMCOMP. They're actually mini-torpedoes designed to seek out the enemy fish and destroy it before it gets you. They're not powerful enough to sink a ship or another sub, but when they catch up with another torp, you'd better clear out of the area fast."

"Well, most of what you've shown me seems like it should help, Admiral. Frankly, I'm not convinced about the soundproof tiles."

And that was exactly what Willis was leading up to. He said, "Ever hear of fox and hounds?"

"A kids' game. I seem to vaguely recall it."

Willis activated a wall switch, and a chart slowly descended from the ceiling against the side wall. "Tomorrow at 0500, you will fire a deactivated rocket from the *Newport* at a target selected by yourself, and get the hell out of there. You have free reign of these four quadrants." His hands indicated an area on othe chart covering a two-hundred-mile radius around Oahu. "The Third Fleet will send its ASW unit after you," Willis said. "And we shall learn firsthand just how well the new equipment performs."

"Yes, sir," Boxer replied. "I guess we sure will."

Boxer was glad to have most of his regular crew aboard the *Newport*. It helped to ease the task of breaking in a new sub for the skipper, and he was glad to see chief of the boat Amos White seated at the diving console and Captain Mark Clemens at his side as exec. The men knew that they were on a practice run. Nonetheless, no one wanted to incur the wrath of their skipper by embarrassing him on this exercise.

Boxer took a position of 21°15′ north by 158° west to launch his strike against a heavily reinforced carrier group on maneuvers north of Oahu. "They'd be expecting us to hit a more isolated target," Boxer told Clemens. "Let's see if we can catch them with their pants down."

Clem grinned and took his seat at the fire control computer.

"Work out a solution for the *Kennedy*. I want a dummy rocket on either side of the carrier."

"Aye, aye, Skipper."

"Whitey, take us down to two zero zero. EO, engines ahead one third."

The diving and engineering officers repeated his commands. The *Newport* slowed appreciably as she settled at the bows. "Passing through five zero feet . . . passing through one zero zero. . . ." Whitey ticked off the depth as Boxer checked the DDRO computer against the manual depth gauge mounted on a bulkhead overhead. ". . . Leveling off at two zero zero, sir. Diving planes coming to null."

"Roger that, DO." Boxer turned to his EXO. "Do you have a solution yet, Clem?"

"Aye, aye, Skipper. The practice missiles are loaded in torpedo tubes one and two and ready to fire."

Boxer nodded and keyed his MC mike. "FTO, prepare to fire one and two."

"Aye, aye, Skipper. One and two ready."

Boxer took his seat at the CIC attack center of the COMMCOMP, adjusted the magnification of the UWIS screen to give him as large an image as possible and said, "Clem, fire one and two."

Clemens twisted the first two dials on a panel before him and pressed the red fire button twice with his thumb. "Missiles away, Skipper."

"Roger that." He keyed the sonar room. "Sonar, conn. Any reason to believe they're on to us yet?"

"Nothing yet, Skipper. They're steaming northwest, away from us."

"Good." Boxer now had the luxury of waiting to see if his attack was successful.

The two missiles broke the surface a thousand feet beyond the *Newport's* bow and arched on a ten-mile trajectory until it homed in on the *USS Kennedy* and the aircraft carrier's support ships. Both projectiles were almost upon them before a radarman broke the news to the *Kennedy's* CO, Captain Ewing. Before a solution on the incoming missiles could be acquired, they exploded above the carrier with a cascade of aluminum foil fragments that sent radar systems haywire and caused defensive rockets to explode against imaginary targets.

"Get that son-of-a-bitch," Ewing instructed his exec. An order was put out immediately, and two destroyers and a missile cruiser were dispatched in Boxer's direction.

"Conn, Sonar. Here they come, Skipper. Three targets approaching," Hi Fi Freedman said. "I place them at zero four three, zero four four and zero four seven. . . . Range one seven zero zero zero yards. . . . Speed four zero to four two knots, Skipper. I make the two faster targets as destroyers and the third as a possible light missile cruiser."

Fox and hounds, Boxer thought. Well, looks like it's time to outfox them. "DO," he commanded, "down to one thousand feet."

"Aye, aye, sir. Diving to one thousand feet."

"Helmsman, hard left rudder. Come to one eight zero." Boxer aimed to head southeast and get lost among the other islands. "EO, engines all ahead full."

Mahoney turned his wheel hard left and took the *Newport* through a hundred-eighty-degree turn. The engineering officer announced, "All ahead full, Skipper."

At fifty knots flank speed, Boxer knew he could simply outrun the pursuing vessels. He'd have to. It would be difficult to mask the cavitation sounds of the twin props that Admiral Willis had ordered him to use. After all, if this exercise were for real and not just a training maneuver, it would be the twin screws of a Soviet *Alfa* that the Third Fleet would be chasing.

"Conn, Sonar. I'm getting pinging from active sonobuoys almost directly above."

"Thanks, Hi Fi." Choppers, Boxer cursed. The carrier had wasted no time in sending its ASW helicopters after him. And they had quickly outpaced the destroyers and the cruiser in their search for the *Newport*. Apparently, a chopper was dragging an active sonobuoy in the water above them, hoping to make contact. Whether or not the *Newport* had been detected, Boxer had no way of knowing. He ordered a change in course.

"Skipper, there's a line of active and passive sonobuoys dead ahead about three thousand yards, at varying depths."

"Roger that, Hi Fi." So they were trying to cordon him off. In a wartime situation, Boxer might slip back in and try to sink the ships chasing him, something he couldn't do against his own navy. Besides, his task was to outrun, outwit, outmaneuver the surface vessels, and to test his new equipment, if it became possible.

"Torp in the water," Sonar announced. "On our tail. Range two thousand yards. . . . Speed seven zero and closing, Skipper. Depth seven five zero."

"Clem, fire off a noisemaker. Mahoney hard right. Come

to zero nine zero. Whitey, down to twelve hundred."

"Aye, aye," they said, almost in unison. The *Newport* turned hard right and dived another two hundred feet within a minute and a half.

"Conn, Sonar. The torp didn't take the bait. It's still following us."

"Range?"

"Fifteen hundred yards, Skipper."

Time to try out another of Willis's toys, Boxer figured. "Clem, fire off the blaster when the torp gets to within five hundred yards."

"Aye, aye, Skipper."

"Whitey, when that fish explodes, take us down to two thousand feet."

"Yes, sir."

"Conn, Sonar. Torp closing fast to five hundred yards, Skipper."

"Fire blaster."

Clemens triggered the new addition to their arsenal, and a half dozen three-foot-long projectiles popped out of their housing at the stern with a hiss of compressed air and zeroed in on the lone torpedo following the sub. At least three of them made contact, and the torpedo detonated with a roar.

"Dive, Whitey."

"Aye, aye, sir." Chief White pushed forward on the diving yoke, and the *Newport* tilted sharply downward to the sounds of seawater rushing in to fill the forward ballast tanks. "Don't have to ask me twice," Whitey muttered under his breath.

"Clem, jettison some garbage. Make them think they got us by the flotsam and jetsam we send up."

While his exec was complying with this order, Boxer keyed the engine room. "EO, cut power to one-third."

There was silence for about fifteen minutes. All crew members not specifically assigned to a task at hand were ordered to climb into their bunks and lie still. The *Newport*

25

was barely making steerageway. Boxer hoped he'd seen the last of the carrier's escort group.

Finally, Hi Fi reported, "Conn, Sonar. I have multiple targets surrounding us. I make it a destroyer at zero six four. . . . Range four thousand. . . . Speed twelve knots. A second destroyer at two seven five. . . . Range just over five thousand yards with a speed of ten knots. The cruiser is at one nine five at a range of twenty-three hundred and steaming in our direction at fifteen knots. Also, they're dropping sonobuoys within the triangle, Skipper."

Boxer worked out his options. He couldn't fight back, he couldn't outrun, and the time he'd spent trying to fool them had given them the opportunity to close in on him. It was as if they knew his location all the time. They weren't fooled by the explosion one bit. He walked over to the water temperature display on the CIC. "Clem, we've got to find a temperature gradient and slip beneath the thermal layer if we're to get out of here." His finger traced the color variations on the monitor until he spotted what he was looking for.

"Whitey, bring us up slowly to four hundred. Steady as she goes. Mahoney, make good course two seven zero. EO keep to five knots till we reach four hundred feet."

"Aye, aye, Skipper," they responded. Slowly, silently, the *Newport* began its ascent. Boxer had them heading straight for one of the destroyers, hoping to slip beneath it undetected, out into open water. He was sure the three escort ships were expecting him to continue his run southeast, between the cruiser and the other destroyer.

"Conn, Sonar. I have the destroyer directly overhead. So far, no sign that she hears us."

So far, so good, Boxer thought. We're almost out of here. "Helmsman, head due west. Make good course two seven zero. EO, steady at five knots."

After ten more minutes of silent running, Hi Fi reported all three ships were behind them. Suddenly a violent pinging echoed throughout the *Newport's* hull. For a submariner, there was no mistaking that awful sound. In a wartime situation, it could mean sudden death.

"Torp in the water," Sonar reported.

No subs nearby, Boxer mused. Must have been dropped by a chopper.

"Torp coming in dead ahead, Skipper. Range four five zero zero. . . . Speed seven zero and closing."

Trying to chase us back inside the trap, Boxer cursed. No way.

"Multiple targets ahead, Skipper. ASROCS. Five of them . . . no, make that six, repeat six ASROCS heading in."

"Dive, Whitey. Dive. Down to one thousand feet."

"Aye, aye, Skipper."

"Clem, fire off a decoy. Mahoney, hard left rudder. Come to zero nine zero."

An explosion rocked the *Newport.*

"ASROCS detonated at one five zero feet, Skipper. Wait . . . Six new targets at one nine zero, heading our way."

"More ASROCS?"

"Aye, aye, Skipper."

A second set of explosions sent shock waves through the hull of the *Newport.* Whose side are they on? Boxer asked himself.

"Conn, Sonar. I have just received a message for you from that chopper pilot."

Boxer paced to the tiny listening room. Hi Fi handed him a headset.

"Ahoy, *Newport.* This is *Pebble-one* from the destroyer *Plymouth Rock.* I am instructed by Captain Ewing aboard the *Kennedy* to score that as a hit by our side. Sorry, Skipper. You done pretty good."

"Ahoy, *Pebble-one.* This is Admiral Boxer aboard the *Newport.* Acknowledge. We are surfacing. Instruct the fleet to hold fire."

"Aye, aye, sir."

"Oh, and *Pebble-one* . . . you've done pretty good, yourself, son. Damn good."


At the meeting aboard the *USS Kennedy* that followed, Admiral Willis was comparing the ships' logs of all the vessels involved in the fox and hounds exercise. Captain Ted Williams was at a chalkboard, plotting out the chase.

"Well, Jack, what do you think went wrong?" Willis asked him. "The new equipment work out okay?"

Boxer replied, "Well, I was pleased with the blaster, sir. That took a torpedo off our tail. The decoys didn't seem to help us much, and as for the soundproofing job on the hull, Admiral, well, I'm just not sure how good it was."

"Not very good at all, if you ask me, Admiral Willis."

CINCPACFLT turned to look at Captain Ewing, commander of the aircraft carrier. "I didn't ask, Carl, but since you're determined to enlighten us with your views, go ahead."

"We had Boxer dead in the water several times, sir. Why, we had the *Newport* surrounded by two destroyers and the cruiser, *Santa Fe*. We knew her whereabouts at all times."

Willis looked at each of the escort ship captains around the table. "That so? Smitty? Golden? McHugh?"

The three captains neither confirmed nor denied Ewing's appraisal.

Boxer said, "This is important, Admiral. I've got to know how well we eluded the hounds today." He glared at the four captains seated on either side of him. "Today was only a game of hounds, sir. Next time, I may be up against bears, and we'll be playing for keeps. If you don't mind, I'd like to get the opinion of the chopper pilot who tagged us."

Willis turned toward Captain Ewing. "Well, Carl, who is he, and why isn't he here with us?"

"Who, Surf? He just got lucky today, Admiral. My three

28

escorts had Boxer all along."

Boxer sat there steaming. Ewing was a pompous ass who was trying to make himself look good at Boxer's expense, and then taking the credit himself, instead of giving it to the people who deserved it. Admiral Willis sensed the same thing and came down hard on Ewing. "Let me remind you, Carl, that the *Newport* scored two direct hits on the *Kennedy*, and that you did nothing to prevent it. Had that sub been the enemy instead of Admiral Boxer, your ship and most of your crew would have perished.

"Furthermore, had Admiral Boxer's orders not been to evade your pursuit, I'm convinced he could easily have sunk at least one of your escorts, if not more. Now, I'll ask you this last time, Carl, why isn't the chopper pilot here?"

Ewing's face went pale. He turned on an aide behind him and barked, "Tell Murphy to get his ass up here on the double."

The young lieutenant saluted and left the Admiral's bridge, returning shortly with a chopper pilot, still in orange jumpsuit, in tow. Lieutenant Murphy was a little over-whelmed by all the brass and stood there fidgeting uneasily.

"Please have a seat over there, son," Willis said, motioning to a chair with his hand. "Admiral Boxer has requested that you tell us exactly how you caught him this morning."

Boxer interjected, "That was a really fine job you did, Lieutenant. I congratulate you."

Murphy grinned. "Thank you, sir. You really had me fooled there for a while."

"Lieutenant," Willis cut in, "we're interested in how well the sound-deadening tiles on the submarine's hull performed."

Murphy glanced over at his CO, Ewing, then back at Willis. "I . . . uh, we couldn't find the *Newport* for at least fifteen minutes, Admiral. We knew she had to be within the perimeter of our three ASW ships. We even laid down a network of sonobuoys that failed to detect the sub. It wasn't until she made a run for it that I got lucky and picked up the cavitation sounds. Those twin screws are a dead giveaway, even at low speed."

Murphy glanced at the commanders of the escort ships and back at Willis. "The *Newport* seemed to shoot out from underneath the hull of the *Plymouth Rock*, sir. I had just about given up the search and was headed back to my ship when I picked up the sounds and went after her."

"Thank you, Lieutenant. That answers my question." Willis turned to Boxer. "What do you think, Jack? Can we make use of the new hull tiles?"

"If what Lieutenant Murphy says is accurate, Admiral, I'll go with them. But we've got to do something to cut back the cavitation sounds of the screws."

Admiral Willis's face took on a stern expression. "Everybody concur with Lieutenant Murphy's appraisal? How about it, Smitty?"

Captain Smith of the destroyer *Plymouth Rock* nodded. "Yes, Admiral. We lost the sub for a while."

"You did more than lose her, Smitty. Had Boxer been a Russkie submariner, you and your ship would have been blown to hell."

Boxer watched Smith's Adams apple pump as the hapless captain tried to swallow his wounded pride. He was very fortunate that Willis didn't relieve him of his command.

"Golden?"

Dave Golden was skipper of the cruiser *Santa Fe*. "Well, we thought we were closing in on the *Newport*, sir. Surf, that is, Lieutenant Murphy here, had a bead on him for a while, and we figured we had her boxed in."

"You did, Captain. You had me corralled there for fifteen or twenty minutes. Lucky for me, I found a thermal gradient to hide under. I almost made it free of you."

"What about it, Mac?"

Captain Mac McHugh shook his head. "Boxer slipped right past us, Admiral. Was it the man, or the machine?"

"The question is," Willis put in, "Was Boxer that good, or were you all that bad?"

"With all respect, Admiral Willis, the way I see it, if I was a Russkie *Alfa* the Third Fleet would be minus a carrier and one or two escorts, but the sub would have been a casualty, too."

Willis dismissed the skippers of the escort ships, then relieved Ewing of his command of the *Kennedy*. "I can't have a man who won't learn from his mistakes in charge of a carrier, Carl. You can command a desk or retire, your choice. Your exec is temporarily the new CO."

When they were alone, Boxer confided in Willis, "I sure admire that chopper pilot, sir. If he's ever looking for a tough, thankless job, I'd like to talk him into joining my crew. The *Manta* can use good men."

"I'll pass it along, Jack. By the way, you did real well today."

Boxer shook his head. "Not good enough, sir. It's a small consolation to have sunk two enemy ships if I lose my sub and crew in the bargain. We still have a lot of work to do."

# Chapter 4

"Wake up, sleepyhead."

"Hunh?"

Ona was on top of Boxer, her thighs straddling his waist, her naked bottom teasing, coaxing his manhood to attention. She leaned forward to plant a kiss on his face. Her bare breasts caressed his chest, nipples hardening to the touch, while a cascade of her long, black hair spilled over his pillow. "Rise and shine, darling. It's almost 0600."

Boxer smiled at the beautiful Hawaiian woman whose bed he'd shared these last few months, and put an arm around her waist, drawing her to him. "You sure know how to get a guy up in the morning," he grinned.

Her hand went behind her and found his throbbing manhood, helping guide him into her. "I'd have to agree that it's been a big success."

Waves of pleasure rolled through his body. He let the good feelings take over, driving away the tensions of the previous day. At least for the moment, he could concentrate on the pleasure that Ona brought to his life. For the moment, he could store his troubles in the farthest recesses of his mind, troubles that had been sidestepped by his involvement in the Pearl Harbor Day ceremony last month. Problems that he had to deal with sooner or later, and considering what Admiral Willis had told him was in store for him, sooner was the more likely. He had some unfinished business to attend to, but for now, for the moment, he belonged to Ona.

"Did I wear you out last night, darling?" She was smiling down at him, timing her movements precisely, coming down onto his final thrust, using all her muscle control to squeeze the last bit of pleasure out of him. "Mmmm," she purred. "You're such a wonderful lover. I could do this with you forever."

Boxer held her to his chest, but didn't respond to her verbally. Perhaps the time had come for some serious discussion of their future.

Ona lifted her head and smiled at him. "Sometimes you can say a lot by saying nothing, darling."

Boxer took her hand in his. "On the one hand, Ona, I could think of nothing I'd rather do than be with you like this."

"And on the other hand," she said softly, "there's a wedding band. That's an old song, Jack. I know all about your Francine Wheeler. That's why I was so standoffish when I first met you. But look what's happened to us. I couldn't help myself."

"Me either. My future with Francine is uncertain. You know she's in a sanitarium in Italy trying to recover from a severe mental trauma."

"I know that she'd been severely beaten and gang-raped, Jack. That's common knowledge among the folks I run around with. The CIA knows all." She closed her eyes and put her fingertips to her forehead, mimicking a psychic. "I'm really sorry for her, darling, as one woman to another. And I knew from the start what your situation was. But a girl can dream, can't she?"

Boxer looked into her eyes. "Frankly, I don't know if she'll

34

ever recover. On my last visit, she was extremely withdrawn, afraid of the very sight of me. The doctors had to take her away and calm her down. I guess what I'm saying is, well, I'll always make sure she's well taken care of . . . ."

"Jack."

"I'd marry you if you wanted me to, Ona."

Ona smiled at him and brushed a tear from her eye with the back of her hand. "Oh, Jack, you're a sweet, wonderful man, a great lover, and you've made me happier than I've ever been before. But . . . no thanks, darling. I don't want to marry you. For several reasons."

Boxer was perplexed. How can you figure women? He shook his head.

"It's not that I don't love you, Jack. I do, more than any man I've ever known. But marriage doesn't seem to work out for me. I've been down that road before, and careers got in the way. The company's a hard master to work for, darling, just as the Navy's a tough mistress. I couldn't stand to become that attached to you, knowing how easily I could lose you."

Boxer didn't know what to say. He knew what Ona said made sense. A submariner's life was not his own, nor was a CIA agent's. And there would always be the problem of Francine, and a score to settle with Henry Tysin, Ona's former boss at the company.

"I'll always be here for you, Jack, if you'll take me on those terms. But I can see that faraway look in your eyes that means you have to get on with your life, and that I won't always be able to be a part of it." She leaned forward and kissed his lips. "So go, darling. Do what you must. I understand."

Boxer placed his hands on her face and drew her into another kiss. "I hate to say good-bye like this."

She wiped away another tear and said, "We have a wonderful tradition here in Hawaii, Jack. We don't say goodbye. We say Aloha. And Mahalo: thanks for everything."

Igor Borodine shivered against the early morning chill as he lay huddled under a thin blanket on a hard wooden platform that had served as his bed these last three months. It wasn't that dampness and cold were new to a submariner's life; it had been his very existence for a good part of his military career. His eight-by-twelve-foot cell was in the subbasement of General Sacholinsk Prison in Vladivostok, an important naval base on the Sea of Japan. Ordinary political prisoners were housed on the level above him, and the KGB had their easternmost headquarters on the main level. But far underground, Borodine's own personal hell never warmed up enough for him to feel anything close to comfortable, and the dankess seemed to permeate his bones.

This morning, he was wondering how his exec, make that former executive officer, Viktor, was faring. Thinking, perhaps, that his closest associate might even be dead by now. He rolled over on his back and tucked his hands behind his head. Funny, he thought, listening to the sound of his jack-booted jailer walking down the long stone corridor bearing his breakfast. I'd have sworn that it was closer to 0500 than 0600. Solitary confinement does strange things to a man's mind, even a man used to tight quarters.

Borodine sat up on his bunk in anticipation of his morning meal. Wonder what it'll be today? The cold porridge of kasha wasn't half bad, and he actually looked foward to the cabbage soup as a warming treat. Add a boiled potato and a piece of dark bread and he was satisfied. And so on the good days, the meal carried him over. More days than not, it was a hunk of bread and water. What would it be today, he mused. What do the bastards have in store for me today?

Borodine heard the key in the lock and the sound of

scraping metal while the heavy door was slid open. He didn't look up. It didn't matter. His jailer was under strict orders not to converse with him or offer any other civilities. The boots shuffled on the concrete floor, and a plastic tray clinked onto the wooden bench along the far wall, but a long moment went by and still his guard hadn't left him. "You'd better go, Corporal, before your superiors punish you for fraternizing with a prisoner," he said, shaking his head.

"I've come to share breakfast with you today, Igor Alexandrovich."

Borodine's head shot up at the sound of the strange yet familiar voice. "Pasha?" An eyebrow was raised. "What brings the chief deputy of the second directorate to the jail cell of a man whose future is measured in days?" A thought went through Borodine's mind. Maybe he is here because my life may last only a few more hours.

Feodor Doneck shrugged. "I wanted to try out the prison food firsthand, comrade. Tell me, is it any good?"

Borodine glanced at the food tray. "Is that soup? The soup is good. They are probably trying to impress you. Admiral Igor Borodine's final meal, eh, comrade?"

"You have nothing to fear, today, Igor." Doneck pulled up the solitary chair and moved it closer to the bunk. Then he lifted the wooden bench and food tray and moved it between them. He broke off a piece of bread and dunked it into the hot soup. "Eat, comrade. You need to keep up your strength."

Borodine brought a spoonful of cabbage soup to his lips, blew on it, and took a sip. "It's very good today." He finished off one spoonful, then another. Looking Doneck squarely in the eye, he said, "I don't fear death, comrade. If you've come to gloat over my predicament, you've wasted your morning. If you've come to have me killed, there's nothing I can do about it."

"Have you any idea why you're still alive, my friend? Why

you weren't shot soon after you arrived here?"

Borodine seemed unconcerned, almost nonchalant for a man in the presence of one of the most feared KGB men in the Motherland. He shrugged and continued to eat his meal.

"Do you think that I don't know it was you who killed my predecessor, Comrade Kacusky?"

A chunk of bread stuck in Borodine's throat, almost causing him to gag. He coughed to open his airway, his spoon still poised over the soup bowl, spilling its contents.

"Surprised, Igor Alexandrovich? I thought you might be. That is the reason that I've kept you alive against the wishes of the minister of defense and some of his cronies."

Doneck chuckled. "I was rotting in that stinkhole Afghanistan when Comrade Kacusky met his untimely demise and I was elevated to his job. For that, I thank you."

"But how . . . ?"

"By reading Kacusky's file on you, I learned that he had been trying to wrest you from Comrade Admiral Gorshkov's protection, and have you killed by his own people. He almost succeeded. Too bad for him that you killed him first."

"There is no proof."

Doneck laughed heartily at that. "I need no proof, comrade. You are sitting in this cell charged with serious crimes against the state, for having a nuclear submarine stolen from beneath your nose, no less, and you still think I need proof of what you've done? Hah. One word from me and you're a dead man."

"Is that what you've come to tell me?" Borodine returned to eating his meal.

"Don't be so brash, comrade. The time will come when you will do a favor for me, and you will be free once more. Perhaps even a hero again. Who knows?"

Borodine wiped out his bowl with a last hunk of bread and looked over the other man before putting the food in his mouth. "And what kind of favor would it take to restore me to my former station, Pasha? Kill another of your superiors for you?" He popped the morsel in his mouth while awaiting Doneck's reply.

The KGB man got up to leave. "We shall see, Igor. We shall see. Meanwhile, I'm having you moved to more comfortable quarters upstairs. You will be given more freedom and company, and I'm told the cold isn't as damaging to the body." Doneck walked through the door opening, then stuck his head back inside. "I'll be in touch, comrade." Then he was gone.

# Chapter 5

The American Airlines L-1011 jumbo jet touched down at Dulles Airport as the sun rose over the nation's capital. For Boxer, it was the culmination of an eighteen-hour odyssey which had begun half a world away in Hawaii yesterday. After a quiet afternoon with Ona and a brief meeting with Admiral Willis, where his request for a four-week leave was kicked upstairs, he spent the following day-and-a-half squeezed between fidgety kids and their cranky parents during the unpleasant flight to Washington, DC.

Talk about jet lag. The trip involved three legs, with two layovers and plane changes. Boxer was exhausted. He hailed the first taxi in line, tossed in his garment bag, and hopped in after it. He gave the driver the Georgetown address that he called home when in DC and dozed for a half hour in the back seat.

He was awakened by the blare of car horns and the screams of several women pedestrians. "What's happening?" he asked the cabbie.

The driver turned his head. "We just missed an accident. That sucker over there got creamed in a hit-and-run just as I got to the intersection."

Boxer was fully alert now and craned his head for a better view.

"Guy in a van came barrel-assing through the red light and smashed right into the driver's door of the Mercedes. I think the sucker's a goner."

"Wait here," Boxer ordered. He fished a fifty out of his wallet and tore it in half. He gave a piece to the driver and tucked the remainder in his pocket. "The other half is yours when I get back."

Boxer got out of the taxi and made his way closer to the wreck. "Someone call the police and an ambulance," he yelled to the crowd and hurried to the Mercedes. Gasoline was leaking from the chassis and spreading on the street below.

Boxer knew the car could explode at any moment and raced to the vehicle and tried to pry the driver's door open. It wouldn't budge. As he circled to the passenger side, someone cried out, "Fire, fire!"

A police cruiser pulled into the intersection with siren blaring. "Hey, you," one of the cops shouted. "Get the hell out of there. You crazy or something?"

Flames licked the front end of the vehicle and started to spread under the driver's seat. "Shit," Boxer muttered to himself and wrenched at the passenger door and pulled it open. The driver was unconscious and slumped forward against the wheel. Boxer managed to undo the seat belt and slid his arm under the man's chest, grabbing a handful of his coat. With all his strength, he pulled the driver to safety as the wreck burst into flames.

One of the policemen got out of the cruiser and stood there watching Boxer. Boxer shouted, "Help me move him out of here. *Now,* damnit."

Boxer struggled to drag the portly driver out of harm's way. The well-dressed white-haired man was dead weight, and the policeman offered no assistance, instead staring at the flaming automobile. Then the car exploded with such force that Boxer was thrown off his feet by the concussion.

When he came to, he found himself strapped to a gurney alongside the accident victim, in the rear of a racing ambulance. He hurt all over.

Amid screaming sirens, the two of them were carried on stretchers into the emergency room of a hospital. The elderly man was curtained off while a team of medics and nurses worked over him. Boxer thought he counted at least six or seven in all. Meanwhile, he was largely ignored.

"Five-W-D," a doctor ordered. "Two units of blood. Somebody type him."

Policemen, both in and out of uniform, soon filled the emergency room, and the hospital tried in vain to keep them back. One tall, muscular man elbowed his way through the mob and held up a black wallet with an ID photo. "Secret Service," he told the police inspector on the scene.

Boxer wondered who the old gent might be to garner so much attention. And while they were all tending to the man, Boxer noted that his own clothes were charred and that his face and hands seemed to be scraped or burned. Just then, an orderly came by, took one look at Boxer, and said, "Hey, man. What happened to you? You look like shit."

Before Boxer could respond, the young man walked over to a sink and began to wash his hands. "I better fix you up. They all too busy with the old guy."

Boxer struggled out of his blazer jacket, but a throbbing pain in his shoulder prevented him from removing it. The orderly picked up surgical scissors and began cutting open the back of the jacket. "You ain't gonna wear this no more, anyways," he said.

Together, they removed the jacket in two halves, along with Boxer's shirt and tie. "Okay, now let me take a look at you." The man walked around Boxer, scrunching his eyes whenever he noticed an especially nasty-looking wound. He put on latex gloves and touched an abrasion on the bad shoulder.

43

Boxer winced.

"Do it hurt? Shit. I'll fix it up."

While Boxer sat there at the edge of the examining table, the orderly carefully applied Betadine antiseptic to all the abrasions and cuts with a long cotton swab, and smeared the burned and blistered areas with a bland, white cream. "What's your name, son?"

"Lemmon. First name's Oliver, but I don't like it, so everyone just call me Lemmon."

"Well, thanks for all your help, Lemmon. How come you know so much about this?"

Lemmon shrugged. "I dunno. I watch the nurses, what they do. Sometimes I help out when they really busy, like right now."

Boxer was covered with bandages now, and feeling more comfortable. "Ever think of becoming a nurse or a paramedic? You'd be a natural."

Lemmon helped himself to a pale green hospital scrub shirt from the laundry cart and managed to get it over Boxer's head without causing too much discomfort. "Your shirt ain't goin' nowhere, either," he chuckled. Then he got serious. "Black dude like me come here looking for work, they don't think of no nurse or paramedic. Black dude like me, you be an orderly."

Boxer didn't know what to say. He slid down off the table and started out of the emergency room. "Could you just point me in the direction of the exit? It doesn't look as if anyone will miss me here."

"Down that hallway and to the left. You can't miss it."

Boxer looked up to find his way blocked by a secret service man, who looked as big and tough as any linebacker, and another man, somewhat shorter, but as rugged looking as the first. "Not so fast, buddy. I need some ID, and a statement."

Boxer saw that he couldn't muscle his way past them, but

44

he was pissed that they only showed any interest in him when he tried to leave. He flipped open a flap to reveal his service identification. "Rear Admiral Jack Boxer, US Navy. I'm here in town for a meeting with Admiral Mason, the chief of naval ops. You can check it out if you'd like."

The taller man looked over Boxer, then his ID, before turning to his companion. "Looks like we've got us a genuine hero, Dave. The guy who saved Senator Burke's life is an admiral. Wouldn't you know it?"

"Senator Burke?" Boxer looked over at the crowd milling around the cubicle next to his. "That's Senator Burke from Texas? He's a one-man dynamo when it comes to arms procurement. All the military chiefs are crazy about him."

The Secret Serviceman handed Boxer back his wallet. "Well, someone sure wasn't. That accident was no accident." The secret service man quickly caught himself. "That's off the record, Admiral."

"Relax," Boxer told him. "We're both on the same side. Do you need me for anything else now? I still have to meet with the CNO."

"I'll still need a statement from you, but it can wait. Here's my card. Give me a call when you finish with your boss."

Boxer glanced at the card. It read *Steven Ross* and had a downtown number. "Sure, Ross." Boxer tucked the card away. "Now, if you'll excuse me . . . ?"

"Hey, will ya lemme in now? Geez, come on, give a guy a break, will ya?" Someone was trying to shove his way into the already cramped quarters.

Ross turned toward the noise. "Hey, it's the cabbie who witnessed the accident. Let him in."

"See?" he told the two agents. "I told you my fare was the guy that saved the senator's ass." He turned to Boxer. "I waited for you like I said, mister." He dangled the torn

45

fifty-dollar bill in front of him. "Now can I have the other half?"

Boxer broke up and laughed so hard he hurt.


"What the hell happened to you, Boxer?" The short, squat CNO took a pull of his big cigar and blew the smoke toward the ceiling. "You look like shit."

"I've been hearing that a lot today," Boxer replied. "It's too long a story to bore you with now."

"Well, try to remember you're an officer and a gentleman." He blew another puff of smoke out of the side of his mouth. "You have to set an example for the men."

What a pompous ass, Boxer fumed. As far as he was concerned, Mason wasn't fit to shine Admiral Stark's shoes. Though he and the former CNO didn't always see eye to eye, they always shared mutual respect. And in his retirement, Stark had become almost a father to him. Boxer realized he would never respect Admiral Mason, whom he considered an ass-kisser who'd gotten to his present position through political pressure, rather than on his ability and leadership. Nontheless, he realized, Mason was the CNO, and therefore his boss. He held his tongue.

"What's this about you taking a month off, Boxer? This is the Navy we're in, not the Boy Scouts."

"I've got the time coming to me, Admiral. I've finished with my assignment in Pearl Harbor, and the *Manta* is in dry dock for repairs and upgrading. I have some unfinished business to attend to."

"Your ladyfriend? You think that will consume all of a month, do you?"

Boxer's face reddened. "Francine Wheeler is my fiancée, Admiral, and solely my concern, not the Navy's. Besides, there is another matter to take care of."

"Yeah, I understand you've got some kind of hard-on for Henry Tysin. That you think Henry had something to do with what happened to your ladyfriend, and you'd like to go chasing all over the world looking for him. I think you're barking up the wrong tree."

"I know for sure that Tysin is responsible for what happened, that he hired the people who did it. I also know that he's responsible for the attack on the *Barracuda* and the loss of a lot of very good submariners, Admiral. And I know he had help. He couldn't have pulled off an assault on an American submarine within the confines of Norfolk Harbor without some very high-ranking assistance from the Navy or Coast Guard."

"That case is closed, Boxer," Mason barked.

"All due respect, Admiral, that case isn't closed until I bring the guilty parties to justice. And I mean all of them." He let that sink in. "And as for Henry Tysin, I'd travel to hell to bring him in."

"Request denied. I can't spare you for a month."

"Then you leave me no choice, sir." Boxer reached into a coat pocket and took out a long white envelope. "This is my resignation, Admiral Mason. Effective immediately."

Mason slammed his palms hard on his desk. "Sixty days. I have the right to demand sixty days' notice. And until that time, you'll follow orders. Do you understand?"

Boxer sighed. "I have over three months accumulated leave due me, Admiral, so that deals me out. You can take it up with the president or the secretary of defense if you'd like."

Mason was on his feet. He stubbed out his cigar in the ashtray and shouted, "Don't you play with me on this, Boxer. You work for the CIA, too, and Director Cultrain has told me in no uncertain terms that you're not to continue with your vindictive witch-hunt for Henry Tysin."

"Ah, the good-ol'-boy network at work, is it? Protect your own? It wouldn't surprise me if Cultrain and Tysin were old fraternity buddies."

"You're in over your head, Boxer. You'd just better watch your ass." Mason was screaming at him.

No sense trying to talk sense to him, Boxer figured, and got to his feet. "Well, if you'll excuse me, I'll be filing my papers with personnel and be on my way." With that, he turned and headed for the door. As he stepped into the hallway, he could hear Mason shouting after him.

"Damn you, Boxer. I never did like you."

Boxer shook his head in disgust and went outside.

# Chapter 6

"Visitor to see you, Francine. Come on, now."

"Go away."

"Please, dear. It's Admiral Boxer. You know, Jack . . . Jack Boxer."

"I don't want to see him." Francine Wheeler lay curled in a fetal position on her bed, rocking back and forth. A bowl of oatmeal sat untouched, a plastic spoon handle protruding from the gruel.

The middle-aged attendant in starched white uniform leaned over Francine. "You haven't touched a drop of food, dear. How are we going to get you well again, if you don't help us?"

Francine's arm swung out and sent the bowl and its contents flying. "Don't want any."

The attendant tsk-tsked and placed a gentle hand on her shoulder. "Come, dear. Your fiancé has come all the way from America just to spend a little time with you. And Dr. Garipalli feels seeing him will do you a world of good."

Reluctantly, Francine sat up on her bed. Her hair was disheveled, and the shapeless hospital gown just hung on her ever-thinning frame. The attendant helped her into a robe and managed a few strokes with a brush in Francine's hair before Wheeler pushed her hand away and stood up.

49

Boxer's first sight of her was as she shuffled out onto the spacious balcony overlooking the Swiss Alps across Lake Lugano. Could this be the beautiful, vivacious young lawyer that he'd been in love with at least the last three years? The thought of what Tysin's hired rapists did to her caused the bile to rise in his craw. He stood there in his Navy blazer, gray slacks, and a tie that set off his salt-and-pepper hair and beard. Francine used to tell him that he looked dashing in that outfit, causing him to blush.

Dr. Garipalli stood at Boxer's side. "Look, Francine. See what Jack brought for you. Aren't the flowers lovely?" He handed a beautiful bouquet to the attendant, who went to put them in a crystal vase on a low table.

Boxer handed over a gold foil-wrapped box. Garipalli said, holding the offering in front of him, "Swiss chocolates. You'll be the envy of everyone on the floor."

Francine didn't respond.

Boxer held back, then said, "Francine, I . . . . It's nice to see you again, darling. How are you doing?"

Francine inched closer to the middle-aged attendant. "Don't let them touch me. They're never going to touch me again."

The woman put her arm around Francine and hugged her close. "No one's going to bother you here, dear. These are friends. Don't you recognize Dr. Garipalli and your fiancé Jack Boxer? There's no need to worry."

Boxer looked at Garipalli as if to say, What the hell is going on here? Isn't she ever going to get better? It's been a year already, and she looks worse than ever.

Dr. Garipalli must have read his expression, and tried to intercede. "Francine, Jack has come a long way to be with you, and do you know why? Because he loves you."

Something must have pulled a trigger in Francine's brain, and she became very agitated. "I know what he wants." Her arms began to flail at her sides. "He wants to fuck me. Don't you?"

Boxer stood there too stunned to move.

Francine's right hand slipped into the V-neck of her hospital gown, and she began squeezing her breast. Her voice seemed to screech, "Is this what you want?" She tried hard to pull her breast up out of the garment, and when she couldn't manage, she screamed and ripped the gown diagonally from her neck down to her waist, revealing the left side of her chest.

Boxer thought, well, at least she looks physically healthy, though a little too thin. But she seems to be flipping out. He turned to the doctor, and in a quiet voice said, "Can't you do something? Give her something?"

Garipalli made a head movement that the attendant seemed to understand, because she left them at once and scurried off down the long terrazzo hallway.

Boxer said, "Francine, please, I . . . ."

"You want to fuck me? I thought so, you dirty bastard." She reached down and pulled up the front of her gown, revealing her naked body from the waist down. Her hand slid over the thick thatch that covered her mound, and she began to finger herself. "Come on, do it to me, do it to me."

Boxer's hands went out toward her. "Francine, please . . . ."

"Don't come any nearer," she was shouting now, her fingers still at work between her thighs. She started backing toward the balcony railing.

Boxer and Garipalli began to close in on her, pleading with her to settle down, trying to buy time until the attendant returned with some medication.

The attendant came hustling down the hall as quickly as her cumbersome body could move. She arrived at the visitor's area with a large syringe in one hand, a plug of cotton dripping alcohol in the other. "I have the Haldol, Doctor Garipalli. Do you want . . . ?" She stopped in mid-sentence, having caught Francine's sudden movement out of the corner of her eye.

51

As the three of them moved in, Francine Wheeler tore off the remains of her clothing, made a dash for the edge of the balcony, and hurled her naked body over the rail, still screaming, "Don't touch me, don't touch me, don't touch me. . . ."

At a small cemetery in the Virginia countryside, Boxer stood with head bowed while a cleric eulogized Francine Wheeler, exhorting the small gathering of family and friends to remember her as she was in life, and not the way she died. He fought back the tears and the hurt as her body was lowered into the ground, feeling a very deep sadness in his heart for losing her, and a rekindled hatred for those who broke her mind and forced her over the edge.

He felt a consoling hand on his shoulder. It was Granville "Slick" Wilkins, Francine's mentor and friend at Georgetown Law. He'd already told Boxer that Francine had left most of her estate to him, including the brownstone that they'd live in in DC. In turn, Boxer insisted that a scholarship fund be set up in her name at her alma mater, and that the remaining funds be disbursed among her relatives. The townhouse would serve as home for Admiral Stark and his adopted son, Chuck.

The morning chill was followed by a light rain that dispersed the mourners even as the mound of earth was being shoveled into the grave. Boxer stood there alone until the workmen finished the job. He walked slowly back to the parking area, deep in thought, oblivious to his surroundings. At the edge of the graveled surface, he looked up to see a big black Mercedes stretch limo waiting for him. He recognized the vehicle, and a visceral rage fired up in him. It was time for him to kill Julio Sanchez.

A blackened rear window opened, and to Boxer's surprise, the occupant was a mild-mannered business type whom he didn't know. Before Boxer could react, the man said,

"Admiral Boxer, I've come on behalf of my client, Señor Sanchez, to offer his condolences. I am asked to . . . ."

Boxer had the man's neck in a powerful grasp that threatened to choke the life out of him. "You tell your boss that the next time he crosses my path, he's a dead man. Do you understand me?"

The man tried to nod Yes; he understood. The fear in his eyes told Boxer that his point was well made. The sound of doors opening caused Boxer to loosen his grasp and turn to face the driver and bodyguard who emerged from the front seat. He noticed the hulk on his side of the car reaching inside his jacket. Just like Julio to send his goons along for protection. Now it was two armed thugs against him. Well, so be it. He wheeled to face his closest assailant.

"Wait, Hugo. Not yet." The businessman in the back seat gasped out his order in time to stop the lumbering giant from shooting Boxer with a small, nickel-chromed automatic.

"Admiral Boxer, please. Come inside and listen to what Señor Sanchez has asked me to say, and then, if you are not interested, I'll be on my way. And, Señor Sanchez will stay out of your way, to be sure."

Boxer tossed the idea around for a moment, then noticed the BMW he'd driven to the cemetery was still waiting for him in the parking area. He told the man in the business suit to wait a minute, and went to let Admiral Stark and Chuck know what was going on.

Chuck had gotten a one-day pass from the Naval Academy at Annapolis to join his father at the funeral. Boxer thought he looked dashing in his dress grays, his hair close-cropped in plebe fashion. "Son, Admiral Stark, I'm going to be a few minutes with those people Julio Sanchez sent over to see me. If I'm not out in fifteen minutes, drive to the nearest police station as fast as you can and have them arrested. By that time, I'm sure there'll be something to charge them with."

Boxer returned to the limo and got into the back seat.

"Thank you, Señor. I am Samuel Da Silva, Julio Sanchez's attorney." He held out his hand to Boxer.

Boxer ignored the hand and said, "Say what you were sent here to say, Da Silva. And skip the phony condolences. I don't want to hear it from you or Sanchez."

Da Silva rearranged his tie and cleared his throat. "Very well, then. Señor Sanchez does not want to be your enemy, though he respects your reasons for hating him. He says that the kidnaping of Miss Wheeler was a contract between him and Henry Tysin, and that it was never meant to get so out of his control, and to cause the disrepair to the lady."

Boxer stifled the urge to strangle the pompous little bastard and forced himself to settle down. "Get to the point, Da Silva."

"The man who is at the root of your problem, Henry Tysin, has taken over Bruno Morell's crime empire, and is considerably more dangerous than while he was the head of your CIA."

"That's debatable," Boxer interrupted. "But go on."

"Señor Sanchez is willing to help you capture or kill Tysin for your word that you won't pursue my client any longer on the matter of your Miss Wheeler."

"I'll consider it," Boxer growled. "But don't ever mention her name in my presence again. It sounds foul coming from your mouth. Understand?"

Indeed he did. Da Silva nodded his agreement and reached into his jacket pocket. He handed Boxer a packet of papers. "Here is your plane ticket to Spain. When you arrive in Torremolinos, call this number and a limo will be dispatched to take you to Señor Sanchez's estate on the Costa del Sol. Travel light. Everything you need will be provided to you by my client."

Boxer took the packet and opened the rear door. "I'll give it some thought, Da Silva. Tell Sanchez that he'll hear from me if I decide to take him up on his offer."

*　　*　　*

Iberia Flight 756 touched down on the tarmac in the south of Spain under a bright, sunny Mediterranean sky. There was a crisp breeze coming in over the water, and Boxer felt invigorated. He was ready for action, to settle an old score or two, depending on how things worked out. He told the immigration officials that he was in Spain on a vacation and found a phone to call Sanchez's number. Within minutes, he was once again in the back seat of a limo, this time speeding through the countryside along the Mediterranean coast. They passed a new development of luxury condos put up to attract expatriate Americans and rich Europeans to the pleasant climate. Further on, the area became more sparsely populated, until they finally came to a vast, hedged-in villa estate that ambled down to the shore. A high seawall offered privacy from the public.

Sanchez's property stretched out over a dozen acres, with wooded borders camouflaging chain-link fences topped with barbed wire, remote security cameras, and armed guards and dogs which roamed the perimeter. Boxer's driver passed through the main gate unchallenged, and meandered down to a spacious white stucco building topped with red-orange clay tiles. Sanchez greeted Boxer in a cedar paneled den, with floor-to-ceiling windows that provided a magnificent view of the sea. He carried two snifters of brandy and handed one to Boxer.

"A peace offering," Sanchez said. He hoisted his glass. "To peace and friendship." Then he swirled the amber liquid in the snifter, brought it to his nose to capture the bouquet, and sipped it.

Boxer drained off an inch of the brandy, savored it in his mouth for a moment, and swallowed. "A truce, Julio. We shall see about peace between us. But never friendship. Now, why don't you tell me what you've got in mind?"

Sanchez said, "Come inside, where we can enjoy the view. I have ordered dinner tonight aboard the *Sea Princess*, which is moored just beyond the seawall to our south." The two of them made themselves comfortable on overstuffed chairs on either side of a coffee table. "Ah, life holds so many pleasures, if one only knows where to seek them."

Boxer took another swallow of brandy. "The point, Julio. You didn't bring me all the way to Spain to chat about your boat or your brandy."

"Ah, forgive me. Well, it seems that our old friend Henry Tysin is what you call 'pussyfooting' around with the Soviets these days."

"What? Henry in bed with the Russkies?"

"Yes. It seems that they have something, rather, someone he wants. And he's willing to trade secrets in exchange for this person."

Boxer frowned. "By secrets, I assume you mean US military and CIA stuff. He's willing to sell out the US to fulfill what seems to be a personal vendetta?"

Sanchez swirled and sipped some more of the amber liquid. "Seems that way. You remember the incident that cost Henry Tysin his CIA position?"

"Yes. I knew Lori Ann Collins, Tysin's secretary. And lover. She turned out to be a Russian mole who was using him to gain inside information. The Feds think that Henry killed her. In fact, I was a suspect, myself, for a while, till I explained my whereabouts to them."

Julio chuckled. "Yes, I remember. Your president told the DC police that you were with him in Texas while the girl was being murdered. That set them on their fat asses."

Boxer nodded. "That left her husband, who had an alibi; Henry Tysin; and Lori Ann's control. Seems the guy has been over here for ages, and was using a bookstore as his cover in Washington. He disappeared about the same time that Henry did. Coincidence?"

That brought a smile to Sanchez's lips. "My informants tell me that this fellow Frumpkin was using Lori Ann to blackmail Tysin. That either Tysin killed the girl to shut her up, or this Frumpkin killed her to frame Henry Tysin. Rumor has it that Tysin's sworn to get this Russian mole to clear himself of the killing. Either way, they both went underground, Frumpkin back to the Soviet Union, and Tysin to Morell's old hangout on Corsica."

"I'd like to get my hands on Tysin."

"I will help you. I have no love lost there myself."

Boxer glared at Julio. "Get rid of the competition and keep the sleaze-and-squeeze market to yourself, eh?"

"I'm a legitimate businessman."

"And I'm the Pope."

Sanchez's face reddened. "You agree that Henry Tysin has to be stopped? That he's dangerous if he sells out your country for that Russian spy? I'm offering you my assistance, nothing more, nothing less. If Henry finds out, he'll try to kill me, too. I'm taking quite a risk."

Boxer drained his glass. "Still, it wouldn't hurt your business much if Henry were out of the way, would it?"

Sanchez didn't dispute him. The truth was evident. "My informants place him in Trieste as of yesterday. He'd be trying to trade off secret CIA stuff for Frumpkin. Find this Frumpkin, and you may turn up Henry Tysin. If he steps behind the iron curtain, it will make tracking him more difficult." He took a sip of brandy and looked Boxer in the eye. "If I leak word to him that you're on his trail, he may seek you out in order to kill you. What do you think?"

"I think that either way, you win, Julio. When can we shove off? I don't want to give Henry too much of a lead."

Sanchez smiled. "After dinner aboard the *Sea Princess*, tonight, we shall take a leisurely cruise through the Mediterranean, around the tip of Italy, and up into the Adriatic. We'll moor in Trieste Harbor. You should be able to put ashore in a small, fast speedboat with a few good men and go after Tysin."

"I'm sure that he'll just be sitting there waiting for me to catch up with him," Boxer said sarcastically.

"My sources are usually accurate, and they tell me that the Soviets are going to turn this Frumpkin over to Tysin in the north of Yugoslavia, not far from Trieste. He'll be waiting all right, but not for you, Boxer."

Boxer shrugged.

Julio said, "It's your move. What do you want to do?"

Boxer took a deep breath and let it out. He didn't trust Julio Sanchez a bit. He was probably heading into a trap, possibly a double trap. He stood the chance of being killed by Tysin or by Julio's men. He had no legitimate business in Yugoslavia, and as an American naval officer, his ass was in deep trouble if he got caught trying to kidnap Henry Tysin. Yet, it was the best opportunity he'd had in a long time, and future prospects looked even worse. "Okay, Julio, let's do it."

"Fine. We dine aboard the yacht at eight. Meanwhile, you have free run of my estate. If you stop off at the dark brown building down the road to the right, ask Hernando to fix you up with whatever weapons you'd like. He's our armorer."

"All the comforts of home?"

Sanchez smiled. "We aim to please. Meet me here at 7:30 and we'll share the tender to the yacht. Till then." He hoisted his snifter and drained it.

# Chapter 7

Henry Tysin sat alone at a tiny table under the awning of a sidewalk cafe in Trieste. A chubby waiter wearing a white apron appeared from within the eatery carrying a tray of pastries and a coffee service. "Espresso, signor," he said and placed his burden on the table. Tysin ignored the man, who left, muttering under his breath. Henry chuckled, for his knowledge of the Italian language was far greater than the servant had given him credit for. "Stinking pig," he'd said. "Go and eat the lot of it, for all I care."

A stranger approached the table and said, "I hear the espresso is excellent here."

Tysin eyed the newcomer, a man in his thirties, of medium build and sporting a full mustache and dark-rimmed glasses: his contact with the KGB. "I understand the pastries are even better. Have a seat and join me."

Tysin poured the steamy black brew into two demitasse cups and offered one to the Russian. He picked out a spongy cake laced with rum and filled with a rich, creamy custard and bit into it. "Delicious. You should try one."

The Russian looked about him, noticing the middle-aged couple at a table between them and the cafe itself, and a pair of pretty young women apparently taking a break from a shopping spree, judging from the parcels set on the ground at their feet. A few other diners occupied tables within the building. Nothing to fear from them, he decided. So far, so good. "These are my favorites," he replied, selecting a rich cannoli tipped with green pistachio morsels. He greedily consumed it in two bites, washing it down with coffee. "So," he wiped his mouth with a napkin. "You have something for me?"

Tysin smiled and sipped his espresso. With his peripheral vision, he spotted a black Fiat idling on the far side of the square, a driver behind the wheel. Two other men paced the sidewalk nearby, pretending to be studying the merchandise displayed in several of the shops. Funny, he thought, how the rigid dress code policies of the US and the Soviets caused their FBI and KGB agents to stand out as cops, no matter how hard they tried to look otherwise. "Do you take me for a country bumpkin, Ivan, to bring all my cards to the table while you have offered nothing in return?"

The Russian took another pastry and ate half of it before asking, "Ivan? My name is Feodor. Of course, I don't expect you to hand over a list of CIA agents without getting what you came for, the whereabouts of a certain party who caused you some embarrassment in your own country."

"Look, Ivan, or Feodor, whatever you want to call yourself, I want the bastard who used the name Frumpkin delivered to me bound and gagged at a place of my choosing. Then I will deliver you the list. *Capisco?*"

"Not so loud." Feodor looked around to see if any of the other patrons had turned to notice their conversation. Satisfied that no one seemed to care a whit about them, he lowered his voice and said, "How can I be sure that you'll keep your part of the bargain?"

Tysin sipped his coffee. "You don't, asshole. You're giving up one man who has outlived his usefulness to your country in exchange for two dozen embassy personnel who are now active CIA agents in eastern bloc countries."

The Russian swallowed the insult. "I am authorized to

disclose only Frumpkin's location to you. You will have to take him yourself."

"But I am alone and unarmed, in a country alien to me."

"That is your problem. I can do only what I can."

"Where is he?"

"Further down the coast, in Montenegro, the south of Yugoslavia. At the mouth of the Bay of Kotor, in the town of the same name, he has taken a room at the Tivat Hotel, posing as a tourist. In truth, he is our station chief there, with an eye on the tourists who visit from all over Europe. He will suspect nothing."

Tysin nodded and wiped his lips with his napkin. He removed a bill from his wallet and placed it on the table beside the espresso pot. "My treat," he said. "And now, if you'll excuse me . . . ?"

"Not so fast, my friend," the Russian spoke. "You have yet to fulfill your part of the agreement. The list, please."

"I'll get it to you." Henry rose to leave the table. As he did, he noticed that the two KGB men had crossed the square and were almost upon him. They branched out on either side of him, hands wrapped around automatic pistols inside their jacket pockets.

"Now you take me for the country bumpkin, eh? The list please. Now. Or else my associates here will make sure that you never use the information I gave you."

Tysin registered surprise. "Do you think I would come here alone like this with the papers in my pocket? What protection would that give me?"

"Trust, asshole," the Russian sneered. "You have a short memory."

The other patrons sensed something was about to happen. An elderly couple left their meal half eaten, tossed a bill on the table, and hurried away. Two women shoppers showed more composure. They neatly folded their napkins on the table and gathered up their packages. One of them opened her purse to fish for money to pay the tab, all the while chatting away about the shopping that they'd done all morning and the high price of everything.

"One last chance, asshole." The Russian stood glaring at Tysin, clearly enjoying the superiority of his position now. "Give me the list or you will die right here in the square." The two goons closed in on them.

Henry shrugged. "Looks like you win this round, Ivan." He sat down and began rummaging through his pockets. He produced a white envelope from an inside jacket pocket and laid it on the serving tray.

The Russian smiled and nodded to his men. As Feodor reached for the envelope, the other two stepped closer to the table. Without warning, a staccato of gunfire shattered Feodor's face and riddled the two gunmen with high-caliber rounds. One of the women shoppers covered Tysin with an UZI machine pistol still smoking from the shootout. The other had already dashed across the street and was firing at the black Fiat with her automatic assault weapon. The driver was hit repeatedly and slumped over the wheel. The woman returned to Tysin and her accomplice.

"Well done," Henry said. "Let's get out of here."

They slipped into the cafe, covering the patrons with their weapons, backing out of the rear exit behind the kitchen and onto two waiting motorcycles. Tysin sat behind one of the women, arms wrapped around her, holding on, feeling the round fullness of her breasts against his arms and hands. He smiled. He'd gotten at least part of what he'd come for, and gotten out alive. And all he'd left behind was a white envelope containing a list of two dozen of the finest restaurants in northern Italy.


It was 0500 and Boxer couldn't sleep. After tossing and turning for a half hour, the effects of last night's heavy eating and drinking and the concern about a double cross by Sanchez had gotten to him. He'd spent many days with too little sleep to know it was time to give it up and plan for what was ahead. He slipped into sweat pants and a heavy sweater, sneakers on his feet, and went out on deck.

The *Sea Princess* was almost two hundred feet long and five decks high, the topmost being the private realm of Julio Sanchez and his most honored guests, Boxer not being one of them. It contained a private bath including sauna and whirlpool, a sun deck, a pool, a well-stocked bar, and private access to the master suite one level below. Sanchez lived in high style on land and sea. The master bedroom contained hidden passageways useful for shepherding out one female guest as another came in through the main entrance to take her place. The passageways also served as an escape route for Sanchez, if need be, or a convenient place to spy on one's associates who borrowed the special quarters for a secret tête-à-tête.

Boxer decided to have a look around the yacht, to stretch his legs and get some clean sea air into his lungs. He quietly walked to the stern and climbed a metal ladder to the third level, where the bridge was located, as well as the galley and many of the services on board. No one stopped him, so he continued upward another level. He decided to walk around the deck to get some exercise. On the foredeck was the speedboat he was to use getting into Trieste. As he turned aft, he could see a Bell Ranger helicopter fastened to the uppermost deck, a fast getaway, if need be. He continued his tour walking aft on the port side of the yacht. About midships, he thought he heard the sharp cries of a woman and inched forward quietly to investigate. Yes, there it was again, the distinct sound of a woman in pain, pleading for mercy. He headed for the passageway that sectioned off the deck fore and aft.

A massive forearm came out of nowhere and slammed against Boxer's head, sending him sprawling to the teak deck. He had barely regained his senses when a giant paw grabbed his neck, hoisted him to his feet, and smashed him hard into a bulkhead. "Get the hell out of here, wiseguy. You don't belong here."

Boxer looked up, dazed by the beating, seeing, who was it? Hugo, the ape from the cemetery in Virginia. Well, no sense trying to be nice to this guy. He said, "Hey, take it easy. I was just getting some exercise, okay?"

The giant stood his ground, shaking his head and blocking Boxer's access to the rear half of the deck, which constituted Sanchez's private quarters. Hugo's hands were balled into fists at his sides. He said, "You were nosing around where you had no business being. You've got a lot of explaining to do to Sanchez."

The cries became more distinctive now. Boxer said, "Well, if you'll just step aside, I'll go back down below, the way I came up."

"How's that?"

Boxer held onto the port rail, apparently having difficulty walking. "Come on, I'll show you." He led the way to the stern, where two lifeboats, which also served as tenders, were carried on twin davits. He lulled the giant to the edge, saying, gently as he could, "You should know about this if you're in charge of security."

Hugo glanced over the stern rail at the ladder. In that split second, Boxer mustered up all his strength and came up with an uppercut into the giant's groin.

Hugo moaned and bent forward, clutching his battered testicles. "Why, you . . ."

Boxer's knee smashed into Hugo's face, cutting him short, and setting him up for more punishment. A left jab closed an eye. A hard right cross knocked Hugo's head backward and sent him sprawling back against the rail.

Boxer kneed him hard in the groin. Hugo screamed in pain, then in terror as Boxer pushed him backward over the rail. The big man's cries woke some of the crew and guests, and they ran to the gunwales to look down on Hugo trying to keep afloat in the sea below.

Boxer shook off his pain and headed for the master cabin. The cries became louder. He tried the door, and when he found it locked, stepped back and kicked below the doorknob. The door shattered inward. Boxer was taken up short by the sight of a young woman, hands tied above her head to the bedposts, her legs spread-eagled and pulled back behind her head, attached to the same bedposts by silk tie-sashes. Her thighs and belly were covered with welts. A riding crop lay on the bedspread alongside her bent figure. She was crying, and pleading, "Don't hit me, please, no more. I'll do anything you want."

"Relax," Boxer told her. "I'm not going to hurt you." He looked about the room. "Who did this to you?"

She whimpered, moving her head toward what appeared to be a closet behind the head of the bed. "In there. He . . . he went in there. Please, don't let them hurt me any more."

Boxer dashed for the closet, finding it empty. He pushed aside several silk suits, a linen dinner jacket, and a silk robe. There, behind them, was a hidden doorway. Boxer pushed it open and stood aside. Though the passageway was still dark, he heard footsteps and proceeded after them.

Boxer burst out onto the deck from a bulkhead a few feet from where he'd shoved Hugo overboard a few minutes ago. There, trying to catch his breath, was Julio Sanchez, shivering in his red-and-blue-striped french-cut jockey shorts. Boxer went after him.

Julio realized that his bodyguard was going to be no help to him. He said, "Please, let's be civilized about this, eh?"

Boxer backed Sanchez closer to the rail. "Still up to your old tricks, Julio? Once a slave trader, always one, it seems."

Julio tried to cover himself with his arms, sidestepping to keep away from Boxer. "The girl's here under her own free will. A nympho. That's how she gets her rocks off. I was just giving her what she wants."

"You slime." Boxer rushed Julio and hoisted him over the side.

65

"Wait, don't."

Boxer saw several armed crewmen converge on him from two sides. He held Julio's flailing body further outboard. "They'll shoot you if you drop me," Sanchez warned.

"Let the girl go. Go ahead, tell them to let her go. I want her set free and flown to a hospital in that chopper. Go ahead, now. Tell them, or I swear you'll die right here."

Sanchez sensed that Boxer meant it. At any rate, he wasn't man enough to call his bluff. "Okay, pull me up," he told Boxer. And to his men, he called, "It's okay. Let the girl loose and fly her to the hospital."

When the crew had put their weapons away, Boxer hauled Sanchez back aboard the yacht. "You lost one testicle already, Julio. Keep that up and you may be singing soprano for the rest of your miserable life."

Sanchez tried to retain his composure. "I . . . I thought we were allies on this venture."

Boxer shook his head. "We happen to be on the same side this time, Julio. I despise the likes of you, but I'll tolerate you till the finish of this mission. Just don't flaunt your whorish ways in my presence. It brings back too many painful memories."

Julio Sanchez wheeled and stalked off to his quarters, cursing under his breath. He was not used to being made a fool of, especially in front of his own men, aboard his own yacht. Yet he knew that Boxer would kill him if provoked. For now, Julio would just have to hold his peace.

Boxer stood there in the crisp morning breeze watching Julio slither off, knowing the man wasn't to be trusted. He shook his head in wonderment. Strange bedfellows fate makes of us, he mused. He turned his back and looked out to sea.

Rimmed by mountains, the ancient city of Kotor lies at the head of the gulf of the same name in southern Yugoslavia.

The buildings, dating back to the Venetian occupation from the 1400s till 1797, are of aging stucco, topped with ubiquitous orange tiled roofs. As the *Sea Princess* rounded a bend, the city unveiled itself to them, and Sanchez had his yacht tied up at a modern wharf designed to accommodate the many cruise ships that stop at Kotor.

Waiting until evening, Boxer donned dark blue coveralls and a peaked cap. He set out, with two of Sanchez's men who were similarly dressed, for the Metropole Hotel. The Metropole was an ultramodern glass and concrete building, a stark contrast to the surrounding buildings. They pulled up in a small panel truck at the delivery entrance behind the hotel. With much aplomb, Boxer and the smaller of his backup team, a Yugoslav named Johny Lehaic, unloaded two heavy shipping chests onto a handtruck and manhandled them into the bellman's station.

Not wanting to give away his nationality, Boxer let Lehaic do the talking with the chief bellman in their native tongue. After checking the bill of lading and delivery instructions, the hotel's baggage handler rang up room 312 in full view of Boxer, to make sure Frumpkin was available to take delivery.

"I'm sorry," he told Lehaic. "Nobody there. He may still be out with those TV ladies. They were making some sort of documentary for an Italian television program, and Mr. Frumpkin had his eye on one of them. I think he had more than his eye on the cute blonde." He chuckled. "You can leave those with me and I'll bring it up when he gets back."

Boxer shot his accomplice a sharp look to tell him, No way do we leave this stuff. Johnny Lehaic was no fool. He told the bellman, "Sorry, but Mr. Frumpkin left strict instructions for me to personally deliver his belongings to the room. I could get fired if I don't bring this up myself."

"And I could get fired if I let you."

Johnny Lehaic reached into a pocket of his coveralls and took out the equivalent of a hundred dollars in local currency. "I understand, my friend. Mr. Frumpkin told us this might happen, and instructed me to pay you a bonus for helping me make sure he got his stuff all right." He waved the bills under the bellman's face.

The bell captain glanced furtively up and down the corridor. Convinced that his superiors weren't nearby, he plucked the money from Lehaic's hand and said, "Follow me. We'll use the freight elevator in the rear."

Johnny Lehaic motioned Boxer to follow, and the three of them headed for the elevator, with Boxer bringing up the rear, in charge of moving the heavy chests.

They disembarked on the third floor, with the bellman leading the way. He knocked on the door to 312, getting no response at all. He shrugged and let them in with his passkey. Boxer pulled in the cargo and set it down in the sitting room. Lehaic went ahead into the bedroom, followed by the bellman. There were cries from inside the room, and the bellman ran out in panic.

Boxer blocked his access and delivered two sharp slaps across the man's face. When Johnny followed, Boxer made the payoff sign with his fingers, and the wiry Lehaic took out some more money. "Look," he said. "Take this and keep your mouth shut. Tell your bosses you brought this stuff up here yourself, and found Frumpkin lying dead on the bed. Understand?"

The bellman understood. He took the money, at least two hundred dollars more. With Lehaic blocking the door now, Boxer went in to see for himself what had happened.

Blood stained the off-white plush carpeting and bedspread. Frumpkin's mutilated body lay on top, his throat slit and his dismembered penis stuffed in his mouth. Whoever had done this had to be crazed, and Boxer figured Henry Tysin fit the bill.

When Boxer returned to the sitting room, Lehaic was patting the bellman on the shoulder and telling him to sneak them out and give them a ten-minute head start before turning in the alarm. The bell captain nodded like a marionette, the bribery money clutched in his greedy hand. He led them to a scarcely used stairway and gave directions to the exit.

In the delivery area, Boxer shook the muscular driver to wake him, and he and Johnny went around the small truck to climb into the cargo area. No sense being visible, just in case the bellman decided to disclose all to save his own ass. Stepping up into the truck, Boxer was able to see a white van, identified with the log *TV-27* above some words in Italian, lose itself in the teeming rush hour traffic.

# Chapter 8

"Try to follow that van. I think it's Tysin."

Augusto, Boxer's musclebound driver, said, "It's no use. They have too much of a lead. We'll never catch them in all this traffic."

Boxer became angry, and his voice reflected it. "You'll never know that until you try. Now *move* it."

Augusto started the engine, but didn't move out of the delivery area. He turned his head around. "I don't work for you. My boss is Señor Sanchez."

Boxer turned his fury on Johnny Lehaic. "Tell him. We can't let that bastard Tysin get away."

Johnny shrugged. "Augusto's right, Boxer. Sorry, but the boss said to help you track down and kill Henry Tysin, if we could. But that don't include racing through traffic after some van—we don't even know it's Tysin. We get stopped speeding by the local cops—what're we doing with these nice automatic pistols in our pockets, and then where are we? In jail? Shoot us some cops, maybe? Sorry, we just can't risk it."

The sound of sirens could be heard now, and the wailing seemed to draw closer and closer to the Metropole. "We'd better get out of here, right now, before the police get here."

Lehaic nodded. "I couldn't agree with you more on that score. C'mon, Augusto, you need a special invitation?

Move it."

Augusto pulled out from behind the hotel and eased into the traffic. "We better head inland. They're sure to have the harbor area covered. That's probably the first place the cops would look for someone trying to escape a murder."

"Then that's where Tysin would be headed. I say, head for the waterfront. At very least, we could ditch the van and take the speedboat out to the *Sea Princess*."

"No way, Boxer." Augusto took the first right turn and headed inland. "I'm not about to risk spending the rest of my life in some Yugoslav jail."

"Or die in one," Johnny chimed in. "We can lose ourselves in the farm country."

Though armed, Boxer thought better of shooting it out with these two. After all, they were his link back to Sanchez's yacht, and to civilization. He settled back and endured the ride through fields of winter wheat and hay. After about a half hour, they stopped near a small farm. Near the small farmhouse of stone and wood plank were a score of corncribs woven of willow branches, with thatch roofs. Lehaic said, "Let me go speak to the farmer and try to get some food, in case we have to hide out around here for a while."

He went into the farmhouse and returned in ten minutes with a basket filled with bread and cheese, and several botles of local wine. Boxer noticed some bloodstains on Johnny's coveralls. "What happened? Did you hurt yourself in there?"

"Nah. The old boy was a little too hard nosed . . . didn't want to part with any of this stuff. So I had to convince him."

Boxer got up, feeling anger in his gut. "You didn't . . . ?"

Johnny looked past Boxer at the driver. "Let's go, Augusto—move it."

Boxer grabbed at Johnny's shirt and almost lifted the smaller man off the ground. "You're no damn good, Lehaic. A different time, a different place, I'd kill you for this."

Augusto got out of the driver's seat and came around

72

behind Boxer, his hand in the same pocket as his automatic. Johnny Lehaic said, "C'mon, Boxer. Let's go, and give me a hand with this. It was either him or me. He came after me with a shotgun. Told me to get off his land. I dunno, maybe the old coot was crazy."

Boxer's grip slackened. Lehaic said, "We gotta get out of here, now, before someone comes and finds him like this."

Boxer shook his head and got in. Johnny passed in the food basket and went around to speak with the driver. Then he returned to get in beside Boxer and slam shut the rear door. The panel truck took off down the narrow road, and they drove for over an hour, munching on cheese and bread, and washing it down with the homemade wine. At one point, when they'd gotten to a particularly secluded spot, the engine sputtered and the vehicle rolled to a halt.

Everyone got out. Augusto opened the hood and began fiddling around inside. When Boxer's attention drifted elsewhere, he removed the wire that connected the distributor to the alternator, then made a big play of trying to fix the problem. Several attempts at restarting the engine failed, and Johnny walked off into the scrub brush, saying he had to take a leak. Boxer stood by the driver's side of the truck, in case he was needed to try to start the engine, while Augusto made a big act out of looking for the problem.

Boxer felt that somehow the power supply had been cut off, and thought the distributor would be one of the first places to look, but Augusto assured him he was a good mechanic and would soon find the trouble. Then, while watching Augusto work, Boxer caught Johnny's reflection in the rearview mirror. He was attempting to sneak up behind Boxer, and when he came into range, drew his automatic.

Boxer caught the look in Augusto's eyes when he spotted his partner coming into view behind them, then averted his gaze back to the engine. Boxer nonchalantly opened the driver's door and leaned lazily against it, while keeping an eye on Johnny Lehaic through the rearview mirror. When

73

Johnny raised his gun to take aim, Boxer dived into the front seat and reached across to open the passenger door.

Several rounds smashed into the open driver's side door, breaking glass, tearing up the sheet metal. Boxer chanced raising his head and saw Augusto getting ready to attack from the front. Boxer found his own Walther 9-mm automatic and fired off two shots at the big man. One round found its mark. It entered Augusto's forehead and knocked him backward.

Boxer shoved open the passenger door and dived out headfirst, tumbled head over heels, and landed in a crouch. He ran around the back just as Johnny got to the passenger side. Diving to his right, on his belly, Boxer raised his gun and fired off the rest of the clip at Johnny Lehaic. All the rounds hit within a foot-square area on his chest. The smaller of the two thugs sank to his knees and fell backward. He was dead before he hit the ground.

Boxer made sure that Augusto was dead, then took a look at the engine compartment. It took him only a few minutes to find the problem, once he realized this whole thing had been a setup. He dragged the bodies off the road, got back in the truck, and headed northwest, hopefully to a safer harbor than Kotor must be in at the moment. It didn't take Boxer long to realize that Sanchez's plan all along was to have him killed, and blamed for the deaths of either Frumpkin or Tysin. Or both. Well, now he had one more mission—to work his way back home, to Washington, DC. A stranger in a strange land, it was going to take all the prowess he could muster.

The taxi ride to the townhouse in Georgetown gave Boxer a chance to shake off the horror of the past few weeks and to focus on the future. With his failed quest to find Tysin and bring him to justice, and his resignation from the Navy, he had a lot of thinking to do. He needed to reprioritize his life, to find new meaning, some new incentive.

He paid off the driver and walked the stairs to the second floor, the main living quarters he shared with Francine Wheeler during those few good years. Her office on the ground level would remain sealed as long as he kept this place, in her honor. He was met at the door by Admiral Stark. "Jack, welcome back. Do I have news for you? Wait till I get you something to drink, and I'll fill you in on what's been happening around here."

Boxer shook hands with his old mentor and tossed his topcoat on a chair. "Good to be back," he said, placing his left hand over the admiral's. "Stoli on the rocks, if we still have it. Better make it a double."

"Sure do," Stark said, heading for the dry bar. "Always will, as long as I'm in charge of the booze around here." He poured himself two fingers of Glenfiddich, neat, and carried the drinks back inside.

Boxer accepted the vodka and held up his glass. Before he could say anything, Stark said, "To Francine, a wonderful woman cut down in her prime, never to be forgotten. May she rest in peace."

Boxer nodded and stared into his drink. "You know, I failed in bringing Tysin in."

"I figured that out all by myself when I didn't hear or see anything about it in the media. Well, son, if anybody could have taken him, it would have been you."

"He was so close. I almost had him in my grasp." He sipped some of his drink and looked up at Stark. "You heard what he did to that Russkie spy Frumpkin? The mole who ran Lori-Ann Collins, Tysin's secretary?"

Admiral Stark took a sip of his expensive scotch. "That was Tysin's doing? I should have known."

Boxer drained off half his drink, and sank into an easy chair. "Henry must have duped him, somehow, then killed and mutilated him. I was one step behind." He shook his head, and finished off the Stoli.

75

"Here, let me freshen that up for you." Stark returned in a moment with another double of Boxer's favorite vodka.

"Thanks. You know, Julio Sanchez set me up, taking me along to wipe out his competition, then have his goons kill me and blame me for the other killings. Unfortunately for Julio, I had other plans. And now I'm more sure than ever that Henry Tysin murdered Lori-Ann. All the evidence points to it."

Stark raised an eyebrow. "Then you don't know about Frumpkin's confession?"

Boxer looked perplexed.

"It's been on the tube all week. All the stations carried the video. It was taped and sent to the networks anonymously."

"Figures."

"Frumpkin sat there and told how he let himself into Lori-Ann's flat and waited for her to come home. Then he surprised her and slit her throat before she knew what happened."

Boxer was shaking his head violently. "That's inconsistent with the evidence. Lori-Ann was beaten severely, then slashed as she tried to ward off her attacker. It's all in the coroner's report. I know, because I was accused of doing it. That's what Detective Murphy tried to pin on me."

Now it was Stark's turn to look surprised.

"I think Frumpkin was aware that he was going to die, even if he confessed to killing her. Knowing the kinds of torture that Tysin is capable of, he probably spared himself some agony by appearing to take the rap. But his confession doesn't add up to the facts in the case." Boxer was now halfway through his second drink. "I think I'll give Murphy a call in the morning."

"Oh, speaking of calls, I almost forgot something real important . . . this came in for you while you were in Europe." He handed Boxer an envelope embossed with the Presidential seal.

Boxer studied it, turning it over in his hands.

"Well, aren't you going to open it? It's from the president."

"I know," Boxer said. "Have you ever felt that you were holding your destiny in your hands? Literally?"

Stark smiled and handed over a small penknife to use as a letter opener.

"It's dated last week. Whatever it is, I hope it could wait this long." Boxer opened the envelope and slipped out the one-page letter enclosed. "President Spooner says that he officially turned down my resignation request. That's a laugh on Chi-Chi Mason, the stuffed shirt. He goes on to say that his close friend, Senator Lowell Burke, head of the senate armed services committee, and Admiral Rodgers, commander of the seventh fleet, have requested that I join them and the secretary of state at a summit meeting in Moscow. They're going to try to resolve the problem of the Soviet nuclear plant and submarine bastion in the Arctic." He looked up from the letter. "They want me along as an expert. Well, with good people like Burke and Rodgers there, this thing may turn out all right. I guess I owe it to them to give it a try, though I'll admit, I never think of myself as much of a diplomat."

Admiral Stark smiled. "Maybe that's why they chose you to go along with them. They probably have all the yes-men they'll ever need. What they need is a fighter, a man with balls to call bullshit what it really is."

That made Boxer chuckle. "Well, if you put it like that. . . ."

Admiral Boris Popov stood at the new floating dock, watching the first group of convicts being herded off a troop carrier into this frigid Arctic wasteland. He wondered how many realized they would die here, giving their lives to man the reactor plant, and build a new colony to support it, much the way the Brits populated Australia a hundred and fifty years ago. He let out a frosty breath and rubbed his hands

77

together for warmth.

Popov turned to the younger man beside him. "Well, Sergei, what do you think?"

Captain Sergei Shevchenko, SUBFLT commander of the North Land bastion, eyed the newcomers and shook his head sadly. "I trust they'll have to do, comrade . . . till the next bunch gets here. Do you suppose they'll send some women along?"

Popov stroked his huge white mustache and smiled. "That is part of my master plan, to make North Land a self-sufficient facility. We shall build our base from here, comrade, and our influence will spread throughout the Rodina. We will teach them to play us for fools. They sent us up here in exile—an honorable command, Boris, they said. Hah. I should have been given command of the Northern Fleet, next in line for Gorshkov's job, but the minister of defense had political allies to satisfy, so they gave it to that ninny Smirnov instead."

He clapped his subordinate on the shoulder. "We shall show them the old dog has some new tricks, eh?"

Shevchenko had been counting the prisoners leaving the black and gray ship. Life would be harsh here for those men, who were even being forced to unload supplies and carry them to the command post before they were marched to their quarters. He wondered if they ought to ease up on them somewhat. If a man reaches his breaking point, there's no telling what he might do. And if a hundred men such as this began to feel that death would be preferable to the way they were being treated . . . . He didn't want to think about it. One thing for certain—the waters of North Land would run blood red.

"Sergei?"

"Huh?"

"I said, 'We shall teach them to pass us over for promotion,' eh?"

Shevchenko nodded. There was no use getting on Popov's

78

bad side, was there? The way he saw things, either way, his current command would be his springboard to success. If old Boris has his way, I am second in command. A smile began to form on his lips. Good thing Popov can't read minds. Because if the old man fails, then he, Sergei Shevchenko, will take over as commander of all North Land. A win-win situation. He need only play the game carefully.

"What are you thinking, comrade? You seem deep in thought."

Shevchenko turned to face his superior. "I'm thinking how we have them by their short hairs, Admiral."

Popov broke out in a loud belly laugh. He made a testicle-crunching motion with his hand, and Sergei laughed along with him.

# Chapter 9

Air Force II, a stark white Boeing 727 with the presidential
seal emblazoned on the fuselage, touched down at an off-
limits airfield in Moscow. As the American contingent
climbed down the ramp, they were immediately greeted by
an honor guard and whisked away in long black limousines.
Senator Burke rode in the lead car, along with the secretary
of state and the U.S. Ambassador, who had driven to the
airport to welcome them. Boxer joined Admiral Willis in the
second limo, followed by the support staff, bringing up the
rear. And of course, they were accompanied by the inevitable
KGB escort.

An icy rain slowed their progress, and the drive to the
Kremlin took more than twice as long as usual. That worked
in favor of the Russians, who hoped to pick up interesting
snippets of information while the Americans chatted on the
drive through the city.

Boxer opened a leather attaché case on his lap and
exposed a black and chrome electronic box to Admiral
Willis. With the twist of a few dials, Boxer had the "bug-
detector" working. Moving the device through a 360-degree
azimuth, he pointed out to Willis several hidden receivers
masked by clicking devices and flashing lights on the
instrument. Willis nodded, and they limited their conversa-

tion to comments about the dismal weather they were experiencing.

The Soviets prepared a magnificent luncheon for the U.S. delegation. While they munched on such delicacies as blini, caviar, and smoked fish, each side toasted the other with the ever-present, free-flowing vodka. Then it was off to the meeting rooms. The question of the nuclear plant and submarine bastion was immediately brought up without preamble by the secretary of state, J. Waldon Bushnell.

"Gentlemen, I wish to convey to you the feelings of my president regarding your building a reactor in so environmentally sensitive an area. If there were ever a nuclear accident, God forbid, it could alter the coastlines of every country in the northern hemisphere, and that includes your own.

"Then, there is the atomic fallout factor," Bushnell continued. "And I must point out building the reactor is in direct violation of our mutual Murmansk agreement."

With a nudge from Defense Minister Charkov, the minister of the interior, Vladimir Nemsky, cleared his throat and made his appeal. "What right has your president to deny us the use of our own land, comrades? We are determined to open our northern frontier, to colonize it and bring in the most viable source of energy. Besides," he sipped from a glass of ice water, "your fears about a nuclear accident are unjustified. We already operate twenty-two such facilities throughout our country."

The U.S. ambassador, Lyndon Douglass, interjected, "You and your colleagues have very short memories, Minister Nemsky. Has it been so long that you've forgotten the Chernobyl disaster? Hell, that fallout cloud covered most of northern Europe. Some of that mess even wound up over parts of the U.S. And that North Land facility of yours is four times as large as Chernobyl."

"That is incorrect, comrade." This time it was Foreign Minister Leonid Grumpke who took the floor. A portly man in his sixties, Grumpke had his thinning hair slicked straight back on his head, and he wore thick glasses. "We deny that the nuclear plant in the Arctic is even as large as Chernobyl. Your intelligence people must be lying to you. And besides, today's technology is vastly improved over the primitive designs of the Chernobyl era."

Ambassador Douglass nudged Admiral Willis, who removed a large manila envelope from his briefcase. The envelope had an inch-wide red border, signifying a top-secret document. The Russians strained to see the contents.

"Let me save you the trouble, gentlemen," Douglass said. He opened the envelope and shuffled out a stack of 8 × 10 glossies. "Perhaps you'd like to see some satellite photos of your North Land facility, comrades. Apparently your own people don't keep you informed."

Defense Minister Charkov greedily spread the photographs in front of him. This did not please him. How did they get such good pictures? he wondered. They are even superior to our own. "This proves nothing," he grunted.

Grumpke moved in closer and looked over the incriminating evidence. The proof was indisputable, and he knew it. He now had the task of shoring up his side's point of view. "The Soviet Union has sovereign rights over the North Land group. It is our right to administer it in any way we deem necessary. What you are asking is equivalent to our asking you to dismantle the Alaskan pipeline for fear of polluting the environmentally fragile Beaufort and Chukchi seas." He almost sneered at Ambassador Douglass. Glancing at his colleagues, he was bolstered by their nods of approval. "I fear that you are unwarranted in your request for closing down our new facility. It is simply a matter of our own internal affairs, and it doesn't concern you at all." His fist came down hard on the table for emphasis.

Senator Lowell Burke had taken about all of this crap that he could handle. He rose to his feet. "That's bull, Leonid. Let me make our position perfectly clear to you and your comrades here."

Grumpke was taken aback by Burke's outburst.

Burke said, "Read my lips, gentlemen. Take down your damn nuclear plant and find somewhere else for your submarine base, and do it soon, or you can forget about any more wheat deals with us and Canada. And that goes for the delivery you're expecting from us next month. Got that? No more wheat. You'll be trading the health, or the lives, of a lot of little Russian babies for your hard-nosed approach to *Glasnost*."

While they bickered back and forth, Boxer kept to himself, as he wasn't called upon by his superiors. But he couldn't help notice that one of the Russian interpreters, a tall, full-figured blonde in her late twenties, thirty at the most, directed most of her remarks toward him. And she continued to make eye contact with him as she waited her turn to speak.

After the meeting broke up, with plans to try again the next day, the Americans were free to tour the nonsensitive areas of the Kremlin. To Boxer's surprise and gratification, the blonde interpreter walked over to him. He smiled at the young woman, who was dressed conservatively in a blue serge suit that was tailored to show off her great figure.

She returned his smile and held out her hand. "Hello. I'm Luba. I would be pleased to show you around, if you'd like. I was trained as a tourist guide before I became an interpreter. And I have permission."

"How can I turn down an offer like that?" he replied. "I'd be delighted." He returned her firm handshake. "I'm Admiral Boxer, Admiral Willis's aide."

"Let us begin in the Gold Room down the hall. Some of the paintings are world famous. They were expropriated from the Nazis after the war."

They entered a magnificent hall with a cathedral ceiling adorned with ornate moldings and carvings. The walls were hung with masterpieces of the Dutch, French, and Flemish schools, some of them pieces commonly thought destroyed during the war. "The Nazis stole them for their own personal use. Now we protect them for all mankind."

Boxer said, "Please spare me the party-line rhetoric. They rightfully belong to the original owners."

Luba turned to look at him. "You do not approve? Some of these were from private collections. The previous owners are now dead. The art treasures live on."

"Sure, at least they're safe here in the Kremlin. Is that what they teach you at the Intourist training centers?"

"Please, Jack . . . let's not bicker. This is supposed to be a pleasant interlude for you. I don't want to spoil it."

Boxer took her arm and turned her to face him directly. "Wait a minute. How did you know my first name? I didn't give it to you."

"I . . . I was briefed on all the participants before your arrival."

"No way." Boxer was shaking his head. "I was a last-minute addition. You couldn't have known."

Luba's face turned red. "Please, keep your voice down. Don't call attention to us." Her eyes darted furtively around the room. They were the only ones present. "We have a mutual friend. I can't say any more now."

Boxer was puzzled. "Can we go for a walk outside?"

"It's cold."

"Your answers will warm me up," he smiled.

"Okay with me. I'm used to the cold. Let me get our coats."

They walked downstairs and outside the Kremlin walls, until they reached the Lenin Mausoleum in Red Square. Standing before the famous landmark, Luba said, "I was a friend of Comrade Admiral Borodine."

"Igor? You . . . ? You were . . ."

"Lovers? That is none of your business. We were dear friends. He spoke often about you."

"I'll bet."

"Don't underrate yourself. Comrade Igor told me about the American submarine commander who was his greatest nemesis, the only man who could ever best him at his game." Her face took on a look of admiration. "He said that you would kill him in an instant if your paths crossed in combat, but . . . that you have risked your life several times to save his, and those of his men."

Boxer began to blush.

"For that, I . . . we both want to thank you." She leaned forward and kissed him lightly on the lips. "I'm sorry."

Boxer studied her classic Scandinavian features. A Viking princess, he mused. More than likely, she hails from the Kola Peninsula, adjacent to Finland and Norway. "Don't be sorry. That was very nice. It's easy to see why Comrade Igor was fond of you." He chuckled. "We have similar tastes in women."

Now it was her turn to blush. "Oh, do you, now?"

They stood there looking at each other for a moment. "It's getting late. Would you like to come to my flat for a drink, or some tea?"

"Tea would be nice, thanks. Besides, if we stand here like this any longer, old Lenin might just turn over in his grave."

"That's not to joke about," she admonished him. "Come, we have a ten-block walk. It will be more pleasant while it is still daylight, now that the rain has ended."

"Can't we take a cab? Taxi?"

She put her arm through his. "It's better if we walk. I can show you some sights."

Boxer figured she had her reasons for turning down a ride. He shrugged and followed her lead.

She explained, "The main thoroughfares are laid out in concentric rings, with the Kremlin in the center. The streets are like the spokes of a wheel."

They passed an ornate church topped with many bulbous gilt domes. "That is St. Basil's Cathedral," she said. "It is a museum now." She pointed across the street. "I live down that way, past the concert hall, close to the river. It's a very good apartment for a single working girl."

Twenty minutes later, they were climbing the stairs to the second floor of a fairly modern concrete apartment building in what seemed to be a decent neighborhood. Luba unlocked her door and stood aside for Boxer to let them in. "Let me take your coat. I'll turn up the heat, and we'll be warm in no time."

She disappeared into a back room with his coat and returned wearing only a white silky blouse, now opened a bit to reveal the swell of her cleavage, and the blue skirt. She had left her jacket and black pumps inside. "Why don't you make yourself comfortable, Jack? May I call you that?"

"Why not?" He removed his navy blue uniform jacket and folded it neatly over a kitchen chair. He loosened his tie and opened his top shirt button.

"Have a seat inside while I put up tea. I'll only be a minute."

Boxer stepped into the somewhat small living room adjacent to the eat-in kitchen. It was Spartan by American middle-class suburban standards, but neat and immaculately clean. There was an upholstered sofa in a floral print and two occasional chairs, a coffee table over an imitation Persian rug, and on the wall a print of one of the paintings he had seen earlier at the Kremlin. He figured that a closed door led to a single bedroom, where she had hung their coats.

"Well, how do you like my place? I was really very lucky to get it."

"Very nice," he said, trying to voice more enthusiasm than he felt. He wondered what she'd had to do to procure her prized apartment.

His thoughts were broken by the whistling of a teapot. In a moment, Luba came into the living room bearing a tray with a metal teapot and two tea glasses set in silver holders. He'd seen Borodine purchase a set like that for his first wife, Galena, many years ago in DC, when Igor was an aide to the

Soviet ambassador. He smiled. It seemed that Borodine and Luba were more than just friends.

When she bent to pour the tea, he couldn't help noticing the full lushness of her breasts, which seemed to strain against the thin fabric of her blouse, barely constrained by her bra. He admired her fine body, which she seemed bent on flaunting to him.

She sat beside him and asked, "Would you like milk and sugar?"

"This will be just fine," he said, raising his glass. "I'm a purist."

She stirred a spoonful of sugar into hers and sipped it. "Ah, perfect. My grandfather used to place a sugar cube in his mouth while drinking his tea. My mother taught my sister and me that it was old-fashioned, so we don't do that anymore."

Boxer grinned. "My uncle did the same thing. See, we have something in common already."

"Two things we share. That, and our friendship with Igor Borodine. That's a good step toward East–West relations, wouldn't you say?"

"And your pleasant company this afternoon. I can see why Igor befriended you."

Luba took a sip of her tea and put the glass down on the coffee table. "Igor and I were lovers. You were quite correct when you guessed that." She leaned closer to him. "How did you know?"

He put down his glass. "As I said, we both admire the same things in a woman. He'd have to be blind for you not to appeal to him. And you're very warm and friendly in a land as cold and bleak as this. I'd be surprised if he didn't fall in love with you."

Luba place her hands on his. "Let me be frank. I also see in you the qualities that I liked in Igor. That is why I was attracted to you so soon. I . . . asked you to my flat hoping that you . . . that we could . . ."

Boxer lifted her chin with his fingertips and leaned forward to meet her lips with his. They kissed gently, tenderly, then came together with a passion that had been building in both of them. When they came apart, he touched her cheek, and with a tear in her eye, she said, "I'd like you to make love to me."

He took her hands and they stood up. "Well, I guess that's what détente is all about." He followed her into the bedroom and closed the door behind them.

Luba turned on a small table lamp and began to undress. While Boxer removed his own clothes, his eyes never left Luba. He watched her unbutton her blouse and undo her skirt, which she let drop to the floor. When she unhooked her bra, her magnificent breasts came free, seeming to have a life of their own. She hooked her thumbs into the top of her panties and provocatively slid them down inch by inch. She kicked them aside and did a little pirouette. "You like?"

"Very much."

He was still in his skivvies. She giggled and pointed to his underpants. "You'd better take those off. They look like they're ready to burst apart."

Boxer removed his shorts and went to her. They embraced and kissed again, feeling the warmth building within them. He lifted Luba and carried her to the bed, then climbed in next to her. He licked her tan, almost pink nipples, teasing them with his teeth and tongue until they became rigid.

"That feels good, Jack." She was wiggling beneath him, her hand groping, finally finding what she was after. "I want to do something to make you feel good, too."

She stroked his manhood until he was fully erect. Then she turned around and took him into her mouth. Boxer felt tinges of pleasure radiating from his groin. His hands played on her body, over the silky soft skin of her legs and thighs, caressing the swell of her bottom and delving into her secret places with his fingers.

She moaned and positioned her love mound, with its silky

blond thatch, closer to his face. Boxer didn't need an invitation.

His face dived between her thighs, his knowing tongue titillating her clit and her labia. She writhed with pleasure. They went on like that for several long minutes, caught up in each other, enjoying the other's ministrations, each responding in kind. Boxer was driven to the point of explosion and it was an exquisite pleasure for him to constrain himself.

For Luba, it was a period of multiple orgasms, each one more intense than the previous. When she could stand it no longer, she said to him, "I want you inside me now, Jack." Then she spread her thighs to invite him in. As he moved in over her, she reached down and took his turgid member in her hand, helping to guide his shaft into her. "Ahhh." She leaned her head back on the pillow and wrapped her legs around his waist.

Soon she was pushing up to meet his ever-deepening and quickening thrusts. She began to moan. Her head thrust from side to side, her breathing became harder, more forceful. Twice she caught her breath as orgasms rippled through her. "Now," she pleaded. "I want you to come in me now."

Boxer was caught up in his own pleasure, while holding back to prolong Luba's enjoyment as well. Now, with a final mighty thrust, he arched his back and drove deeply into her at the same time she pulled up to meet him. He felt the intense heat as her vaginal muscles pulsed along his shaft, alternately tightening and relaxing, squeezing the very essence from him. When he exploded, he sensed that she had her final orgasm at that precise moment, timing it to his. Pleasure given, pleasure received. They collapsed in each other's arms, completely spent.

They lay there together for an hour, gently stroking each other, exchanging small talk and endearments. Finally they showered in what to Boxer was a rather primitive shower, which consisted of a showerhead suspended overhead by a tubular ring attached to the wall.

"I must get back to the others," he told her. He was dressed again, and anxious not to be missed by his superiors in the delegation.

"I know. Perhaps tomorrow I can give you a better tour of the city, after our meeting."

"Are you sure your accompanying me won't be frowned upon by the authorities?"

She smiled and shook her head. "You Americans . . . you all think we live in a police state, without any personal freedoms. It's not like that here at all."

Boxer didn't want to argue with her. Every defector, even Igor Borodine, had told a different story, much to the contrary. He merely said, "I'd better go. Thank you for the tea."

His smile told her the thanks were meant for much more. She leaned close to him and turned her face up to kiss him. When he walked out the door and down the stairs, Luba primped her hair and sat down on the sofa to reflect on what she'd accomplished today. All in all, not bad. She was certain that KGB Deputy Director Doneck would be very proud of her, snaring the famous Admiral Jack Boxer on the first try. Yes, she had done very well indeed.

# Chapter 10

The American delegation filed into the conference room to begin their second and last day of negotiations. Both sides realized that if a compromise wasn't pending, they could be at the brink of a major war. And this time, everyone realized, there would be no real winners. Both countries would lose, leaving the door open for a third power to attain world hegemony by default.

After the formalities were dispensed with, it was Secretary of State J. W. Bushnell who got things off and rolling. "Gentlemen," he opened, "let me be frank and lay all my cards on the table. It is in the best interests of my government to have your nuclearized submarine base closed down. I've already told you of the president's fears of a nuclear accident in the Arctic, and his determination to end, at all costs, a ballistic missile enclave located so strategically near our borders.

"And on the other hand," he continued, "we recognize your country's need for long-term, low-priced grain sales to feed your people. What I'm proposing, then, is a compromise, a trade-off of wheat for peace. Think about that for a moment, gentlemen. Consider the consequences you face, either way."

Soviet Foreign Minister Grumpke knew the options very

well. He would try to get the best deal he could, and give up nothing. "The cost of our nuclear plants in North Land exceeds the equivalent of several billion American dollars. To dismantle such a project could bankrupt our economy, and it is not negotiable."

Ambassador Douglass cleared his throat and interjected, "We'd be willing to agree to a scaled-down power plant used for peaceful purposes, Minister Grumpke. But the submarine bastion has got to go."

Yuri Charkov, the defense minister, stood up and shouted, "Nyet. We are excercising our rights to defend our nation as we see best. And that includes our fortress in the north. We need a means of countering your Star Wars weaponry."

Luba directed the tirade at the American ambassador and the secretary of state. Up until then, she had been looking in Boxer's direction, her face a pleasant smile for his benefit, no matter what the subject. She felt she'd won him over to her side.

Senator Burke countered with, "No way that submarine bastion of yours stays, Charkov. How can you equate that to Star Wars Initiative? Star Wars is purely defensive. It destroys ICBMs fired at us. Your sub base is a threat to the entire northern hemisphere, and we won't have it."

Charkov began slamming his fist on the conference table.

Lowell Burke shook his head and said, "Your shenanigans won't do you any good here, Yuri. My government is adamant."

For the first time, Interior Minister Nemsky broke forces with Defense. He knew that he himself would have to bear the brunt of the Politburo's ire if the grain deal fell through. "Just suppose we agree to the nonmilitary use of North Land. What assurance would you give us regarding grain sales?"

Charkov glared at his counterpart in Interior, but Nemsky would not meet his eyes, instead looking straight ahead at Senator Burke, who seemed the most militant of the Americans.

Burke smiled slightly. "We're talking about yearly guaranteed sales of six million metric tons each of wheat, corn, and soybeans, with most-favorable-nation conditions for the next ten years. And there's more available if you should need it. In return, we want the dismantling of your sub base, with regularly scheduled inspections. That's where Admiral Boxer, here, comes in. He'd be in charge there." He turned to Boxer. "Jack, why don't you brief the gentlemen here on that?"

Boxer rose and stood at attention in his best military bearing. He was a little surprised, although prepared for his new role. "We would propose an initial inspection, preferably before we leave for home, and again after three-, six- and twelve-month intervals. At that time we'd expect all traces of a military installation to be removed, and a scaling down of half your nuclear capacity." He noted the anger and hostility in Luba's voice as she translated his demands.

The Secretary of State rose from his comfortable seat. "So there you have it, gentlemen. I hope you'll consider our offer and accept it as a fair one. It allows us all to advance your policy of *Glasnost,* and live in peace."

Grumpke said, "We'll consider your offer, comrades, and if you'll be our guests for another day, you'll have your answer late tomorrow, after the full Politburo has a chance to review and vote on it."

Vladimir Nemsky, the minister of the interior added, "For your pleasure, we'd like you to be our guests at a special performance of the Bolshoi ballet this evening. I'm sure you'll find it most interesting and enjoyable."

Ambassador Douglass extended a hand of friendship to Nemsky. "Thank you, gentlemen. On behalf of the American delegation, I'd like to accept your hospitality."

Boxer looked across the table at Luba, wondering if she'd agree to accompany him to the ballet. Despite her outward resentment of his remarks earlier, somehow he was sure she'd find a way.

After flying through total darkness for several hours, one of Nemsky's aides pointed out a glow on the horizon to Boxer and Admiral Rodgers. "That is Ostrov Komsomolets. You can see how the nuclear plant provides energy to light up the sky during the winter months. Normally, the sun doesn't set at all up here during the summer, and it never rises above the horizon during the winter. Now, here on North Land, we have finally changed all that."

Boxer and Rodgers were openly impressed. The Soviets had the capacity to provide light and warmth to the area twelve months a year. Inhabitants could live and work in sub-Arctic conditions. A fishing industry could be developed, and some game and farming might be introduced. Not a bad way to harness the atom . . . not bad at all.

The Soviet military transport set down on a cleared ice field on the northwest shore of the island. Everyone climbed into waiting snow vans and were towed the mile or so to the headquarters building, a long, one-story reinforced concrete structure facing the waterfront, just south of the power plant. Boxer had noticed during the landing that adjacent to the land mass was an opening in the ice cap several square miles wide.

"That's due to the circulation of the seawater by the plant," Boxer was told. "The temperature of the effluent is ninety to ninety-five degrees Celsius along the shoreline, and dissipates farther out. This gives us an ice-free area of about twenty-two square miles."

Once inside the headquarters building, Boxer and Rodgers, as well as the Russian contingent that accompanied them, were able to remove the massive red parkas that were needed to ward off the extreme cold. Boxer thought the interior felt comfortable, and indeed, it was set for seventy-six degrees. An escort ushered them to Admiral Popov's suite.

Interior Minister Nemsky made the introductions, keeping the real cause of the meeting from the military heads of the North Land project, for the time being. "Comrades, may I present Admiral Rodgers and Admiral Boxer of the American Navy. They are in the Soviet Union as part of the mutual military exchange program our general secretary has championed. All for the betterment of *Glasnost* and *Perestroika.*"

Nemsky turned to the Americans. "This is Comrade Admiral Boris Popov, who has overall command of the North Land Fleet, and his chief of staff for submarine affairs, Captain Sergei Shevchenko."

The four officers saluted, and Popov waved them all into their seats. He pressed a switch and gave an order into his intercom. In a minute, two stewards carried in trays laden with tableware and food. They set them down on Popov's long desk and left the room. Popov looked over the spread and, satisfied, smacked his lips. "Good. And let us not forget the vodka, eh?"

They snacked on the ever-present caviar and kippered herring and salmon, and toasted each other with an incredibly smooth vodka. It was the finest Boxer had ever tasted, and he complimented Popov on it.

"Yes, Admiral Boxer . . . we receive the finest of everything. The best food, the best vodka, anything we want, in fact. Women, television, movies. This is all in exchange for our working under such harsh conditions." He clapped Shevchenko on the shoulder. "I am even assigned the finest submarine commander in the entire fleet, now that Comrade Borodine is no longer with us, eh, Sergei?"

Shevchenko nodded, apparently taking his boss seriously. "Yes. I have learned everything the master had to offer, and now no one ranks above me. Sorry if I'm not humble, comrades. I fought long and hard for this moment. And if . . . when I am finished with my tour of duty up here, I am in line for Borodine's old job. I shall . . ."

"That is quite enough for now, Sergei," Popov cut him off. "Have some more vodka. Then we shall give the interior minister and his guests a tour of the facilities." He refilled everyone's glasses. Come, comrades, let us put more antifreeze in our blood before the visit to the power plant. Drink up." He raised his glass. Outwardly, he was the perfect host; inwardly, he was seething. How dare the fools on the Politburo bring the enemy up here to his kingdom? Those responsible for this reprehensible act would be made to pay. He downed his drink. Yes, they would all have to pay.


"Impenetrable," Boxer declared, once he was alone again with Rodgers on the flight back to the States.

"I agree, Jack. Had we not broken their will by holding the grain deal over their heads, they'd have created a monster that no force on this earth could unseat."

Boxer nodded. "It was at least as formidable as the Soviet bastion in the White Sea, behind the Kola Peninsula, judging from recent satellite photos, and from what I've learned firsthand during a mission that almost failed, I'll be glad to see it dismantled when I return in the spring."

A cute stewardess came by to remind both men to buckle their seat belts, and for Rodgers to put out his cigarette. They were arriving at Dulles International in five minutes.

"Will you be staying in DC for long, Jack? How about dinner tonight? I know some great restaurants." Rodgers patted the slight bulge that age and fine dining had added to his otherwise trim figure.

"Thank you, but I was due back in Hawaii yesterday. They've patched up the *Manta*, and it's ready for sea trials."

They shook hands and separated at the terminal. There was nothing to keep Boxer in the nation's capital any longer. With Chuck at Annapolis, Stark back on Oahu, and Francine . . . Boxer headed for the American Airlines desk and booked a one-hop to Honolulu, with a stopover in LA. After what seemed like an entire day in the air, Boxer reported in with Admiral Willis on Pearl Harbor.

"Welcome back, Jack. The CNO wants you to move your operation to Alaska, to train your strike force with the Snow Troopers. Some of the new men could use the experience of fighting in a frigid climate. And it will place you closer to North Land in time for your reinspection visit."

Boxer saluted. "Well, I'll be sorry to leave here, Admiral. It's been a good tour of duty for me and my men. But the chief has a good point. Just in case the Russkies try to play hardball, we'll be more prepared to handle the trouble." Boxer lowered his voice a bit. "Frankly, sir, I'm a bit worried that if we ever *did* have to fight it out with them, we'd never get close enough to do any good before they'd intercept us."

"Well, hopefully," Willis said, adding his cigarette butt to the ever-mounting pile in his ashtray, "we won't have to put it to the test. I understand you came back from Moscow with the deal you were hoping for."

Boxer nodded. "We traded wheat for peace, as Senator Burke put it to the Russkies. The general secretary agreed to close the submarine base and cut back on their power plant. They really don't need so much power if they're not supporting the subs."

Willis agreed. "I understand our farmers make out well, also. They get a guaranteed buyer for their crops for the next ten years. That's something they can take to the bank."

Willis fidgeted with another cigarette for himself, and then offered the pack to Boxer. "Smoke?"

"I'll stick with my pipe, if you don't mind." When he had the bowl of his meerschaum-lined briar filled and tapped down, he accepted a light from Admiral Willis. The pipe, a Christmas present from his son, John, several years back, acted like a pacifier to Boxer. It reminded him of all the good things that a family meant to him. It also carried a little sadness, for with his folks and Francine gone, and his ex-wife Gwen keeping herself and John as distant from him as possible, he realized he'd probably never get to enjoy the comforts of home that most men had. Well, he was a submariner by choice, and that meant he had to make certain decisions. . . .

"Jack, why don't you take a week of R&R in Hawaii before shoving off? You've got it coming to you."

Boxer blew a puff of smoke toward the ceilng and smiled. "Thank you, Admiral. I'll do the same for my men before we shove off."

"Good idea. Rolly and his men are over on Maui, cross-training with the Marine garrison stationed there."

Boxer borrowed a jeep and driver and got dropped off at the Kaneohe Marine Corps Air Station, where he hitched a ride on a flight to Maui. At Marine hadquarters, Boxer asked the whereabouts of Major Roland Jones and his rangers. A corporal pointed out an isolated concrete-block building in a remote corner of the base.

Boxer found the Rangers' complex fenced in with barbed wire and patrolled by armed guards with K-9 companions. Inside the main building, he was immediately challenged by an MP. "Tell Major Jones that Admiral Boxer is here."

The guard gave a precise salute, but did not give ground. "He's out in the field." He clicked on a walkie-talkie and spoke rapidly into it. Then his face reddened, he said, "Yes sir" several time and put the radio down on the desk. Snapping to rigid attention, the MP said, "I apologize for the inconvenience, Admiral Boxer. Major Jones said for me to escort you directly to the training grounds, if you wish, sir. Otherwise, he'll meet you here."

"No need to apologize, son. You were doing your job. Now if you'll just point out the major's whereabouts, I'll be out of your way."

Boxer found Rolly on a low wooden platform at the head of a group of about thirty men who were doing push-ups.

Facing each column of ten commandos was a squad leader. Mean Gene, Turk, and Long John Silverman were shouting encouragement to their charges, while Rolly kept count. As Boxer approached he could hear, "One ten, one eleven, one twelve . . . . Come on now, girls, you can do it. Keep pumping."

Some of the men noticed an admiral in dress blues watching their progress and started to rise. Rolly began to shout, "What the hell's the matter with you, Powers? And you two? I didn't order you to stop. What's the matter, the mud too messy for you? Okay, then, we'll do two hundred."

Slowly, more of the men quit their exercises and pulled themselves upright. Rolly turned to see what they were staring at, only to see Boxer standing there grinning at him. "Ten-*hut,*" he ordered, and saluted his boss.

The Rangers stood there, mud dripping from their fatigues, T-shirts, and faces, saluting at attention. Every one of them looked rugged enough to play pro football, and tough enough to lick his weight in grizzly bears. Boxer said, "At ease, men."

The men relaxed just slightly. Their major's idea of "at ease" was a lot more rigid than the rest of the service.

"Sorry to interrupt your training, Major. I just came to let you know we shove off in one week for Alaska."

"Yes, sir," Rolly said. "I'll try to have these pussies ready by then. And we've got a squad of SEALs joining up with us tomorrow. That'll bring us up to platoon strength by the time we push off."

The Rangers looked as combat ready as any group Boxer had seen, but he deferred to Major Jones's decision to push his men even harder. "I'm taking a few days R&R before we leave. Maybe you'd care to join me for drinks tonight?"

Rolly scratched his head. "Yes, sir. I'd like that."

Boxer smiled. "Bring along some of your men, if you'd like."

"It will be a pleasure." Then he lowered his voice. "Now, if you'll excuse me, I've got to try to make men out of these girl scouts."

Boxer saluted and turned away. "See you tonight, then."

Jones watched him retreat for a minute. Then he turned back to his commandos. "All this standin' around gonna make you soft. Let's start from the beginning. Everybody, push-ups. One . . . two . . . c'mon, get your faces in the mud. . . . Three . . . ."

# Chapter 11

Boxer's party arrived by jeep at Big Alice's, a tavern off the main highway leading out of Lahaina, on the westernmost shore of the island. Maui's hundred-year-old whaling town was a haven for tourists and sun-worshipers, and also for the many drug dealers and users who liked it for its easy, laid-back hippie subculture. Big Alice's saw its share of both worlds.

Mean Gene pulled onto the gravel parking strip, and he, Boxer, Turk, and Rolly climbed out. They noticed a dozen flashy motorcycles lined up at the edge of the lot, mostly Harleys, Suzukis, and Kawasakis, top-of-the-line muscle bikes. The men filed past the noisy crowd of bikers and other locals and found a table near the bar amongst the tourist trade. Above the bar, a giant TV screen was showing the Celts beat the pants off the Lakers.

At precisely nine P.M., a husky, thirtyish woman wearing a sweatshirt bearing the tavern's logo walked to the television and switched on a talk show. "Hey, c'mon, Alice, we were watching the game."

"Aw, shut your face. I'm watchin' Annie Adams."

A biker said, "You can watch that broad all week long. Put back the game."

Big Alice lumbered over to the biker and rested her fists on

103

her ample hips. "You don't like it, get the hell out of here and drink somewheres else. It's nine o'clock, and I'm watchin' the Annie Adams Show." She turned her head toward a three-hundred-pound hulk seated at the far end of the bar. "Ain't that right, Ziggy?"

The huge man got up and made a move toward the offending biker. Boxer could make out that Ziggy was more muscle than fat, and from his appearance, he was one of them, only bigger and badder—the ultimate biker, and obviously Alice's enforcer. Ziggy said, "You got trouble hearing, asshole?"

The complainer sat down and looked into his mug of beer. The big man looked at the others. "Any more complaints?"

No one said anything.

Ziggy straightened his leather vest over his black T-shirt with the familiar Harley-Davidson winged emblem, and returned to his seat.

After several commercials, a vivacious woman in a red dress appeared on screen. She exhorted her all female crowd, "Hi, ladies."

"Hi, Annie," they shouted in unison.

"Last night," she said to her audience, "we had on women who love women."

A cheer rose from the ranks of her supporters.

"Tonight . . . we go one step better. Women who love women . . . who used to love men."

More cheers.

"Our guest this evening is famous author Talia Witherby, and her significant other, and collaborator on their latest novel, *Navy Wife*, Gwen Boxer."

Someone yelled, "C'mon, Alice, turn that crap off."

"Shut your hole before I shut it for ya."

Amid the shouting, Boxer sat there staring at the screen, too stunned to react. The three Rangers looked at each other, embarrassed for him, not wanting to meet his gaze.

The camera closed in on Annie's two guests, a study in

opposites: Gwen, beautiful, tall, and blond, with classic good looks, and the short, dark-haired author with the well-muscled body of a gymnast. Gwen Boxer wore a short royal blue dress that wrapped across her bodice to reveal the swellings of her ample cleavage. Talia wore a gray jumpsuit.

"Is it true, Mrs. Boxer, that you were once married to the captain of a submarine?"

Gwen smiled at her host and said, "Well, actually, Jack is an admiral now."

"Big, macho guy?" Annie prodded, flexing her biceps for the audience.

"He liked to think of himself as macho, yes. Sometimes it can be a bit much. The strong, silent type who keeps everything bottled up inside, never sharing, never caring, afraid to show his emotions."

"That's not true," Boxer muttered to himself.

"And Talia, dear, is it true that you met Gwen while she was a student in your writing class?"

Witherby patted Gwen's hand and looked at her admiringly. "Yes. Gwen was taking a course I teach at a local university. It was love at first sight, at least on my part."

Annie smiled and made the naughty-naughty sign with her fingers, and said to Talia, "Do go on, dear. Give us all the goodies."

Talia ran her hand through her short hair and looked at Gwen, then back to the audience. "Well, it started out innocently enough. I just loved her story, but it needed a professional touch. So . . . I suggested we work on it together, as collaborators, try to get it published and split the fee. She agreed, and, well . . . how long could I work with this luscious creature without falling in love? The rest is history."

As Annie's audience cheered, one of the bikers made a smooching sound and yelled, "Oooh, lez be friends."

"Yeah, I wouldn't mind boffing that big blond bitch."

Someone else shouted, "Yeah, if you could get the other

one's face out of there long enough."

The whole motorcycle gang thought that was funny and laughed and carried on.

Rolly could see that Boxer was on the verge of creating mayhem and shouted over at them, "Hey, knock it off, will ya?"

"Who said that?" someone asked.

A biker pointed in their direction with his beer mug. "That shiny-head nigger over there. Let's teach him a lesson."

"Aw, sit down and drink your beer," one of his friends told him.

"My hero," Gwen was saying, "fictional, of course, goes off to sea to play his silly war games and save the world, while his wife sits alone at home for months on end. While hubby is away, she gets involved in a series of love affairs, the man at the bank, the mailman, you know . . . very sexually unsatisfying."

"And along comes her old college roommate," Talia butted in, buffing her fingernails on her collar. *"Moi,"* she smiled. "And things begin to get *very* interesting."

The two women looked at each other and began to giggle.

"Hey, baby, how'd you like to get interested in this?" A biker was standing for all to see, his hand groping at his crotch.

"How 'bout this one?" a lanky biker with a sleeveless jacket asked.

Boxer had had enough. He rose from his chair and walked toward the two guys clutching their groins. Rolly and his two men were just a few steps behind. "That's enough from you two," Boxer said. He turned his head to Big Alice. "Ma'am, I'd appreciate if you'd turn this off."

Alice said, "What's botherin' you? You know those two goosie-goosie broads?"

"Maybe it's his ol' lady?" someone ventured.

"Hey," Alice said. "One of them queers your ol' lady? I hope not, handsome. You're too good lookin' to waste on those two lezzies."

"Give 'em some of this, see how much they like it." It was one of the two instigators who'd started the commotion.

"You tell 'em, Augie," the sleeveless one prodded.

The few tourist families present tried to find cover behind their tables. The cycle gang backed up Augie.

Boxer said, "I asked you to knock it off."

Augie stood with his legs a foot apart, one arm across his chest, the other hand in Boxer's face, provoking him. "Lookit, Boy Scout. This is our gin mill. If you don't like it here, take the nigger and ape-man and ratchet face and find yourself a milk bar someplace. Now get the hell out of here while we still let you."

Boxer looked at his men and shrugged, then took a step backward.

Augie smirked, and turned his head to show off to his boys. He turned back to face Boxer too late to stop the knee that was arching up into his groin. He doubled up, hands dropping to his battered testicles.

Boxer's uppercut stood Augie back up. A hard right cross to the jaw sent him staggering to the floor.

Rolly grabbed the sleeveless biker by the throat before he could react, and yanked him forward off his feet. A huge black fist smashed the punk's nose, and he crumpled.

The bikers rushed the four of them, enjoying the two-to-one odds in their favor. The first two found out how Mean Gene got his nickname, and Rolly and Boxer each tangled with one of the gang. That left Turk facing six bikers, pretty even odds for someone who'd been the All-Hawaii karate champ three years running.

Turk kicked heads, punched, spun around, and connected with overhead kicks. He shoved three bikers against a wall and moved in on them. Boxer watched Ziggy come to their aid with a baseball bat in his beefy paw. "Behind you," Boxer warned Turk.

Turk caught the bat on the downswing and wrenched it

107

from the big man's grasp. Boxer moved in and pounded Ziggy's face with a combination of punches, and finished him off with a fingertip jab to the Adam's apple, followed by a hard right to the solar plexus. Turk finished off his three opponents, leaving them bloodied and battered.

The two of them turned to find their counterparts. Rolly was slamming someone's face into the bar. Mean Gene was breaking a bar stool over a biker's head. Boxer and Turk took in the room. There were no more challengers. The bikers who could got out of their way. Ziggy sat there on the floor at the end of the bar, clutching his throat, gagging and coughing.

Big Alice looked around the room. The tourists were beginning to find their seats. Some hastily threw money on the table and left the place. Boxer and the Rangers stood there looking at each other, breathing hard, satisfied with their work. Alice drew four frosty mugs of beer and set them on the bar. "Drink up, boys. On the house. In ten years, I've never seen anything like this."

Boxer shrugged and passed the beers to his men. They clinked glasses and drank greedily from the frosty brew. "One more thing, Alice."

"Yeah? Anything you want, mister. Nobody's ever beaten Ziggy since he was a kid."

Boxer smiled and took another sip, then pointed at the TV. "Put the game back on, will you?"


Boris Popov looked out from the front entrance of his headquarters, scanning the horizon with high-powered binoculars, surveying his kingdom. He was pleased with himself. He was supreme commander of one of the three most powerful Soviet naval bases, and *de facto* commissar of North Land. He controlled a fleet of three Yankee-class SSBNs and one of the monstrous Typhoons, all capable of firing ballistic missiles four thousand miles. They were protected by a half dozen modern *Alfa* SSNs, the fastest subs afloat before the advent of the American *Shark*-class super subs, and their newer, Soviet counterparts. A pair of *Sierras*, capable of firing land-attack missiles 1600 nautical miles, rounded out his submarine fleet.

He also controlled a small fleet of surface support ships, spcialized radar- and sonar-equipped patrol crafts, and the nuclear powered icebreaker *Revolution*. And it was *Revolution* that he was searching for on the horizon. It was due home momentarily, escorting a delegation from Moscow on this final merchantman, bearing supplies and labor, until the spring thaw.

Sergei Shevchenko walked up the path to headquarters and greeted his superior. "How goes it, Comrade Admiral? You seem especially contented this morning." He sensed that something big was about to happen.

Popov spread out his arms magnanimously. "Why shouldn't I be? The time has come for Moscow to bestow upon me my just reward. They are coming to announce my promotion." He placed a hand on the younger officer's shoulder. "Don't worry, Sergei. I will put in a good word for you. You will see. They will offer you my current position when I assume my new command."

An aide came out of the building holding a document. "Excuse me, Comrade Admiral." He held the paper forward. "It's from the captain of the icebreaker."

Popov snatched the paper and shooed the radioman away as if he were a mere fly. He read the message, and his smiling face turned grim.

"What is it, Comrade?"

Popov held the paper at his side and stared out to sea. "The *Revolution's* captain wanted me to know that the Moscow delegation is traveling with a platoon of crack troops and a dozen KGB officers. There is hardly a need for them here."

Not a way to hand a man a promotion, Sergei realized, as

he was sure Popov did. "What do you want to do?"

Popov broke off his gaze and said, "Don't let them off the ship."

"What?"

"You heard me. Order the captain of the merchantman to weigh anchor in the channel, and send a small tender out to pick up only the delegation. No KGB. No Arctic Wolves. Keep the troops on board."

Shevchenko saluted. "Yes, Comrade Admiral."

"What is our own troop strength, Sergei?"

Sergei did a quick calculation. "One hundred men, Comrade. They alternate standing guard over the prisoners and protecting the facility."

"Inform our men. The KGB and the storm troopers are not to leave their vessel. Is that clear?"

"Perfectly. Do you think there is a problem, Comrade Admiral?"

Popov shrugged. "It's best to be prepared." He continued looking through his glasses. "Ah, there they are, Sergei. Now, remember your orders."

Shevchenko saluted and moved down to the low block building at the water's edge that was the submarine headquarters. He looked beyond the Yankee-class boomer to the two ships approaching the shore. By now Popov would already have ordered the merchantman to heave to. He went into the radio room and picked up a spare headset, indication to his radioman to continue monitoring the conversations. A tugboat had been sent out to take aboard eight or ten people, at most. He heard the tug's skipper tell them to stay put for the time being, that a larger craft would be dispatched for them.

He overheard them arguing. Finally the delegation from Moscow boarded the tug and met with Popov. As a precaution, Sergei ordered one of the Alfa hunter-killer subs to stand ready to fire on the merchantman at his orders. Satisfied, he returned to command headquarters to see what

Popov wanted him to do.

Popov introduced him to assistant deputies of defense and interior, three civilian administrators, a KGB lieutenant colonel, Dmitri Rubel, and their aides. Before long, Popov had them inside drinking vodka and toasting the motherland and each other's health. With everyone feeling good after their arduous trip north, the group turned to business.

Rubel took a folder from Roskow, the defense deputy, and laid it on Popov's desk. He said to the commandant, "Comrade, you have served the Rodina well. Construction on the power plant is ahead of schedule, with two reactors already working. However, out of economic necessity the submarine bastion is being scrapped, and our other plans are to be cut back. I'm very sorry to bring you this news. You're to return with us to Moscow. Those are your new orders." He pointed to the folder.

Popov glared at the KGB man, drained the vodka from his glass, and flung it against a wall. The sound of shattering glass got everyone's attention. "So, Dmitri . . . I am not good enough to command here any longer, eh? Is that what you've come to tell me?"

Rubel stood his ground. "Since there is no longer any military use of the island, there is no longer reason to have a military commander present." He shrugged. "Of course, we will have surveillance equipment here, and perhaps someday, some missile silos set up. But, it is time to devise a civilian administration over North Land. Comrade Ustinov will be the new overseer."

Ustinov, a fat man with a full, dark beard speckled with gray, smiled and bowed at Popov. He extended his hand to shake.

"And if I refuse?" Popov dared them.

You could almost hear the gasps of the civilians. Rubel stared at Popov, incredulously. "Surely, comrade, you jest? You cannot refuse the government. They will have you shot."

Popov curled his white handlebar mustache between his fingers. The trace of a smile parted his lips. "Oh. I see. I suppose that is why you're here, comrade . . . to see to it that I go peacefully. You don't have to answer that. I've already considered that one day this might happen."

"Please, comrade. You will be promoted to another post."

Popov leaned into the man. "Oh? Have they discovered another naval station in Siberia? Antarctica? Some other godforsaken place? Oh, forgive me, comrade. Has my choice of words offended you?"

The two of them stood there staring at each other for a moment. Rubel finally said, "Please, Comrade Admiral, make the transition an easy one. Come back to the ship with me."

"I refuse."

Rubel's hand went into his parka.

"Before you commit suicide, Comrade Colonel, you'd better have a look around you."

A dozen of Popov's troops stepped into the room and surrounded the visitors, AK-47s at ready.

"B—but this is treason!" Rubel sputtered.

Popov smiled. "Tell me something, comrade. Does Defense Minister Charkov agree with all this?"

"I have no idea."

"I have." It was Roskow, Charkov's assistant deputy.

Popov nodded. "Go on."

"At the Politburo, my superior alone spoke out against this move. He was voted down."

"Well, as long as Minister Charkov has not lost his senses, we shall not capitulate to the weaklings who seek to undercut our military advantage over the west. As for anyone here wishing to join us, you are welcome. The rest of you, consider yourselves under arrest."

Rubel was livid. "Don't be a fool, comrade. My men will cut down this rifraff of yours in a minute. Don't think you can get away with this."

"Hah. Where are your terrible storm troopers now? Ah, they are still aboard the merchantman, are they? You will order them to throw their arms overboard and report to the ship's brig, Comrade Colonel."

"Go to hell."

Popov leaned over and smashed his fist into Rubel's face, knocking him off his feet.

"One word from me and Captain Shevchenko, here, will order the *Alfa* sitting beneath your ship to sink it."

Rubel spat blood. "I will not betray the motherland, as you do. If you want them to surrender, tell them yourself. You'll get no help from me."

"Arrest that man," Popov ordered.

Rubel glared at the admiral and cursed him through bleeding lips. "Bastard. Rot in hell." He reached for his shoulder holster.

As a 9-mm automatic came into view, Popov shouted, "Shoot him."

Rubel was riddled by fire from a half dozen assault rifles. He died before his head hit the floor.

Popov looked at the terror-stricken members of the delegation, one by one. He said simply, "Anybody else?"

# Chapter 12

At 2130 hours Hawaiian time, Boxer saluted and shook hands with Admiral Willis, did a smart about-face, and walked up the prow of his newly refurbished *Manta*. All men and supplies were secure below, and the hatch dogged shut. He glanced up at the *Manta's* retractable sail, routinely kept fully extended until they were dived and under way. Mark Clemens, his EXO, was waiting for him to take over the conn.

"Evening, Skipper. It's a beautiful night."

Boxer climbed the tower and accepted a hand from Clemens while stepping over the bulwark. "Roger that, Clem. Take a good look around. It'll be our last for a while."

Together they checked off all the instruments in the sail's bridge. Satisfied, Boxer announced over the MC system, "All hands, this is Admiral Boxer. I now have the conn. Prepare to get under way."

He watched a bank of ready lights change from flashing red to amber to green, indicating all systems go. "Mahoney, come to one eight five. Engines, all ahead one-third."

"Aye, aye, Skipper," replied the helmsman. "Coming to one eight five."

"All ahead one-third," the EO repeated. And the *Manta* slipped out to sea.

Boxer followed the navigational devices, marking the

channels into and out of the harbor, until he got into deeper water, then ordered a dive. "DO, five degrees down on the planes. Take us down to periscope depth."

Chief Amos White pushed forward on the diving yoke to set the planes and took on enough forward ballast for a shallow dive. The sounds of compressed gas escaping and water running through pipes could be heard throughout the boat while Whitey repeated the orders.

Ten miles offshore, Boxer could still make out the lights of Honolulu and the hotel row at Waikiki Beach. A beautiful sight, one he would never forget. He ordered a change of direction, and the *Manta* rounded the southeast tip of Oahu and headed north.

At twenty miles north of the island, they picked up their first tail. "Conn, sonar. I've got something. Bearing two four zero. . . . Range twenty thousand yards. . . . Depth one zero zero. . . . Making propeller turns for two five knots, skipper. We've got a Russkie sub for company. Twin screws. I think it may be a *Victor*."

"Roger that, Hi Fi. Good work. Keep me informed."

"Aye, aye, Skipper."

Boxer said to Clemens, "We'll let them think we're heading home to San Diego. Retract the sail and prepare to dive." He keyed the MC switch. "Helmsman, change course to zero five seven. Engines ahead one-half. DO, take us down to two zero zero. Steady as she goes."

Over the next five minutes, the *Manta* did a slow slide to two hundred feet and headed east. "Clem, take the conn for the next two hours. Maintain bearing and speed, and let me know if our friend does something unexpected."

"Aye, aye, Skipper. I have the conn."

Boxer walked back to his quarters, a small room with a sleeping cot and a navigation table, the boat's safe, and a mini-version of the COMCOMP, the computer command center, and a smaller version of the UWIS screen that displayed their environment out to a distance of five nautical

116

miles on a 360-degree azimuth. He rolled out a chart of the North Pacific ocean floor and plotted their present position from the COMCOMP. They were entering a fracture zone, a twelve-hundred-mile series of ridges and crevasses occasionally strewn with boulders. He had decided on a plan.

He would lull the skipper of the older class Soviet sub into thinking that tracking the *Manta* would be a milk run. Then, at precisely the right moment, Boxer would lose the *Victor* among the ridges that rose like undersea mountains, then change course and simply outrun the Russkie on a line toward Alaska.

Satisfied, he set a timer to wake him and slept for an hour. Boxer wanted to recharge his energies. It was going to be a very long night.

When he awoke and returned to the bridge, he took over the conn and ordered a deep dive. "All hands secure for angles and dangles. Whitey, dive to fifty feet from the bottom. EO, increase speed to three zero knots."

"Aye, aye, sir," Chief White said. "Diving planes set at one five. Taking on ballast."

"Making three zero knots, Skipper. Engines ahead two-thirds."

"Roger that," Boxer answered. The *Manta* angled forward at forty degrees and raced for the ocean floor.

Hi Fi Freedman manned the sonar and coordinated it with the UWIS. He keyed the bridge. "Conn, sonar. We're losing that *Victor*. She's lagging behind."

"Thanks, sonar."

Whitey had been calling out the soundings as the *Manta* headed for the seafloor. "Passing through four thousand feet, Skipper. Approaching five zero zero from the bottom."

Boxer checked the UWIS. The "bottom" that Whitey's instruments had detected were actually the tops of the north-south running pressure ridges, broken every twenty to two-hundred miles by east-west chasms, appearing on the screen as if a leviathan had swiped its claws along the bottom, trying to destroy what nature had wrought.

Boxer keyed his engineer. "EO, conn. Engines ahead one-third. Slow us down to one five knots. That *Victor* can't follow us down here."

As the *Manta* slowed appreciably, Hi Fi signaled the bridge. "Skipper, we've got a new tail. A new target just leap-frogged the *Victor* at two six zero. . . . Range is six thousand yards. . . . Making turns for four zero. . . . repeat, four zero knots. ID as single screw *Alfa* class."

"Roger that, Hi Fi." Boxer's eyes were glued to the UWIS. He knew it wouldn't be easy shaking the *Alfa*. Racing through a maze of ravines and mountains at forty knots was extremely dangerous. One miscalculation and he could easily demolish his sub, giving the Russkies a victory without even firing a shot. He realized the *Manta* and the lives of all his men were at stake.

Hi Fi called out new coordinates. The *Alfa* was closing fast. Boxer made his decision. "DO, dive to within five zero feet of the bottom. Repeat, five zero from bottom."

"Aye, aye, sir." Whitey, who, as chief of the boat, was the most experienced sailor and highest ranking NCO aboard, still referred to Boxer as sir, rather than Skipper. "Diving to within five zero of bottom."

The *Manta* angled downward. Boxer ordered, "EO, engines ahead two-thirds."

"All ahead two-thirds. Aye, aye, Skipper."

The *Manta* seemed to slide down the rocky face of a pressure ridge, abruptly leveling off near the ocean floor. Boxer ordered, "Mahoney, hard right ten degrees. Come to zero six five."

The sub immediately veered hard right along the course of an east-west running cut in the ridge. They were in a canyon with sheer walls climbing five hundred feet above them. Boxer directed the helmsman to hug the wall of this canyon to throw off the trailing *Alfa*. They would hide in plain sight, knowing the Russkie sonar had its limitations.

The next break between pressure ridges was just up ahead. Boxer ordered, "Mahoney, left rudder ten degrees. Come to zero zero five."

"Aye, aye, Skipper." Mahoney repeated the orders while he trimmed the rudder. The *Manta* swerved north.

Boxer noticed an outcropping up ahead and headed for it. The *Manta* came about and hovered below the overhang facing the direction it had entered from. Boxer keyed the forward torpedo room. "FTO, arm one and two with Mark 48s."

"One and two armed and loaded, Skipper."

Clemens sat at the fire control module, setting dials and calculating a firing solution set at the entrance to the crevasse they were in. "Solution is set for a target dead ahead, Skipper. We can't miss, provided they come our way."

Boxer put his hand on Clem's shoulder and smiled. "Make some noise."

Clemens nodded his head and released a noisemaker from a chamber in the stern. "Hope she takes the bait."

Boxer watched the UWIS screen intently. A fast moving blip appeared near their position at the moment Hi Fi called in the coordinates. "Conn, sonar. Target bearing three five zero. . . . Range two thousand yards. . . . Speed three five and closing fast, Skipper."

The *Alfa* was dead ahead and homing in on them. Perfect. Boxer stood behind his exec. "Fire one, Clem."

A hissing of escaped gas signaled the firing of the torpedo. "One away, Skipper."

Even before the imminent impact, Boxer ordered engines reversed two-thirds, and the *Manta* backed away from under their hiding place.

"Conn, sonar. Torps in the water. Heading our way and closing at six zero knots."

"Whitey, take us up, fast. Blow forward tanks."

"Aye, aye, sir." The *Manta* rose sharply at the bows as

119

compressed air replaced the water in the ballast tanks.

"Torps passing beneath us, Skipper."

"Roger that, sonar."

The Mark 48 torpedo found the *Alfa* before it could react. The resulting explosion blew away the needle-shaped bows, and the Russkie sub sank like a stone. Aboard the *Manta*, Boxer's men could hear the crushing sounds of the sea claiming the Soviet submarine and its crew. There was no chance for survival at that depth.

Something hard pounded the outer hull of the *Manta*. Boxer's head jerked upward. "What was that?"

Clem's eyes were on the UWIS screen. "Looks like we shook loose some boulders, Skipper."

The EXO's remarks were punctuated by the sound of two more impacts against the hull. "We've set off an undersea avalanche," Boxer said. "We'd better get the hell out of here while we can." He keyed the engine room. "All ahead full, EO."

The *Manta* shot upward, above the top of the pressure ridge that they'd hid beneath, taking one more boulder against the rubber-coated hull before coming free. Boxer signaled Damage Control. "DCO, please report."

"We're taking in some water aft of the forward torpedo room, Skipper. I have a welding crew on the way."

"Roger that, DCO." Boxer eyed the panel of lights overhead that indicated the integrity of the submarine. One light was flashing red, while the others remained green. "Clem, that *Victor* class is going to wonder where the *Alfa* is. Let's go back and give it a surprise."


"Clem, take over the conn. I'm going forward to check on Rolly and his strike force." Boxer stepped from behind the COMCOMP, making room for his exec. "Some of his new men have never been in a sub before. That last encounter may have unsettled them."

"Roger that, Skipper."

Boxer made his way forward to the troop carrier compartment, which housed his forty-five-man contingent of Rolly's Rangers, mainly of Marines, SEALs, and Delta and Ranger Special Forces. Boxer thought them one of the most ferocious fighting teams he'd ever fought with.

He stuck his head inside the bulkhead. The men were mostly sitting around on their sleeping cots, or at the galley table drinking coffee or soft drinks. Here and there, a few queasy men lay on their backs on their bunks. Mean Gene Greene spotted Boxer and jumped to attention. "Admiral present," he barked.

Forty men jumped to their feet, stood at rigid attention, and saluted. The few too ill to get down tried their best.

"As you were, men . . . at ease. Major Jones, please instruct your men that hereafter, we'll have none of this aboard any submarine that I command. We can't have everyone jumping to attention every time I go by. Save your strength for the enemy."

One or two Rangers began to stand at ease. Rolly's icy stare cut right through them, and they returned to attention. Boxer shook his head. "That's an order, Major. Stand your men at ease."

"Yes, sir." He stared down his troops. "Well, what the hell you waiting for, a special invitation? As you were."

"Thank you, Major. Let's keep things informal in here. It will make it easier for me to run the sub."

"Yes, sir."

"Goes for you, too, Rolly. How many of the men are sick?"

Jones did a quick check. "Four, maybe five, sir."

"I'll have the quartermaster take a look at them. Doc Calahan's treated hundreds of cases of seasickness. How are the new men doing?"

"So-so. It's mainly them who got sick. Their squad leader is doing okay, though."

Boxer smiled. "Billy Lone Eagle? That's what I'd expect, judging from his folder. He's supposed to be an extremely strong swimmer."

"Could have made the Olympics, but he chose the SEALs instead. He led the swim team at Annapolis."

Boxer nodded. "Reason I stopped in, we're likely to have a go at another Russkie sub before long, one that's been tailing us since we left Oahu. We just sank a Soviet *Alfa*, one of their premier submarines. I think the two are working in tandem."

Rolly said, "I think most of the guys will be all right."

A tall, lanky sailor wearing a blue coverall that was the work garment of the sub crew entered the compartment. "You sent for me, Skipper?"

"Thanks, Doc. Some of Rolly's men need your assistance."

"Seasick?"

Boxer nodded.

Calahan reached into the first aid kit he carried and came up with a black nylon strap. "Latest thing. Pentagon sent them out for a field test. Who's first?"

Rolly pointed out one of his new men, who lay moaning on his bunk, hands clutching his belly. "Orlando," he said.

Doc wafted smelling salts under the hapless Ranger's nose until he perked up. Then he fastened the strap around Orlando's wrist and activated a tiny electronic button on the underside. "Acupressure," he told them. "Can't really explain it, but it usually works." He looked at Boxer and grinned. "Course, if we pull another little maneuver like we did back then, we might all need to try these out."

"Couldn't be helped," Boxer replied. "We could have been a lot worse off than seasick if we didn't get that *Alfa* before she got us. Well, I'll leave you to your work, Doc. Take good care of the boys. We've got at least one more sub to tangle with before we get to Alaska."

Boxer walked back to the bridge just as Hi Fi notified them of a new contact. "I believe it's our *Victor*, Skipper.

122

Sonar image sure fits."

"Let's give the Russkies something to think about," Boxer told his EXO. "Signal all ahead one-third."

Clemens repeated the command. "EO, slow down to five knots."

"Time to try out some more goodies, Clem. Ready to activate the sound signature broadcaster."

A smile broke out on the exec's face. Another new gadget . . . what would they think of next? He toggled a switch, and a speaker mounted in the bow began emanating a laser-disk recording of the underwater sounds of an *Alfa*.

"Conn, sonar. Target bearing two seven zero. . . . Range eight thousand yards. . . . Approaching at two zero knots. It's the *Victor*, Skipper. ETA is one zero minutes."

"FTO, load and arm number one, re-arm number two, and stand by."

"Aye, aye, Skipper. One and two armed and loaded."

Clemens took his seat at the fire control console and began to calculate a firing solution.

"We'll make this one nice and easy, Clem. Set to fire at three thousand yards."

Mark Clemens dialed in the bearing-range-speed coordinates, along with depth of target, and locked in the solution. He used his key to unlock the firing mechanism and rested his right hand on the red trigger button. He would fire at a range of just inside of two miles. "Roger that, Skipper."

The *Manta* stole closer to the more primitive Soviet submarine, which had to rely on a sonar system that was much less sophisticated than the UWIS aboard the super-sub. Hi Fi continued to mark the progress of the *Victor*. "Target bearing two seven seven. . . . Range five thousand yards. . . . Speed two one knots and closing."

Boxer watched the image of the Soviet sub approaching on his monitor. "Time?"

"T minus sixty seconds, Skipper."

123

Suddenly, five distinct sonar pings struck the *Manta's* hull and echoed throughout.

"He knows we're here, and thinks we're the *Alfa*," Clemens said. "Why make all that noise?"

"It's a signal, Clem. The *Victor* and the *Alfa* must have arranged a predetermined signal between them as a means of identification." Boxer keyed sonar. "Hi Fi, reply with five pings, same sequence."

"Aye, aye, Skipper." The sonar sounded five times even as Hi Fi Freedman replied. "Damn. Skipper, torps in the water. Two targets bearing two seven zero and two seven three . . . range two thousand feet . . . speed six zero."

Boxer looked at his exec. "Wrong reply. Fire one and two."

"Aye, aye, firing one and two."

"Whitey, dive. *Dive*. Down to four zero. This is an emergency."

In less than a minute the twin enemy torpedoes were upon them. A sudden rush of compressed gas and seawater heralded a lurching forward of the *Manta*. Boxer found a handhold on the periscope pedestal and hung on.

"Torps passing overhead."

"Thanks, Hi Fi."

The *Victor* didn't fare so well. Both torpedoes struck the Soviet sub. The explosions tore it apart. The shock waves drove the *Manta* toward the bottom. "Hang on," Boxer shouted.

"Conn, sonar. Both Russkie torpedoes are giving chase. Range two five zero zero yards and closing at six zero knots."

"Just great," Boxer muttered to himself. "Sunk by torpedoes from a sub we already destroyed." He keyed the MC mike. "DO, dive, dive, dive."

Once again, Whitey pushed hard on the diving yoke. "Planes at one five degrees, sir. Diving hard and deep."

"Roger that, Whitey. At one zero zero from the bottom, pull up hard."

Both torpedoes pursued them relentlessly, speeding after them at sixty knots. Boxer knew it was impossible to outrun the fish. He could only hope to outsmart them.

Close to the sea floor, the *Manta* suddenly veered up at the bows, sending everyone scrambling for something to hold onto. One torpedo headed for the bottom and exploded, sending up a geyser of debris.

"Skipper, sonar. One of those torps didn't buy our diversion. It's right on our tail."

Beads of sweat ran down Boxer's forehead. He wiped his brow with his sleeve. "Clem, fire off a noisemaker, now." He switched on the MC. "Helmsman, right rudder, hard ten degrees."

The torpedo sped past the noisemaker, slowed, and changed course, once again charging after the *Manta*.

"Damn. She didn't bite," Clemens cursed.

"Must be a heat seeker. That's why it didn't go after the noisemaker. DO, diving planes up one five, repeat, up one five on the planes."

The *Manta* shot upward, even as Whitey repeated Boxer's orders.

"Mahoney, left rudder ten degrees. Come to two seven five."

The *Manta* responded by twisting to port as it continued to climb.

Boxer asked, "Sonar, where's that torp?"

"Still on our tail, Skipper. Two thousand yards. No, wait. It's falling off. Two five zero zero. . . . Three thousand yards. I think we're in the clear."

Boxer checked the UWIS screen. The blip was dropping, wavering, and stalled for a moment, and then did a perfect swan dive off the bottom of the screen. A smile chased the tension off Boxer's face. "Damn if it didn't run out of fuel."

A cheer broke out in the control center, then picked up throughout the sub as the good news spread fore and aft.

Boxer said, "Whitey, take us up to two zero zero. Steady as she goes. We could all use a break about now."

Clemens slouched in his seat, the tension finally easing from his shoulders. "Whew, that was a close one."

"Too close," Boxer said. "Much too close."

# Chapter 13

It was barely 0400 hours when the *Manta* followed the green and red channel marker lights into the Point Barrow coast guard station. Here at the northernmost point in Alaska, it would remain dark until almost noon, when the sun would cast less than an hour of daylight as it barely hovered on the horizon, then slipped out of sight for another day. It was here that Boxer's strike force would begin the rigorous cross-training with the fabled Snow Troopers, who were the eyes and ears of America in the Arctic. Like Rolly's Rangers, the Snow Troopers had to be in a constant state of readiness, able to move out at a moment's notice as a counter-insurgency or first-strike force.

Boxer was met at the mooring slip by an aide to Captain Frank Dawson and taken immediately to headquarters. Dawson stood up and saluted Boxer. "Welcome back, Admiral. How was Hawaii?"

Boxer shivered. "Weatherwise about as different from this as you could get. Do you ever get used to this cold?"

Dawson chuckled. "You learn to dress for it, and I guess your body begins to accept it. I understand your men are going to train with us."

"Right," Boxer said. "The CNO wants us to undergo cold-weather training at least once a year. His thinking is, in the

127

advent of war, the Arctic is where the Soviets will likely try to launch from."

Dawson agreed. "Sure, what with the submarine enclaves in Kola and Okhotsk. And, until very recently, up in North Land, of all godforsaken places. Say, why don't we go inside and get you warmed up over coffee? How about something to eat?"

"Coffee sounds good," Boxer replied, following Dawson down a hallway to a large galley almost devoid of occupants. "I'd like to get my men settled in before I take on breakfast."

Dawson filled two mugs with steaming coffee from an urn and carried them to a small table in the officers' dining area. Boxer turned a wooden rung-back chair around and sat with his arms draped over the back. "My people are already attending to that." Dawson added cream and sugar to his cup.

Boxer sipped his black coffee. "Appreciate that. We've been under for almost a week. That's a long time for the landlubbers on the strike force. Even some of the SEALs had to get used to the confinement, and the motions of the sub underseas. What do you have set up for us?"

Dawson sipped his coffee and fidgeted in his jacket pocket. "Mind if I smoke?" He offered Boxer a pack of Marlboros.

"Go right ahead, Frank. I'll stick to my pipe."

Both men lit up, wafting twin plumes of smoke toward the ceiling of the concrete-block structure. "Well, you'll spend a few days here with us getting acclimated. Then it's off to Anderson for survival training, a mock assault on St. Lawrence Island, that's as close to the Soviet Union you can get without creating an incident. Finally, they'll parachute onto the ice cap, probably over Canada."

Boxer nodded. "Good. I'd also like them to practice storming a mockup of the Soviet base. I'm responsible for coming up with a plan to take over that North Land facility in case of Soviet noncompliance, though that seems remote right now. The Russkies have agreed to our terms, in exchange for a prime wheat deal. Senator Burke put the old carrot and the stick to them, and they decided it was as much in their interest as ours to take down the military base."

"You can never be sure with the Russkies on something like this. They'll try to get away with whatever they can, if they figure we'll take their word for it."

Boxer put his cup down. "That's part of the deal. I've been up there on an initial inspection with Admiral Rodgers, although I don't think the base commander fully realized what we were there for. His people told him we were on a military exchange program, you know, goodwill and all. Show each other our toys and all play nice together. Anyway, I guess he bought it. Admiral Rodgers said that Popov's sort of a maverick, and his people didn't want to set him off by tipping their hand."

Dawson picked up their empty mugs and carried them to the kitchen, where a skeleton crew was working. "How about whipping up some breakfast?" he told them. "We've got eighty-five hungry men about to descend upon us."

He returned to their table. "My cooks are setting up breakfast for your men. How does two hundred and fifty eggs with a whole side of bacon sound?"

Boxer smiled. "You'll be making a lot of friends, Frank."

"Good. Let's get 'em fed and then we'll get them settled in. A couple of days of good food and hot showers, and then it's off to cold-weather survival school and wilderness training."


Midnight. Rolly Jones led his team of ten Rangers, including squad leader Turk Turkell, to the airfield outside of Nome. His counterpart in the Snow Troopers, Captain Richard Dickerson, had his ten-man team already aboard two modified Blackhawk helicopters awaiting takeoff. "Okay, watch your heads, men. Turk, take five men with you aboard BH-2. I'll ride with Double Dick in the lead chopper. Just pay attention to the Snowboys, and follow their lead."

Turk gave a thumbs-up, and trotted to the second chopper, bent low, and held his helmet to his head against the whoosh of the rotors. Turk knew as much about fighting as any man, but he realized that he hadn't had much cold-weather training. He would watch and listen, then go back and teach the others.

The twin choppers hopped over some mountainous terrain and headed west, toward the tip of the Seward Peninsula, the closest point on the mainland to Soviet territory. As they hovered over a particularly secluded valley, Dickerson asked Rolly, "Ready?"

"You bet."

"Okay, strap on your packs, and don't forget the showshoes. We'll have a long walk down to Wales." Cape Prince of Wales was the westernmost outpost on the peninsula.

At his signal, a Snow Trooper got up and stood at the open hatchway of the chopper, locking his jump cord to an overhead cable. Dickerson said to Rolly, "One of my men followed by one of yours. Then you jump, and I'll bring up the rear."

"Got it." He turned to his four charges. "Okay, Garcia, Vegas, O'Malley, Olesnicki, get your gear ready and line up."

One by one, the two white camouflaged choppers dropped their passengers into the valley below, then headed back to Nome. The twenty-two men were on their own now, totally without support except from each other. While the Snow Troopers helped the Rangers into snowshoes and adjusted the seventy-pound rucksacks, Dickerson and his lieutenant, a wiry hundred-and-fifty-pounder named Earl Palmer, walked up and down the line, making sure everyone made the jump without sustaining any injury or loss of gear. So far, so good.

"Wales is that way," Double Dick said, pointing west. "We'll hike to the top of that ridge and camp there in the morning. We reverse the clock up here, sleep during the day and march at night. That way we stay practically invisible to the enemy."

Rolly said, "I can understand moving at night, but how do we remain hidden during the day?"

"You'll see," Dickerson replied.

They moved on in two single lines, Dickerson and Rolly at the head of the lead group, Turk and Palmer bringing up the rear. "Damn, it's cold," Turk complained.

Palmer looked at the big man, ice frosting his protective face mask. "About thirty below. You fart now and it'll freeze and fall to the ground."

"You ever get used to it?"

"Everybody asks that," Palmer replied. "Just make sure you're dressed right. From time to time we do a digit count, make sure nobody's frostbitten."

"A what?"

"Count your fingers and toes. Make sure they're all still there."

Turk involuntarily flexed his fingers inside his heavy mittens. All there. He leaned into the wind and followed Palmer up the mountain ridge.

At the top, Dickerson signaled a halt. "We'll set up shop here." Several of his men put together a listening station, complete with satellite dish and long-range receivers. "We stay put and listen for the Russkies. Sometimes they send out sorties into our territory, to try to spy on our installations. One of our jobs is to see that they don't."

Rolly set down his heavy pack. "I guess we pitch our tents here, then."

Double Dick was smiling and shaking his head. He loved to see the look on their faces when he told them. "No tents, Major. We dig ourselves into snow caves. The snow insulates against the cold, and we blend in real nice with the surroundings."

"Snow caves. Damn."

"Can't be too careful, Major. We've already had radio contact with one group, the Russkie Arctic Wolves. They're the Russkie equivalent of our unit. You know, I've never had to fire my M-16 up here, but we still carry them, including night scopes."

Rolly motioned for his men to tighen up their ranks. "We'll take turns on sentry duty with the Snow Troopers," he told them.

"We'll take two-hour shifts at sentry and on the receivers," Dickerson told him. "The rest of the men can start digging in."

Within an hour, the combined group had carved shelters under the deep snow drifts below the peak of the ridge, and had dragged branches along their trail to erase any signs of their camp. Their white snowsuits and parkas kept them invisible from sight. Dickerson taught them to lie curled up in fetal positions, to make their heat signatures seem to imitate those of sleeping moose calves to an enemy using sophisticated thermal-imaging spy gear.

Double Dick told Rolly, "We'll stay here until 1600. Then the sun will be well enough below the horizon to keep us in darkness for our descent down to the coast. We should reach Wales in two days."

From seemingly out of nowhere, Earl Palmer interrupted their conversation. "'Scuse me Captain, Major, but Harry's got something on the radio, and your Russian's a heap better than ours. Care to give a listen?"

Dickerson nodded. He clapped Rolly's arm. "Coming?"

"Sure, why not?"

The three of them made their way to the listening post. Harry was wearing a headset, and intently taking notes on a small notepad. Dickerson asked, "What's up?"

"We got us some Russkie visitors, Cap'n. Signal's pretty strong to be coming from Chukchi. I make them somewheres between here and Cape of Wales."

"What the hell they doin' here?" Rolly asked.

132

Dickerson shrugged. "Whatever it is, they're up to no good. We'd better try to cut them off before they reach the shoreline."

Rolly nodded. "If we radio for help, our men can fly on ahead and cut them off as they approach the coast."

"You have to figure," Dickerson was shaking his head, "that they're here to spy on one of our facilities. That means they'll have the best listening equipment they can get." He was listening in on the Russian conversation with one earphone against his head as he spoke. "We're only invisible when we're silent. If we transmit, those Russkies will pick it up for damn sure, and we run the risk of losing them. There's too many places for them to hide out in."

"So we have to do it ourselves. Then we'd better get moving, or we'll lose them anyway."

Double Dick checked the luminous dial of his chronograph. "It's almost 1100 hours. We'll rest the men here until the sunlight fades in three hours and try to cut them off. I know some shortcuts."

At 1415 hours, the gear was packed and the campsite abandoned. Twenty-two men set out after an unknown band of Soviet infiltrators. Dickerson had the men switch to skis for the descent down the mountain, and they more than doubled their speed climbing up.

Using the radio signals to monitor the Soviets' progress, Dickerson led them along an abandoned trail leading toward the coastline along the Bering Strait, just short of Cape Prince of Wales. Limiting sleep to four hours daily, they might just get there ahead of the Soviets.

It was on the second night that they realized that they had made better progress than their Soviet counterparts. While the unit went ahead to set up an ambush, Lt. Palmer fell behind to personally try to assess the enemy's strength. Since any radio transmission would tip off the Russians to his presence, Palmer realized that he was entirely on his own. He could listen, but he couldn't call for help.

He ventured off the trail and circled back around the area the Soviet radio traffic was emanating from. He traveled on snowshoes and pulled a branch tied to his waist to remove his trail. It took him the better part of four hours until he came upon a group of ten or twelve white-clad Soviet soldiers sitting on their packs in a circle, eating a meal. Probably the fabled Arctic Wolves. A lone sentry kept watch.

Good. That meant the Americans had a two-to-one advantage. They might even be able to take prisoners. That would be some political coup, catching Soviet troops on American soil. Palmer felt good. He didn't go in much for politics outside his home state of Tennessee, but he knew the state department could stretch this incident into enough clout to really mean something in the cold war against the Russkies. Especially with their so-called *Glasnost* policy of friendship with the West.

As far as Earl Palmer was concerned, he didn't trust them one bit. He did a compass check, marked the area on a field map, and had started to rejoin his unit when his receiver started squawking. He squatted low. Keeping out of sight, he recorded as much of the brief conversation as he could. There was a second, larger group coming up behind this one, which was now obviously acting as a scouting party for the main troop.

He had to get back to warn his men. Dickerson might mistake this small band for the entire enemy forces, and be caught off guard by the larger unit.

Palmer was already tired from the four-hour trek back up the slope. Now he had to outrace these fresh, well-rested troops who began to assemble before pulling out. He'd never make it. But he sure as hell was going to try.

Earl removed his pack and buried it in the heavy snow, keeping just his weapons and a small fanny pack containing survival gear and a high-energy snack. Then he began his race down the mountain against time, and against the enemy. His only advantage over the enemy was that he already knew his way back.

The Arctic Wolves moved out in single file, allowing the lead man to break a trail for the remainder. Palmer figured if their tactics were similar to the Snow Troopers', they would alternate the lead to allow the trailblazer a bit of rest. He had to break ground the entire trip back.

Keeping beyond visual range of the Soviets, Earl ran a parallel course along the same abandoned trail as he'd been down earlier, traveling faster than he knew good survival practice dictated. He had no options; he had to reach his men well before the enemy. When he reached the area where he split off from them to double back, he could pick out some telltale signs that someone had passed through here. He hoped the Soviets missed it. He was too close now.

Palmer ran the next mile or so, breathing laboriously, near exhaustion. He could sense that the lead Soviet unit was upon him, though he couldn't make visual contact when he chanced to turn around. He came to a small rise ahead and made an end run for it, keeping off the pristine snow ahead. No sense giving himself away. He was beyond tree cover out here, and keeping out of sight became more difficult.

Just beyond the rise he chanced a look back at his pursuers. A mighty hand came out of nowhere and pulled him off his feet. Another hand muffled his cries of astonishment. When his eyes focused, he saw the massive body of Turk Turkell hovering over him.

Earl pulled Turk's mitt off his face and gasped, "Tell the captain, more on the way . . . first unit, squad strength." Palmer was gasping for air now. "Rest of platoon behind."

Turk turned to another, smaller man huddled in the snowdrift alongside him. "Harry, tell Double Dick and the major. We got company and then more company."

As Harry crawled out of the shelter, Earl Palmer said, "Harry."

The man turned around.

135

"Stay low. They were right behind me."

"Right, Lieutenant." He was off.

A half hour went by. Turk and Palmer heard scraping sounds outside, and some talk in Russian. Earl pointed directly overhead, and Turk nodded his agreement. The Arctic Wolves were making camp right on top of them, using the snowdrift to rest against while they paused to get their bearings, and perhaps to have some refreshment.

To Turk, it was both exciting to have the enemy that close overhead and frightening to be buried in a snowbank beneath them. One slip, and he realized they would both be dead.

To Earl Palmer, though exciting, this was also fairly routine stuff, a maneuver practiced many times over during war games. He put a reassuring hand on his partner's shoulder, and they sat tight. Fifteen minutes later, the Soviets were gone. Earl hoped that Harry got through in time to Dickerson and Jones. He waited another ten minutes before venturing a peek out from their snowbank.

From the lee of the protective rise, he could make out another group of white-garbed troops heading their way. It was too late now to break out of their cover. They could only stay put and hope that the second group of Arctic Wolves failed to find them, too.

The main body of Arctic Wolves passed right on over them without taking time to stop. Palmer figured they must have bivouacked back a ways and descended the slope on a signal from the lead squad. He was grateful for that.

A half mile below, Captain Dickerson had ordered his men to let the Soviet scouting party pass by them without firing. He would deal with them later. When the second force marched in two files through his ambush, Double Dick brought his night glasses to his eyes and counted off thirty Soviet soldiers in this group and ten in the first. He knew then there would be no quarter given. He recognized the uniforms of the elite Arctic Wolves, and he knew he risked losing too many men if he gave them the opportunity to surrender. They would die first, and take as many of their enemies as they could with them. No: he had the bloody task of killing them all.

Dickerson took aim at the soldier who seemed to command the troop, drew a deep breath, and fired a short burst. The victim's body jerked and limply fell. More shots were fired from both sides of the Soviet columns. The air was filled with the stench of gunpowder and the sounds of men dying. Amid the cacophony, bodies jumped and jerked in a grim *danse macabre*.

Amid the slaughter, one of the Soviets managed to fire off a flare, and the area became illuminated. Now the Arctic Wolves had targets to fire upon, and they began shooting down the Americans. Soon the snow-covered ground was awash with blood.

Farther down the slope, the advance party heard the shooting and rushed back to the aid of their comrades. Amid the glare of rockets, they charged into the melee. Rolly Jones and three men lay in wait for them.

Outnumbered two to one, the Americans had to rely on ambush, and Rolly's men were positioned on either side of the path back to the fighting zone. As soon as the scouting party passed by, Rolly began firing long bursts at the enemy. His three men followed suit. The Soviets could either turn and fight or rush ahead to join with their main force. Either option was grim. They fired off a few rounds at Rolly's men and headed for their main force, thinking that in unity they would find strength.

As Rolly and his small band pushed upward from below, the Arctic Wolves closest to the top of the slope tried to fight their way back up, away from the ambush. They were shocked to see two Americans leap out from a snowbank and fire down on them. They were caught in an ever-tightening trap.

When there were fewer than a dozen of the Soviet fighters

left standing, Dickerson called a cease-fire. Immediately the American M-16s stopped. Dickerson called out in his choppy Russian dialect, "Lay down your arms and we will not harm you. You are prisoners and entitled to be treated according to . . ."

A Soviet flare lit up the sky and a Soviet round broke the silence and caught Dickerson in the side. His left arm hung at an awkward angle. Immediately his men took up their weapons and the fighting became fierce once more. They would not surrender and fought gallantly to the last man.

Rolly Jones ran to where Dickerson had fallen. Two Snow Troopers were already attending to their leader. "How is he?"

The trooper serving as medic looked up for a moment to see who was asking. "He took one in his upper arm. It missed the shoulder by a few inches." He went back to his task.

Rolly got up and looked at the carnage all around him. "Okay, troops. I want a head count, now."

He was not pleased by what he learned. Out of twenty-two, five of the Americans died; two more were badly wounded and would have to be airlifted back to Nome. Captain Dickerson had narrowly escaped death. On the other hand, the Soviet troops had all been slaughtered. And for what, he wondered. An incursion into enemy territory? For what purpose? Rolly Jones shook his head. Perhaps they'd never know.

What he did know was that he had to get some critically wounded men to a hospital quickly. He and his men would have to lick their wounds another time and get their fallen comrades back safely. He summoned up his strength and assumed command. "All right, men, let's move out."

# Chapter 14

Boxer and some of his strike force had been airlifted to the northern warfare training center in Fort Greely, Alaska, for a special briefing on the Soviet reactor plant on North Land. They were escorted to a two-story concrete structure crowned by a dome which resembled the top half of a golf ball.

Boxer was joined by Mean Gene Green and his squad of ten rangers of mixed backgrounds: SEALs, deltas, marines, and special forces, and by Sergeant Billy Lone Eagle and his squad of SEALs. They were ushered into a spacious, circular room with a huge mock-up of a nuclear reactor at the center. A smiling man dressed in blue slacks and a shirt and tie, his sleeves rolled up to his elbows, stood next to the display. He was bald, with only a fringe of dark hair around the back of his head.

"I'm Dr. Sylvan Arnold," he told them. "You gentlemen must have lots of clout to have me flown all the way up here from DC. The president said it was very necessary for me to brief you in person."

Boxer introduced himself and his men. He'd heard of Arnold, one of the nation's leading experts on nuclear energy, and, Boxer guessed, on nuclear weapons. "I've been up to the Russkie reactor on North Land, Dr. Arnold, and the powers that be feel it's important for me to gain some expertise. But with the new trade agreement, I'll probably never have to make use of what you teach us here today."

"One never knows, Admiral Boxer. Meanwhile, I'll give you all the facts you can assimilate. As you can see, this is a pretty good replica of a Soviet plant. I had it flown up here with me. It's based on Chernobyl. We got a pretty good glimpse of that one during the cleanup procedures. We're counting on this being a prototype."

"Let's hope it is, if we ever have to go up there and do something about it."

Arnold walked to the front of the architect's model of the plant. It was at least twelve feet on each side, and gave the appearance of a wedding cake. "We'll start here, at the heart of the reactor." He removed a layer of styrofoam made up to resemble poured concrete. "This is the reactor core. As we move down and out from this, we come to the miles of water pipes which flow up into the core. There the water is superheated and sent up here, to these separator drums, where the steam is siphoned off to power these turbines, way out here." He pointed to a horizontal series of cylinders along the right side of the reactor. "It's really very simple," he said, grinning from ear to ear.

Boxer's men looked at each other as if to say, Is he serious?

"Say, Doc, lemme see if I got this right, okay?" It was Mean Gene who rose and walked up to the model. His arms spread out to touch the twin rows of water pumps that stood on either side of the core. "You mean these pumps move the water through these pipes up into the core right here?"

"So far, so good," Arnold acknowledged.

Green went on. "Then, when the water flows through this hot core, it turns into steam and these drums here send it out to the turbines. That right?"

"Excellent."

Mean Gene asked, "How do they turn it on and off?"

It was Boxer's turn to smile. Gene had asked the sixty-four-dollar question.

Arnold placed his hand on top of the core area. "The nuclear reaction is controlled by these boron control rods in a typical Soviet plant. Quite simply, they lower these control rods to slow down the reaction. When the power drops to two hundred megawatts, a trip signal shuts down the reactor."

"Where is the control room, Dr. Arnold?" Boxer asked.

"This building to my left, Admiral." Arnold patted a low structure running the length of the reactor on the side opposite the turbines. "The computers that control every facet of operations are housed in here."

Boxer rubbed his salt-and-pepper beard. "Then that's our objective, if we ever have to intervene?"

"Let's hope we never have to, but yes, that would be your objective. And if you gentlemen will follow me into the next room, I'll show you what the computer room looks like in one of these babies."

"Comrade Admiral Popov." The young lieutenant was clearly upset with the news he was sent to bring to the commandant. "I have something to . . ."

Popov slammed a beefy fist onto his desktop. "Then say it, damn it! Tell me what you've come to say, and stop quaking in your boots. You're acting like a woman."

The lieutenant bowed slightly, and stuttered, "I am ordered to . . . that is . . ." Popov's glare cut him off. "The platoon of Arctic Wolves has escaped from the merchantman overnight. We . . . they cannot be found. I'm sorry to . . ."

Popov was around the desk before the hapless soldier could finish. A slap across the face brought him up short. "Please, Comrade Admiral. I am just the messenger, not . . ."

A backhand to the face shut him up. "Who is responsible

141

for this outrage?"

The soldier was afraid to speak. He envisioned his career, no, perhaps his very life, at stake at this moment. He hesitated, but knew he couldn't refuse a direct question. "Comrade Major Sverdlov, Comrade Admiral."

Popov's private bodyguard was never more than a room away. Popov shouted a command and a dozen heavily armed guards burst into his office. "Arrest this man and get him out of my sight. Then I want you to send for Major Sverdlov, who is in charge of guarding the merchantman with our friends from Moscow."

A half hour later, Sverdlov and three of the KGB officers from the ship were dragged into Popov's headquarters, bound hand and foot, and gagged. "Bring that one to me." Popov pointed to the major in charge of guarding the prisoners.

"Remove his gag."

"Thank you, Comrade Admiral," Sverdlov gasped, as soon as the restraint was removed from his mouth.

Popov stepped up to him. The two burly guards holding Sverdlov tightened their grip, forcing their prisoner to stand at attention despite his bonds. The commandant looked the man in the eye, staring him down. "Are you a traitor, Comrade Major, or just the most incompetent officer up here?"

The major said nothing, afraid to spark his commander's ire even more.

Popov slammed a fist into the prisoner's face, smashing the major's nose. Blood streamed down his face while Popov declared him a traitor. "I knew it. No officer could be so stupid. You had to want them to escape." Popov unholstered a sleek 9-mm automatic pistol and stuck its tapered barrel into Sverdlov's ear, twisting it to inflict pain. "Do you have anything more to say, comrade?"

The major, though a seasoned veteran, was afraid to speak, and found himself unable to control his bladder. As the front of his trousers became wet, he felt the warmness spreading over his thighs. Though his superior declared him guilty of high treason against the state, in actuality it was the base commandant who was guilty of this crime. When his fate became clear to him, he felt gladdened that he'd looked the other way as the Arctic Wolves under his surveillance climbed over the side of the merchantman using rope ladders and escaped on inflatable rafts. He tried to recapture his dignity and was straightening up, when he heard the cylinder pulled back on the automatic that was inserted in his ear. And then came the deafening explosion that ended his life in an instant.

The three KGB officers who hadn't escaped with the troopers stared at the dead man bleeding below them, and then at each other. Perhaps it had been a mistake to remain behind. Perhaps.

"Take them around the back and shoot them," Popov barked.

The KGB men struggled against the ropes that bound them, but to no avail, and were dragged outside to their doom.

Popov shouted to his men, "Send for the captain of the guards, now."

In minutes the captain was driven to the headquarters compound, past the firing squad as they cut down the three KGB officers, and he strode briskly into his commander's office. He couldn't help but notice the sticky pool of blood congealing at his feet. He came to attention.

"A platoon of Arctic Wolves escaped from the merchant ship that brought them here. Find them. Kill them. We control access to all the food and shelter on the island. Sooner or later, they will have to come in, or else they will surely die out there. You must stop them. Is that clear, comrade?"

"Yes, Admiral." The captain of the guard understood perfectly. It was suicide to go after crack storm troopers in the kind of environment where they fought best. He didn't stand a chance of survival, unless his men took them by surprise. On the other hand, one look at his half-crazed commander told him that to refuse was suicide as well. He thought about being crushed between a rock and a hard place. This was it.

"Take fifty men, and bring them back, dead or alive. And double up the guard at the plant and at my headquarters."

The captain saluted and went out, glad to escape Popov's wrath for the time being.

Popov summoned Sergei Shevchenko, his chief of the submarine fleet. COMSUBFLT was at his side in ten minutes. "When our deceased comrades fail to report back within a prescribed period of time, their friends in Moscow will no doubt come looking for them. Make sure that you and your fleet are ready for them."

Shevchenko smiled. He and Popov were holding all the aces in this game. The high command wouldn't fire on their position for fear of causing a nuclear accident. That meant they'd have to come by sea, and his fleet could handle that. Or they could try to drop paratroopers behind their lines, to fight their way to the base, hand to hand. No problems there, either. Planes could be shot down as easily as ships could be sunk . . . and with no worry about reprisal by heavy artillery or missiles. "Have no fear, Comrade Admiral. If and when they come, we will be ready."

Admiral Gorshkov, admiral of the fleet, the chief of staff for naval operations, hadn't left his headquarters suite for a week. He'd been frantically trying to find out the fate of the replacement committee for North Land. The merchantman they'd left on hadn't returned, nor had it been heard from since the one and only message, which stated that Comrade Rubel and the newly appointed administrators had gone ashore to relieve Popov.

Gorshkov was one of the few individuals who knew that the captain of that vessel was a naval officer of the same rank, and not of the merchant marine. And Captain Lubeck was charged with keeping him up to date on what was happening, his eyes and ears in the north. To make matters worse, the damned KGB was harassing him. After all, they kept telling him, a dozen of their agents were aboard that ship.

His thoughts were broken by an announcement on his intercom. "Comrade Admiral, excuse me, but Comrade General Doneck is here to see you."

Speak of the devil himself, Gorshkov cursed. "Please do not keep the Comrade General waiting. Send him right through."

Gorshkov was already out of his seat when Doneck entered his office. "Ah, Pasha, how good of you to join me. Sit. What can I do for you today?"

After shaking hands, Doneck looked around the walnut-paneled room replete with naval prints and oil paintings. The largest one, holding the place of honor behind the desk, between the hammer-and-sickle and the navy emblems, was a glamorized oil painting of the carrier *Leningrad*, fighter planes catapulting from the flight deck and guns flaring at some imaginary enemy. Who will be the holder of this office next, he wondered. "You can begin by cutting out all the usual crap with me, Comrade Admiral. Tell me what has become of the *Kirov*, and my men aboard."

Gorshkov shook his head. "I have had no word yet."

"Tell me, comrade, so that I may testify at your trial, what are you doing about it?"

"Ah, Pasha, I am an old man, so you can't threaten me with death. I have no family, so you can't even hold that over my head. But because of our long association, I will tell you anyway. I have sent out an *Alfa* submarine commanded by one of my most experienced captains to find out what's going on. I haven't heard from him for two days. He was

145

getting very close to the bastion."

Doneck said, "I was against putting Popov in charge of North Land, but he has friends in high places. Or at least, he *had.*"

The old admiral's head swayed from side to side. "Hindsight is wonderful, eh, Pasha? It gives you twenty-twenty vision." He pushed an ashtray toward the KGB deputy to catch the ash falling from his fancy Italian cigarette. The KGB always gets the best of everything, mused Gorshkov, especially foreign goods. Oh, well. "I was in favor of sending my *best* submariner up to North Land, but he is in some prison in Siberia, or perhaps dead by now."

"Ah, you speak of Comrade Borodine. Yes, he is . . . or was the very best. Too bad he couldn't even keep his own submarine from being stolen out from under him while he was out carousing with the Yankee pigs."

"You judge him too harshly, Comrade. Had he been aboard, he would have been just another victim of that Japanese Red Army gang."

*"Red Army."* Doneck almost spat out the words. "Those anarchists are against all governments. How can they steal the name of our Red Army, which embodies the spirit of communism, of purity of soul, of . . ."

Gorshkov was waving a hand in front of his face. "I know all about that, comrade, as well as you do. The point is, Igor Borodine is the best man for this job. And if he's still alive and well, he should be sent to North Land to find out what's going on up there, and to put a stop to Popov's abuse of power."

Doneck lit another imported cigarette and offered one to the admiral. Gorshkov was about to decline, but decided, what the hell, let's see what the big deal is. He allowed the KGB man to light him up, and drew deeply, exhaling the smoke through his nose. Not bad.

"The Minister of Defense feels otherwise, comrade. He is opposed to sending your Comrade Borodine up against

Popov, and Comrade Charkov has the Politburo's ear on the matter."

Gorshkov took another drag from the cigarette. One could get to like these little pleasures, but . . . no sense getting hung up on them. This would be his one and only opportunity to smoke one. He let the smoke slowly waft to the ceiling before speaking. "I know that, Pasha. Minister Charkov has ordered me to send a fleet up to North Land and take it by force if my submarine doesn't return, or at least contact me in the next forty-eight hours. The base at Polyarnyy is alerted and is making preparations this very minute. They sail the moment I give the word." He crushed out the stub and said, "Pasha, if Admiral Popov has kept control of North Land for himself, he has to be stopped. You know, I've always felt Boris was a little crazy, and unfit for any command, but as you said, he has high-ranking friends."

"Then, we'd better hope that your man comes back safely, and with Admiral Popov in tow, eh, comrade?" With that, Doneck tossed the almost-full pack of cigarettes on the admiral's desk, and left without looking back.

Langley, Virginia, 2300 hours. A bleary-eyed chief of naval operations, Admiral Charles "Chi-Chi" Mason, blustered past the skeleton staff at CIA headquarters, shooed off a young security guard who didn't instantly recognize him, and pushed his way into the director's office. Cultrain looked up from a pile of folders on his desk and waved hello. "Glad you could make it on such short notice. Have a seat."

Mason slammed his leather briefcase on the long teak desk and sputtered, "This better be good, Cultrain, dragging me out here at this hour."

"I think we've got trouble, Mason, with a capital T."

The CNO immediately removed a big, expensive cigar from a breast pocket and tore away the protective cellophane wrapper. He bit off the tip and leaned forward to accept a light from Cultrain. "Get to the point, please. What the hell's so important?"

The director tossed a packet of 8 × 10 glossies in Mason's direction. "Have a look at these satellite photos, Chi-Chi."

Mason flipped through them, letting out a long, low whistle. "Damn. The Russkies have half their North Fleet heading east toward North Land. Why are they reinforcing the base there, when they should be dismantling it?"

"Exactly. Our agreement goes into effect in a month. We gave them all winter to dismantle the damned military base. We've got an inspection scheduled for the beginning of March. And now this."

Mason slid the pack of photos back to Cultrain, all but one. "Mind if I keep this one?" It showed a phalanx of a dozen large surface ships streaming through the Barents Sea, heading northeast. "This'll update my own data."

"Keep it. Those shots are only six hours old."

Mason tucked his prize into his briefcase. "Somebody ought to notify the president."

"In the morning."

Mason disagreed. "That's too late. The future of the world could rest on this movement of ships. Don't you remember the Cuban missile crisis?"

Cultrain smiled. "That was thirty some odd years ago, Chi-Chi. I was barely out of college."

"And still wet behind the ears. Well, I was aboard a cruiser taking part in the blockade. We were all shitting bricks until the Russkies turned tail and ran back home. Good old Johnny boy called Krushchev's bluff, he did. And a good thing for all of us. Well, I look at this as another Cuban missile crisis, only now we're playing for higher stakes. The president has to know about this right away."

Cultrain sat back in his seat, his hands steepled in front of him, fingertips drumming nervously. "Okay, go tell him."

"You just better get off your fat ass and go with me,

Cultrain. This is your data."

"And your responsibility as CNO." He tried to stare down Mason, but the CNO didn't waver. "I suppose I'd better come with you to keep you from overwhelming Spooner with bullshit instead of facts." He rubbed his weary eyes, replaced his glasses, and slowly got up. "Let's go see the old man. We'll take my limo."


President Spooner had the Soviet Ambassador on the carpet within an hour. Secretary of State Bushnell was present, along with Cultrain and Mason. "I demand an explanation right now, Gregori. You can cut right through the party-line rhetoric and tell me why half your Northern Fleet is heading toward North Land at this very moment when just the opposite should be happening."

Cultrain and Mason shared a smile. The president wasn't wasting words on this.

"I'm sorry, Mr. President, but I know nothing about which you speak."

Spooner nodded, and Bushnell handed the ambassador two of the 8 × 10s. "Anything there look familiar to you?"

The Russian was flustered. "Some ships. So?"

Mason said, "We've identified the *Lubovich*, here," he said, pointing to a heavy cruiser, "and the *Ashkenatze*. We're working on the others now."

"I demand an explanation from your government now, Gregori. The lessons of your Cuban fiasco were not lost on us here."

The Soviet ambassador was seething. The satellite photos were excellent, and he was certain that the ID was correct. But what the hell *was* going on up north? He'd better find out, and fast. These crazy Yankees were breathing hellfire.

# Chapter 15

Captain Andre Grodsky was happy for the opportunity to prove his abilities on his own. Until recently, all submarine commanders were subordinated to his former mentor, Igor Borodine, and his special submarine, the *Sea Demon*. But now, since Cmorade Borodine had disgraced himself and been sent to prison, he himself had become number one. He, Andre Ivanovich Grodsky, would have the honor of bringing that traitor Popov home in chains.

It had been two days since he'd transmitted his whereabouts to headquarters via extremely low-frequency ELF signals. Grodsky knew his main adversary, Shevchenko, was a worthy opponent, and realized the need to maintain radio silence. Now, at less than fifty miles from his target, his task was to slip into the bastion undetected, send his ten-man scuba team ashore to rendezvous with the KGB officers, arrest Popov, if necessary, and sprint him off to Polyarnyy.

"Comrade Captain," the sonar officer keyed the bridge. "It looks like a minefield ahead. The bearing is zero five seven . . . range five kilometers . . . depth two zero meters."

Grodsky lifted the MC mike to his lips. "Engineer, engines ahead one-third. DO, dive to five zero meters."

"Yes, Comrade Captain." Both officers did as they were ordered.

151

Grodsky realized he was diving precariously close to the bottom, but he had little choice. All the island groups in the Arctic, north of Siberia, were merely the high points of an undersea plateau which was an extension of the Soviet mainland. The sea was shallow for the most part all the way from the Kola Peninsula to the eastern shores of North Land, where the continental shelf fell precipitously down a sharp escarpment to the north and east.

The submariner cursed to himself. Popov had set this trap well. The seafloor was due to rise another twenty meters just ahead. An unwary skipper might be lulled into the minefield while he was intent on keeping well above the bottom. He checked his charts of the area: this quadrant was fairly well known to him, as he had trained in the region. He decided to play it safe and circle the area cautiously, looking out for further limpet minefields. The problem, of course, was that he had to use his active sonar to positively establish the coordinates. The mines didn't emit any sounds for his passive sonar to pick up.

*Bastard.* Grodsky cursed Popov's efficiency as he changed course and took a more northeasterly route to the reactor site. Finally, a breakthrough. He marked his position on the chart, noted the longitude and latitude in the ship's log, and picked his way through the slot formed by tiny Shmidta Island to the west, and the larger Komsomolets Island, which housed the reactor plant and the submarine bastion on its northwest shore. He would use the reciprocal route for his return to Polyarnyy.

"Comrade Captain, excuse me, but we are entering shallow water."

Grodsky nodded to his EXO, and noted that the depth gauge on the bulkhead read thirty meters, almost periscope depth for the *Alfa*. Now comes the tricky part, he said to himself. Fifty kilometers to go. He told his exec, "Misha, have the men rig for silence."

"Yes, comrade." The EXO passed the word down the line,

and every man not specifically assigned a task in running the boat got into his bunk. The toilets were turned off, and the garbage disposal system was shut down.

Grodsky keyed his chief engineer. "Slow down to zero five knots. I only need to make steerageway until we enter the harbor."

"Aye, aye, Comrade Captain."

The *Alfa* crawled along uneventfully at five knots for the next ten miles. Grodsky felt that Popov must have considered the line of limpet mines to be sufficient discouragement for any approaching submarines or large surface ships. At any rate, he was feeling lucky. The thermography screen in the CIC showed a rise of almost ten degrees in the ambient water temperature, signifying his approach to the ice-free zone surrounding the power plant. He was almost there. He could almost feel it.

The scuba team was advised to stand ready to go ashore in a rigid-hull inflatable submersible vessel designed after an American model. It could travel up to ten kilometers underwater, at speeds of thirty knots on the surface. The divers wore heavyweight cold weather wetsuits to protect against the usually freezing waters of the Arctic.

Just then, a distinct pinging sound reverberated throughout the *Alfa's* hull. Grodsky got a sickly feeling in his gut, but tried not to show any emotion to his crew. He picked up the mike. "Sonar, report in."

"Comrade, there is a series of five sonobuoys running north-south on our port flank. We are approximately five meters from the third buoy in the chain."

"Very well. Helmsman, right rudder five degrees. . . . Come to zero three five."

The helmsman repeated the orders even as the sub shifted to a northeasterly course.

"Steady as she goes. Engineer, reduce speed to zero three knots."

"Aye, aye, comrade. Making zero three."

The next fifteen minutes were nerveracking for Grodsky. Detection meant certain death. The minutes ticked away. The sonar sounds became more faint, until finally he felt he'd lost contact.

Captain Sergei Shevchenko had been following the progress of the *Alfa* with a sadistic glee from the bridge of his command submarine, the *Yankee*-class ballistic missile sub *Hornet*. That fool, Sergei thought. He believes he's eluded us by turning away from our active sonobuoys. Hah . . . right into the path of our passive sonar line! In fact, Shevchenko had personally been following Grodsky's progress from the moment the *Alfa* tripped off the sonar ground array sensors, which were coordinated with the mine fields at the fifty-mile perimeter.

Sergei was proud of that system, which he'd designed himself. It was set so that a vessel would either be sunk by the limpet mines, or trip off the sonar system if it managed to avoid the underwater explosive devices. Everything else from that point had been designed to funnel an enemy sub, or surface vessel, for that matter, into a trap that left no margin for escape. It was now simply a matter of time. He watched the image of the enemy sub intently on the sonar screen. His snare was about to spring shut.

"Comrade Captain, I hear hydraulic hatch noises. Something is happening."

Sergei grabbed a spare headset and placed a receiver over one ear. Sure enough, a hatch opening. "Arm tubes two and four."

The torpedo room replied, "Two and four armed, Comrade Captain."

"Conn, sonar. I am picking up sounds of a small motor coming from the direction of the target."

"Alert the patrol craft to stand ready to intercept a small surface craft." He said to his second in command, "I'll bet they're using one of those American sub-skimmers. That will give our surface craft something to practice on."

The *Hornet's* fire control officer called out, "Comrade Captain, the target is dead ahead, range one kilometer. We have prepared a firing solution."

Sergei smiled and said to his exec, "I could put one right up his ass now. The fool wouldn't even know what hit him."

The EXO allowed himself a chuckle. He realized that a sub's sonar didn't function directly aft, and that it had to occasionally veer from side to side to "clear its baffles," as they called the procedure of checking behind themselves. And, he also knew that they'd bullied the target sub's skipper into concentrating on where it was heading, rather than checking what was behind it. His captain was quite right . . . they could bugger the bastard right now, just as smoothly as they pleased.

Shevchenko keyed his sonar officer. "Sonar, hammer him hard. Really let him know we've got him."

"Yes, comrade."

Sergei put a hand on his exec's shoulder as the EXO took his place at the firing controls. "Fire when I tell you." He picked up the ship-to-ship radio and held it to his lips. Then, "Sonar, *now.*"

A staccato blast of sonar pings rang out against the target, and echoed back inside the *Hornet.* There was no mistaking the message to the *Alfa.* He'd been had. Shevchenko gave his demands to the target sub. "Ahoy, *Alfa* captain. You have exactly ten seconds to acknowledge your surrender and to surface your boat. We give you a chance to save your crew."

Grodsky listened to the heavy sonar percussions ringing through his hull. He froze in his tracks, surprised—no, shocked. Where did it come from? How did he miss it? What to do?

"*Alfa*, you have five seconds left to surrender. Acknowledge, or die."

Behind them. Of course. "Why didn't I . . ."

Every hand in the *Alfa's* attack center stared incredulously at Grodsky. Why didn't he say it? Surrender, damn it, or we're all dead, their faces seemed to say.

Instead, the *Alfa's* skipper went through his evasion procedure by rote, just as taught at the training center. "Helmsman, right rudder ten degrees. DO, up planes one five degrees. . . . Engineer . . . ."

No one moved, too stunned at their captain's inability to react properly. The EXO made a grab for the ship-to-ship radio to yell out, we accept, we surrender. His words were drowned out by an explosion. A torpedo hit the stern and blew it away. The sea flooded the engine room, instantly killing that crew. A bulkhead folded. The hull crumpled, severing the pipes that cooled the engine's nuclear power plant.

More bulkheads cracked from the pressure of the sea, and the *Alfa* lurched to the bottom. Captain Grodsky tumbled forward and hit his skull on the deck. As he lay dying, the *Alfa's* reactor began its meltdown, blasting through the hatches protecting the forward compartments from the onslaught.

Aboard the *Hornet*, Sergei listened in fascination to the sounds of the *Alfa* sub and its crew dying less than a mile away. He knew there'd be no survivors. Time to move on. "DO, prepare to surface."

A siren sounded, and compressed air forced ballast from the forward and midships compartments. The *Hornet* rose rapidly to the surface. Shevchenko told his exec, "Take the conn. I'm going up top."

A noncom scurried up ahead of Sergei to open the conning tower's hatch, then followed his captain into the outside bridge. The two of them watched the wetsuit-clad scuba divers come to the surface in their inflatable raft, bewildered by what was happening. A moment ago they had sneaked up to within a few kilometers of shore and were leaving the submarine to start their part of the mission. Now they were bobbing on the surface, with ten divers armed with AK-47s looking up at two patrol boats equipped with heavy machine guns aiming down at them.

For a moment nobody moved. Then Sergei Shevchenko decided their fate for them. He keyed the patrol craft and gave the order. "Fire," he said. And almost as an afterthought, "No survivors."

"So, Gregori, what did you tell them?"

The ambassador to the United States looked nervously from one inquisitor to another. He knew his career was on the line, or worse. Here he was being raked over by five top-ranking Politburo members who realized as much as he that the wrong answer could provoke a war with the West. He swallowed, and said as evenly as he could, "Comrade General Secretary, I assured President Spooner that our fleet was merely engaged in war-game maneuvers in the Barents Sea, and for them not to be concerned."

Defense said, "And he believed you, eh, Gregori?"

The ambassador said nothing.

Foreign Minister Grumpke said, "Well, at least Gregori held them off, comrades." He didn't admit to an offensive against North Land on our part, he thought. And if the Americans don't like it, let them protest at the UN, for all the good it will do them.

The somber-faced general secretary asked, "Are we so sure that this offensive against Popov is the only way to handle this? I have my doubts. Admiral Gorshkov is in favor of sending in a super sub with a strike force of commandos."

"That's already been tried, comrade," Defense Minister Charkov put in. "We've tried to reason with the man. We've sent up a team to wrest control from him. They haven't been heard from since. Furthermore, Gorshkov has already sent one of his best submariners up there. And he hasn't reported back." He chuckled softly. "Perhaps Comrade Admiral

157

Popov has the right attitude? Don't give in to the Yankee imperialist pigs. North Land is rightfully ours, to do with what we please. Maybe we've given in too much to their demands. It's obvious that it can be defended by a very small force of determined men."

KGB Director Plotnick slammed his fist down hard on the table. "Enough of this foolishness, comrades. I sent a dozen good men to North Land with the sole purpose of relieving Popov of his command. He's probably killed them. I have no intention of allowing an outlaw to determine policy by default. Popov must be controlled. And," he added, "in such a way that anyone with such anarchist views will be sure to get our message. I say, have the fleet continue on to North Land. Gregori can continue to tell the Americans whatever he wants. Just stall them off till we crush that bastard."

Charkov shrugged. He wasn't about to take on the KGB openly.

The general secretary said, "Comrade Plotnick is correct. We must use sufficient force to crush the resistance so that no other fools try to get away with something like this. Anyone opposed?"

No one was.

"Good. Then it's settled." He turned to the minister of defense. "Yuri, have Gorshkov order the fleet on to North Land. Tell him . . . tell him that failure will not be tolerated."

# Chapter 16

It was settled, then. Gorshkov ordered the North Fleet to proceed forthwith to North Land. Admiral Kasimov, the fleet commander, was airlifted to the carrier *Leningrad* to personally oversee this engagement from the flag bridge. The armada set off with the flagship at its center, flanked by the cruisers *Lubovich* and *Ashkenatze*, with a destroyer riding point and two others protecting the supply ships, tankers, and troop transports that made up the support group. Five *Alfas* were temporarily removed from protecting the submarine bastion off the Kola Peninsula, and sailed as the advance guard.

On the fifth day out, the fleet rounded the horn of the big island, Novaya Zemlya, and began its passage across the open water to North Land. At three hundred kilometers out, Kasimov ordered two of the carrier's Badgers to fly over the target area and bring back aerial photographs of the site. The admiral was interested in the condition of the airstrip, missile battery placements, and possible drop sites for his *Spaeznaz* paratroops.

His was a difficult job. If Popov chose to fight it out, Kasimov didn't have the option of using missile bombardment, or of sending in fighter-bombers, for fear of hitting the reactor and setting off a nuclear accident. On the other hand,

Popov could use any tactics at his disposal to destroy the fleet. What Kasimov hoped to do was to surgically amputate Popov's defenses with lightning pinpoint raids on his facilities. Once he got his forces safely onto the island, they could easily overpower the defenders and shut down the reactor. Without the protection of the reactor to hide behind, Popov could be handily crushed.

Boris Popov twisted his mustache as he went over the communications he'd intercepted via the STARSAT network. Didn't they realize he had access also? "Sergei, look at this." He had his charts spread out in front of him. "There's a lot of radio chatter coming in from somewhere about here. From all indications, there is a sizable naval operation in the vicinity." He pointed to a spot about two hundred miles to the southwest.

Shevchenko nodded. "War-game maneuvers?"

"No." Popov was shaking his head. "More likely they have come searching for their merchant ship and their people. I doubt that the submarine got any messages back to them, or we'd have intercepted them."

Sergei agreed. "I'd like to send out one of the choppers to have a look."

"Good idea. Go ahead." Suddenly Popov jumped up out of his seat, knocking his chair over backward. He kicked at it and shouted, "Bastards. Do they think they can take me by force? Sergei, I'll destroy them first." He began hyperventilating.

Shevchenko stood up. "What would you have me do, Comrade Admiral?"

"Have the missile batteries moved in closer to the plant. From there we can shoot down their aircraft, and they can't retaliate without taking a chance of hitting the reactor. Hah."

Shevchenko was already on the phone calling in orders to

the field commanders.

"Have any of the prisoners not directly needed to man the power plant kept behind barbed wire. It won't do to have them running amuck if we come under attack."

"Good idea. And, Comrade Admiral, I would suggest that you move your command post to the *Hornet*. It has excellent communications facilities, and it would be near impossible for the enemy to fire at you, since they wouldn't know where you were. Besides, if things go against us, we could easily escape."

"Escape? I have no desire to escape, Sergei. I'm staying here until they accede to my demands that I be promoted to admiral of the entire Soviet Fleet."

"Gorshkov's position?"

"Who do you think is responsible for that task force on its way up here?"

"We don't know that yet, comrade. Perhaps . . ."

The whining of an air-raid siren interrupted the discussion. The red phone on Popov's desk rang until the admiral grabbed the handpiece and shouted, "What?"

Shevchenko looked at his mentor.

"Damn it." Popov slammed down the receiver. "Two Badgers flying in from the southwest about fifteen kilometers out. We have them on radar."

"Part of the fleet?"

"Scouting party. Don't give them a chance to report back."

Shevchenko saluted and radioed his artillery colonel. "Take them out as soon as you acquire your targets. Don't give them a chance to signal our defenses back to their carrier."

Sergei moved to the doorway of the command post and peered up at a low-flying aircraft just coming into view. It did a low, slow sweep over the prominence of rocky land that the base was built on, and headed away. A second plane followed at a more discreet altitude. "Fire, damn you, fire!"

Shevchenko shouted out loud.

Almost as if in answer to his command, the lead aircraft took a hit from a SAM missile at its tail section, jinked up and down a moment, and spun out of control trailing a plume of black smoke. The second jet took a direct hit and seemed to disintegrate in a fiery explosion that sent flaming pieces of fuselage cascading down like a fireworks display.

"Good work," Shevchenko said to no one, and reentered the bunker. "Now I'll send out a chopper to pay our friends a call. We'll need to know the fleet strength, if we're going to be able to defend ourselves."

Popov continued to toy with his handlebar mustache, first one side, then the other. "We already know something of their strength, Sergei. Those Badgers had to be launched from a carrier. There is nothing else up here. In the North Fleet, a carrier, probably the *Leningrad*, is always escorted by two cruisers and a complement of destroyers. Next, they need support ships to transport fuel and equipment, and, if I'm not mistaken, they are bringing in troops to overrun our position. They know they can't bomb us out. So they'll try to flush us out on the ground, eh? Mark my word, Sergei. Send your chopper, but remember what I have just told you."

Shevchenko smiled. "And of course, they will send in more submarines to join the fate of the last *Alfa*. Ah, Comrade Admiral, you are a genius. They should have made you commander of the fleet long ago."

"Soon they also will realize that, Sergei. Now, it's time for you to take your battle station. We have work to do."

"Are you sure you won't join me?"

"Go. You know what to do?"

"Rest assured, comrade. Nothing will penetrate our bastion. We have SOSUS sensors out at seventy kilometers, and also at twenty. There are mine fields to lead their subs into our line of fire, and anti-submarine nets to keep them out of where we are exposed the most, from the north. But as you know, they will most likely approach from the west, and

162

we will be ready for them. I have a half dozen *Alfas* arranged to guard the boomers."

"Have your two Sierras choose their targets carefully. The primary target should be the carrier, of course. Next, any cruisers, then troop carriers."

"What about the tankers?"

Popov shook his head. "They're closer to North Land than to home. Better not cut off their fuel supply so they have the option of returning to Polyarnyy. Otherwise, they might feel that there is no way out except to over-run our base, here. No, hit the fighting ships first."

"Aye, aye, Admiral. Good luck."

Sergei was driven to the pier by one of the guards, and immediately took over command of the *Hornet*. "I have the conn," he announced.

"Comrade Captain." A radioman entered the control room. "I have just received this from the chopper pilot. He transmitted barely minutes before being shot down."

Shevchenko took the message from the man. It listed the coordinates of the surface ships as they approached the tiny island, Ostrov Vize, the last bit of land they would pass on their way to North Land. A formidable task force, much as the old man had predicted. And they showed they were serious when they shot down his chopper. Well, they would pay dearly for that.

Sergei took a look around the command center, which he personally had converted to his own specifications. There was a dedicated monitor assigned to each of his subs, and a hotline to Popov in the command bunker. In the event that the admiral had to leave his post, the entire operation could then be controlled from the *Hornet*.

Satisfied that he was as ready as could be, he ordered a dive to five hundred meters, still well within the tolerances for this class of submarine. The diving officer began calling out the depth changes. "Passing through one hundred meters . . . one fifty meters. . . ."

163

The *Hornet* eased itself into the deep water to the north of Komsomolets; at an angle of twenty-five degrees, nice and steady, it would take its place among the others. The monstrous *Typhoon* lay quietly at seven hundred meters, snuggled into a deep canyon at the edge of the continental shelf. The remaining boomers were dispersed in the shallow waters of the ice-free zone, but under the protection of the *Alfas*. Shevchenko felt they were quite secure.

Popov climbed down a flight of stairs to the control room he had set up in a converted bomb shelter. A team of radio operators supervised by a lieutenant manned the computerized communications equipment. He was barely settled in when the call came from the radar officer. "Here they come, Comrade Admiral. About twenty of them."

Popov sat down at the radar console, set the distance for twenty kilometers, and watched almost two dozen blips moving their way in four groups, each forming a V-shaped flight pattern. "Open fire when you have acquired your targets. And remember, no survivors."

The first wave struck at 0900 hours, diving low and firing rockets at the reinforced concrete command bunker. They were easy prey for the SAM battery at the base of the reactor plant. Four Badgers were blasted from the sky before getting their missiles off. Two others managed to release their rockets before being struck by the surface-to-air missiles. One of them spun out of control and splashed into the harbor, joining the other four. The last of them crashed into the rocky shore and burst into flames.

The second phase of the aerial attack came from two squads of six jets each, and they picked out targets in the harbor. One rocket hit the ice breaker, *Revolution*, and a fire broke out at the stern, just abaft the bridge. A team of firefighters rushed out with hoses gushing sea water, trying to put out the flames.

A jet streaked in low, and in four seconds it loosed six hundred rounds of machine-gun fire at the fire control party, cutting them down. The fire raged out of control. A hurried message went out to Admiral Popov from the skipper of the icebreaker. "Comrade Admiral, we are being cut to pieces. Can't you do something?"

"Keep your head down, Captain. I'm going to have the *Revolution* towed alongside of the merchantman. They might not fire on you and risk endangering their own ship."

Popov ordered two of his tugs to shove and pull the icebreaker alongside the *Kirov*, to share the same double slip like two peas in a pod. One of the tugs was destroyed before the task was completed.

Popov was shouting at his AA crew. "Get those damn Badgers. What the hell are you doing up there?"

A SAM battery atop the reactor homed in on the six jets making up the left wing and fired a barrage that hit five of them. A second volley destroyed the remaining Badger and chased off the right flight wing. Fires were raging on the ground. The burning carcasses of several fighter jets floated in the harbor.

Aboard the merchant ship *Kirov*, Captain Lubeck found one of the AK-47 assault rifles left behind by KGB men who went ashore. He shouted for the merchant marine sailors aboard to join him in storming the icebreaker. A few brave souls grabbed weapons and ran to the gunwales and began firing at the crew trying to put out the fire.

The first mate watched his captain being shot down, leaving him in charge of the burning ship. He radioed his dilemma to the command bunker. Popov was furious. He raised Shevchenko aboard the *Hornet* and gave him his orders. "Sink the *Kirov*."

"But comrade, that will leave no way off this island except by submarine."

"Sink it, Sergei. That's an order."

"Aye, aye, Admiral." Sergei switched off the radio. "Damn," he cursed to himself. The old man was losing it. Maybe he *was* going crazy. He turned around to see the

165

radio officer looking at him. "Well, what the hell are you staring at?"

"Sorry, Comrade Captain. Did you want me to notify one of the *Alfas?*"

"No," he shouted. "Yes, yes, of course. Patch me to Captain Troika."

"Yes, Comrade Captain."

In a moment, the *Alfa's* captain was on the line. "Troika here."

"This is Captain Shevchenko. You are ordered to sink the *Kirov.*"

"But . . ."

"Sink the *Kirov,* Captain."

"Yes, of course, sir. At once. Over."

"Out." Sergei toggled his set off, angry with himself.


Aboard the carrier *Leningrad,* eight of the Badger jets that set out a half hour earlier limped back. Two had sustained minor damage.

Admiral Kasimov quickly arranged a meeting of the commanders of the two cruisers, himself and the captain of the *Leningrad,* and the flight leader, who miraculously escaped serious damage from the SAM missile bombardment. "Gentlemen, we're here to reassess the situation. The colonel here will give his evaluation of the first phase of our attack."

The men were arranged around a large table with a three-dimensional chart of Komsomolets Island and the waters offshore. Each of the fleet vessels was indicated by a scale-model replica, and all were arranged in their current positions. The pilot leaned over the table, made a slight adjustment as he saw it, and proceeded. "The missile batteries are here." He placed a replica at the base of the power plant, "and here, right on the roof of the damn thing. How are we supposed to knock them out? We don't dare fire so close to the reactor. I lost four planes trying to get in position to hit the batteries without hitting the building."

"Strafe them."

The fighter pilot looked up at the admiral.

"Strafe the SAM battery atop the building next time. Your machine-gun rounds won't penetrate that concrete. It's almost five meters thick, and reinforced."

For the first time, the flight leader smiled. "Thank you, Comrade Admiral. You are most astute." He toppled the model missile launcher battery on top of the building. Then his hand moved to the low concrete building carved into the rocky ground facing the harbor. "We believe this to be the headquarters building. I personally watched it take one direct hit. I think we should concentrate on that on the next attack."

"I agree," Kasimov said. "Please continue, Comrade Colonel."

"This is housing for the hundreds of prisoners who man the power plant and do most of the menial work around the base. And this compound is their exercise yard. It's encircled with high fences topped with barbed wire. No sense in firing on them. Beyond that, to the north and east, is the guards' quarters. Here is the airstrip, just as it appears in the model. I think if we can take the airstrip, we can fight our way to the coast, here." The colonel was moving imaginary forces with his hands, pushing the enemy toward the harbor.

"Very good, Colonel. On the next wave, we should concentrate on dropping paratroopers along here, at the base of the slope, and have them make a drive for the airstrip." Kasimov slammed a fist into the palm of his other hand. "Damn, I think we have a chance. Colonel, how does the harbor look?"

"Grim. We managed to sink a tug, and I know of a direct hit to the stern of their icebreaker. But as I made a last pass overhead, I saw them maneuvering the ship next to the *Kirov*. We can't fire on it when it's that close to one of ours."

Admiral Kasimov shook his head. "They sank the *Kirov*."

"They *what?*" The pilot couldn't believe his ears.

"No one saw it take a hit, so they must have torpedoed it. At any rate, it dropped like a stone. I doubt that there were any survivors, or else Captain Lubeck would have radioed us by now."

The flight leader scratched his head. "Well, that leaves the icebreaker extremely vulnerable to an air attack. Don't they realize that? They've just forfeited their only surface passage off the island."

"If you're trying to tell me that Admiral Popov has lost his mind, I'd be inclined to agree with you, Colonel. I want you to destroy the *Revolution* during the second wave. Understood?"

"That'd be my pleasure, comrade." Thoughts of revenging his fallen comrades swept through the pilot's mind. He would sink the icebreaker himself.

"Give your men a few hours rest, Comrade Colonel. We strike again at 1500 hours. The sun will be well below the horizon by then, and maybe, just maybe, we can catch them by surprise."

# Chapter 17

Popov realized he'd won the first round. He also knew that his enemies would be back, and in force. He called his officers to the command bunker to plan their defense. "We were lucky the last time," he told them. "I'm sure the pilots had orders not to fire at anything close to the reactor plant. That worked well for us. Merely by hiding our SAM batteries in and around the power plant, we were able to shoot their planes from the sky without fear of retaliation. You can be certain that they won't allow themselves to become a shooting gallery when they strike again."

The artillery commander spoke up. "What would you have us do, comrade?"

"Give us a rundown of your strength, Colonel."

"Well, I have four SAM launchers, each capable of firing up to eight rockets simultaneously. Three are mobile units, and the fourth is atop the plant itself."

Popov nodded. "What about the smaller units?"

"Ah. I have two dozen hand-held German Scorpion rocket launchers. They are operated by one or two men, and are highly mobile. In fact, they can be fired from the back of a jeep."

"Or a foxhole. Or a tugboat. Or the doorway of my bunker."

"Yes, Comrade Admiral. That is correct."

"Ground forces?"

A major stepped forward. "My colonel is personally commanding a troop of fifty men who are searching for the escaped Arctic Wolves, comrade. I have another three platoons at my command."

Not nearly enough, Popov figured. Well, we'll see about that.. Maybe I have a trick or two left up my sleeves. "Captain, what is the situation in the harbor?"

"Not good, Admiral Popov. I fear that with the *Kirov* sunk, the icebreaker *Revolution* will be a prime target. The tugs are almost completely defenseless. The fuel depots are exposed, and the patrol craft are sitting ducks."

Popov looked at his group of field officers, from one to the other. "If I were commanding the task force, here's what I would do," he said. "I'd send in my jets, concentrating on the troop quarters, the command complex, the fuel tanks, and the harbor facilities. I'd sink every vessel I could find. And while the forces here were trying to cope with all that, I'd try to land paratroopers around the perimeter of this base and let them fight their way back to the harbor.

"I'd try to land my troop carriers in the harbor, and that means at least one icebreaker and some support ships, possibly a destroyer or two. And, of course, submarines to clear the way for them. I'd try to destroy everything the forces here would need to fight a prolonged engagement. And I'd wage a war of attrition. The only thing I'd leave standing on the island would be the nuclear plant."

Popov let all that sink in. "So . . . what do we do? What kind of defense shall we put forth, comrades? Anyone?" To the artillery commander, he said, "Colonel, how would you deploy your forces?"

The colonel replied, "I don't have a large enough force to defend against all that, Comrade Admiral."

"Major?" Popov was getting annoyed.

"A hundred and fifty men is no match for what is likely to

be at least a thousand troops aboard the two troop carriers, Comrade Admiral."

"And you, Captain?"

"I would arm my surface ships with some of the missile batteries. At least we wouldn't go down without a fight, comrade."

"Well, at least one of you has balls. Very good, Captain. What you shall do is arm each of the craft with one or two of the hand-held Scorpions, and disperse your fleet."

"Disperse them?"

"Yes, Captain. The next air strike will be looking to the most damage to us in a lightning raid, to help prevent us from stopping them again. Send your craft to the most remote spots on the harbor. Split them up, and fire on any of the jets that comes within range. That should save most of them."

"Excellent, Comrade Admiral."

"Major, I want you to gather up the hostages that tried to take over my command—all except the deputy minister of defense. He may prove to be an ally. I want you to secure each of the others to the tops of the fuel tanks. Have them spread-eagled, so they present the largest target possible. That will at least get the jet pilots thinking before they drop their bombs.

"Next, I want the prisoners dressed in uniforms, or anything that looks like a uniform. Shirts may be all that's necessary, and stand them outside in groups around our troop quarters, in full view. Place small groups of your men among them with machine gun units and Scorpions. From the air, the jet pilots may confuse them with us and make them primary targets. And disperse the remainder of your forces."

"Very good, Admiral Popov."

"Well, now, Comrade Colonel. Have you any idea now how to deploy your artillery?"

"Disperse them," he answered, sure of himself, finally.

"And have them wiped out completely."

"But . . . you just . . ."

Popov stood there twisting his mustache, glaring at his artillery commander. "Do I have to do all of your thinking for you, Colonel? Listen, here is what I want you to do. . . ."

"Comrade Admiral, here they come."

Popov stood before the giant radar screen that he used to monitor the overall situation. Thirty blips representing Badger fighter jets edged into view, three flight wings in V-formation, each streaking toward its own target.

The left wing veered off and headed for the troop quarters. Each of the ten jets carried a pair of rockets cradled under its swept wings. Twenty rockets hurtled into the two-story block buildings, sending chunks of concrete and steel and human parts in all directions. A second pass with machine-guns spitting fire chewed up the ranks of soldiers outside their barracks. Strange, though, the flight leader seemed to think there should be more resistance from them. Most just stood there and were cut down.

The Badgers went into a steep roll to turn back toward the carrier, and suddenly realized they were being shot at with antiaircraft fire from below. Four jets were caught by surprise. Three burst into flames and careened to the ground. The fourth took a few rounds to the tail, lost altitude, and seemed to be fighting its way back up when the pilot lost control and spiraled into the harbor.

The center flight wing streaked hell-bent toward the harbor, and a dozen rockets blew the icebreaker *Revolution* in half. A secondary explosion sent an immense fireball heavenward, incincerating the nominal crew who remained aboard to defend her.

One diesel fuel tank took a direct hit and sent flames shooting skyward before the wing leader realized there were live targets tied to the tops of the fuel tanks. Human shields.

172

It was a cinch that Popov wasn't putting his own men out as bait. The flight leader called a halt to the raid on the tank farm. They'd have to find another way.

Simultaneously, the third wing zoomed in low over the harbor and blasted the headquarters bunker, chipping away at the reinforced concrete, chewing up radar receivers and power lines along the way. This flight, the jets stayed well clear of the nuclear plant. As the center and right phalanxes regrouped overhead, the missile battery atop the power plant went into action. Eight SAM missiles catapulted into the airspace overhead. Six jets took hits and crashed, one spiraling down and spewing burning parts into the prison yard below.

The flight leader signaled his wingman and said, "Follow me. Let's put a stop to that bastard." They swooped in a hundred feet from the ground, chewing up the distance to the reactor in a horizontal plane below the firing line of the SAM battery. At seemingly the last second, they climbed into view and strafed the missile crew and the launcher. They went into a barrel roll, and followed the survivors of this foray back to the fleet.

From out of nowhere, the three mobile SAM batteries were hauled from out of hiding by heavy trucks and fired their volleys of eight SAMs apiece. Several jets broke formation and streaked back overhead. In unison, they dropped projectiles which burst into thousands of strips of aluminum foil. A few of the missiles got through and blasted their targets into fireballs streaming to earth.

Most of the SAMs were confused by the aluminum flak and burst noisily but harmlessly in air. Thirty jets out, nineteen returning . . . not very good, the flight leader reflected as he headed out to sea, but better than the first wave. And there was nothing much left standing on land except for the power plant itself. Funny, though, the ground forces seemed to die without offering much resistance, almost as if they were resigned to giving up their lives. And

173

most of the surface fleet had escaped their wrath.

On the next sweep, he and his crew would provide cover for the troop carriers and the paratroopers. Then this damn war would be somebody else's.

By the time phase two had ended with the return of the fighter jets, an advance segment of the fleet was already within forty miles of Popov's bastion. Three of the *Alfa* subs had triggered off the SOSUS array at the seventy-kilometer perimeter and were wending their way through the mine field that funneled their unknowing skippers exactly where Sergei Shevchenko wanted them.

They were followed on the surface by two of the destroyers and both troop transports. It was almost as if Popov had written their orders.

The transports were capable of carrying a mechanized battalion in their vehicles, ready to roll out the moment the forward loading ramp touched down on the shore. Each of the monster vessels ferried five hundred men and their jeeps, half-tracks, gear, weapons, and supplies ready to overrun Popov's defenses. The destroyers were there to see to it that none of Popov's subs got through to these troop carriers, in the unlikely event that they got past the fleet's *Alfas*.

At forty kilometers out, the Badgers soared overhead once again to sweep the opposition from their defenses, and to litter the skies with more aluminum chaff to thwart the SAM missiles. Two jumbo transport jets raced in after the fighters, thirty men huddled inside of each, ready to parachute onto the airstrip beyond the camp.

At fifteen kilometers out, the three *Alfas* spread out and cut engines, and coasted in making five knots. Their task; to seek and destroy Popov's sub fleet before it got to the troop transports.

At a depth of twelve hundred feet, Sergei Shevchenko monitored their progress from the attack center of the *Hornet*. His own hunter-killers were lying in wait, hidden by the thermal layer produced by the nuclear plant's hot-water recirculation. The trap had been set, and Sergei waited patiently to set it in motion. The real prey was twenty-five klics back, on the surface, fully laden with enemy troops. Patience, he told himself. Be patient.

Three of Sergei Shevchenko's six-sub *Alfa* fleet remained in the harbor as defenders, while the remainder slipped silently through the well-known mine fields to seek out the enemy surface forces. With the use of small sonobuoys strategically placed at various depth, the skippers of the *Riga*, *Luza*, and *Kuga* knew the exact locations of the three submarines sent ahead to establish safe passage for the transports.

As the invaders cruised overhead at a depth of forty meters, the defenders' sonarmen marked their progress from below the safety of the thermal. One by one, the *Riga*, *Luza*, and *Kuga* slipped silently into position behind their unwary foes. The *Riga's* captain followed an *Alfa* that veered to port, apparently to investigate the antisubmarine nets that blocked access to the harbor from the north. He ordered his fire-control team to prepare a firing solution on this target.

"We have a solution, Comrade Captain."

"Torpedo room, load and arm one and eight."

"Yes, Captain, one and eight armed and ready."

With minimal agitation of the sea around them, the skipper guided his sub through the thermal barrier and came up seven hundred meters behind his prey, keeping within the protective void of the dead area of the *Alfa's* passive sonar.

The *Alfa* made a sudden turn to starboard, possibly to clear her baffles. A moment later its highly sensitive sonar picked up the *Riga* on its tail and went into a dive, picking up speed as it dropped.

*Riga's* sonarman followed the *Alfa's* progress, calling out the changing coordinates and speed. The skipper keyed his fire control team. "Reacquire the target."

"We've got it, Comrade."

"Fire one," he ordered.

"Number one launched."

The wire-guided torpedo left the tube with a whoosh of compressed air and dived after the *Alfa*, building speed and very quickly closing the gap between them. Aboard the *Riga*, an officer slaved the torpedo into the sub's own sonar system, and it mimicked every move the *Alfa* made to break away. At forty knots, sub and fish dived toward the shallow bottom and leveled out a few meters off the rocky harbor floor.

"One minute of fuel left in the torpedo, Comrade Captain."

The skipper pushed his peaked cap up high on his head and wiped sweat off his forehead with his sleeve. "Increase the torp's speed to six zero knots."

In seconds the torpedo closed the gap and collided with the *Alfa* just as it tried a desperate lunge to starboard to evade the fish. The sub took the hit almost broadside, breaking in two from the concussion, and sank to the bottom.

Almost at the same time, the *Kuga* unleashed a torpedo at its target, and a second *Alfa* died.

The remaining *Alfa* evaded the torpedo fired at it by the *Luza* and headed out of the harbor. Its skipper hoped to gain more room to maneuver in the open sea. The *Riga* had its escape route blocked to starboard while the *Kuga* converged on it from the port side. Two torpedoes sped after the target sub, and it dived deep to evade them at the mouth of the harbor.

An enormous explosion sent shock waves back to the three defenders. The *Alfa* had run into the mine field and was struck immediately afterward by one of the fish. Its crew never stood a chance. Chunks of the hull and instruments cascaded to the bottom.

The three defending submarines headed back inside the confines of the harbor, circling at three different levels with active sonar pinging away at potential invaders. There were no more to be found. They'd successfully swept the bastion clear of invaders. Their job now was to defend against anything that got by their three counterparts who'd gone off to find the fleet, and to present to them a lethal greeting.

On the first pass, the lead wing of fighter jets flew in low to avoid Popov's radar detection, leaving behind a cloud of metallic foil cluttering up the skies above the base. The second wing bombed the headquarters bunker and took another swipe at the troop quarters. The first wing circled around and laid down a pattern of ground fire aimed at keeping heads indoors. Under this umbrella of coverage, the two jumbo-jet transports flew in overhead and dropped their twin loads of thirty paratroopers each onto the airstrip beyond the fringes of the base, and turned to make the two-hundred-mile flight back to the carrier *Leningrad*.

The two destroyers were churning up the seas, doing twenty knots ahead of the twin troop carriers. They were almost within reach of the mouth of the harbor when the first submarine was detected. They were well prepared. Admiral Kasimov had warned them about this possibility.

A chopper went aloft above the lead destroyer and circled the area of the sub sighting, a sonar detector suspended from a long cable dipping below the surface of the sea. The pilot set the sonobuoy to active, and the pinging ripped through the *Alfa* below.

Aboard the ship, the sonar officer was following the action. "Torp in the water," he radioed his captain. "Bearing one two zero . . . range one hundred ninety-five meters . . . speed four zero."

The destroyer's skipper ordered his ship to turn hard left, away from the speeding torpedo. "Engine ahead full," he ordered his engineer. The crew stood on the starboard rail and watched the silvery fish pass behind their stern, its guidance wires severed when the *Alfa* dived to avoid the chopper's sonar.

The chopper dropped a marker buoy and withdrew to another position. The destroyer fired off an ASROC antisubmarine rocket, which arched into the water near the marker, and began an undersea search for the submarine. The *Alfa* was no match. The projectile's own sonar homed in on the sub and tracked it down, closed the gap, and exploded against the stern.

The chopper dipped its sonobuoy at the site of the explosion. "Score that as a hit, Comrade Captain. We can hear the hull-popping sounds of the *Alfa*. Good shooting."

While there was celebration aboard the first destroyer, two more submarines were stalking its sister ship, which was followed closely behind by a troop carrier. An alert sonar operator sent a warning to his captain. "Sub off the starboard bow, Comrade. Bearing zero six five . . . range three thousand meters . . . speed two five knots . . . depth of seven zero meters."

Another search helicoper was dispatched to the target area.

"Torpedo in the water," sonar warned, and the skipper took evasive action, turning his ship away, while the chopper dipped his sonobuoy above the target.

"Torpedo in the water off the port quarter, Comrade Captain."

The warning came too late. The two *Alfas* had converged on the destroyer from both sides, firing their torpedoes almost simultaneously. The destroyer hadn't a chance from the start. In trying to evade the starboard torpedo, it sped directly into the path of the other streaming toward her from the port side.

One torpedo hit amidships, just above the destroyer's keel, blasting a gaping hole in the hull. As the ship listed heavily, the other torpedo slammed into the exposed underbelly, below the munitions storage magazine. The destroyer exploded with a mighty roar, actually leaping from the water at the bows, and slamming back hard against the surface. There was little time for the crew to escape, but a few lifeboats began to drop from the decks.

Meanwhile, the chopper pilot followed the progress of its target via the sonobuoy suspended from the cockpit. He dropped a torpedo onto the submarine while its skipper was prematurely celebrating his victory. The torp ran true. The *Alfa* took the hit and spiraled to the seafloor. "Bastard," the chopper pilot cursed, and sped to the sinking ship to help rescue any survivors.

High on adrenaline from his decisive kill of the destroyer, the skipper of the surviving submarine, Captain Skolnok, went directly for the troop carrier. He dove to thirty meters and lingered directly in the approach of the oncoming ship. There was nothing Skolnok liked more than a shot at the bows to a submariner, an almost sure kill. He armed two torpedoes and quickly calculated a firing solution. "Fire one."

"One launched."

"Fire two."

"Number two is launched, Comrade Captain."

Both torpedoes caught the troop carrier dead on, blasting gaping holes below the waterline. The immense, squat ship took on water and began to sink at the bows. As the tip of the ship went under, the weight of the vehicles and men aboard shifted forward, dragging the troop carrier down further. Captain Skolnok was jubilant. He would score this one as a kill. The ship would sink slowly, but surely. It was not built to survive this sort of devastation. Now he turned his attention to the remaining transport, forsaking the destroyer's wrath. His mission was made quite clear. Sergei Shevchenko ordered him to stop those troops from coming ashore. If he failed, the bastion could be lost.

The pinging of the chopper's submerged sonar rang throughout the submarine hull. They had located him. Time was of the essence. Skolnok had to reach the troop carrier before the destroyer or its chopper got to him.

"Dive. *Dive*," he ordered. The sub angled toward the target, which had increased speed to escape. He had to cross the path of the destroyer to get to it. "Load and arm one through six."

"Captain, all six tubes for one target."

"I repeat, load and arm one through six."

"Yes, Comrade Captain. Loading and arming all six tubes." The torpedo officer began to think that his captain had lost his mind. What he didn't realize yet, though Skolnok knew, was that they were on a suicide run.

The chopper's sonar was hammering the *Alfa* relentlessly now, and dropping market buoys for the destroyer to follow. The first ASROC was fired at them within minutes. Skolnok ordered a deep dive, and an abrupt change of course to evade it. "Helmsman, hard left rudder ten degrees. EXO, fire off a noisemaker. Planesman, up diving planes one zero."

The highly maneuverable sub jerked, lurched, and pitched, using every trick that Skolnok could come up with. The ASROC missile faltered and lost its target. Now the *Alfa's* skipper had a hard choice to make. He could try to fight off the destroyer, and take a chance on losing the troop carrier, or he could go directly for his main target and sink it, and then worry about his own safety.

Captain Skolnok was handpicked by Sergei Shevchenko for his expertise, as well as his tenacity, dedication, and bravery. He knew his mission, and he would do what it took to accomplish it. He headed directly for the troop carrier making forty knots, the devil be damned. He strode to the fire control computer and checked the sonar image on the screen. All six torpedoes were locked on a track that would discharge them amidships of the target. "Ready one. Fire

180

one," he ordered.

"One launched."

"Ready two, fire two."

The FCO repeated his orders and loosed a second fish.

"Bridge, Sonar. Two rockets chasing us. Bearing is one nine zero . . . range one thousand meters . . . speed is six zero and closing."

"Ready three. Fire three."

"Comrade Captain," the sonar operator was frantic. "I repeat. Two ASROCs directly behind us . . . range five hundred meters."

Skolnok didn't waver for a moment. "Ready four. Fire four."

"Comrade Captain, please do something. We'll be hit. Rockets now three hundred meters behind us. . . ."

"Ready five. Fire five."

The torpedoes streaked toward the troop carrier. Already, one had hit its mark, ripping a hole in the hull above the waterline. With each release of a torpedo, the planesman coolly compensated for the loss of forward ballast. Skolnok was content. He had succeeded in his mission. He had done his job well. If that fool sonarman would only shut his mouth. "Ready six. Fire six."

The ASROC found its mark before the last torpedo was launched. It exploded above the sail, shearing it from the deck at the weld. The second rocket hit the upper deck when the *Alfa* lurched from the initial impact. The sea flooded the main compartment, slamming seaman and officer alike to the deck. When the icy waters reached the engine room, the steam generated burst the reactor's coolant pipes. The nuclear fuel was freed of its constraints and burned out of control, overpowering the screams of the dying, as Captain Skolnok's *Alfa* plunged to the bottom, finally settling alongside the wreck of the troop carrier that was its own target. The sea claimed both victor and victim alike.

# Chapter 18

Captain Sergei Shevchenko had received Skolnok's final message before the submariner's own *Alfa* was fired upon and downed. Two destroyers and two troop carriers had set out to deliver a ground-attack force against Popov. One of each had been sunk, and the second transport ship was listing badly, limping toward the harbor under the protection of the remaining destroyer.

Sergei passed along the news to headquarters, and also to his own *Alfas* safeguarding the harbor. As COMSUBFLT, he told his skippers in no uncertain terms that the reinforcements must not get to shore. The defense of the harbor was in his hands. Admiral Popov had other problems to tend to.

The paratroopers had overrun the airstrip and set up a defensive perimeter. They set up a series of mortar units around the field, and with a lieutenant and his radioman calling out firing coordinates from a high point overlooking the base, they laid down a devastating barrage of rockets on the headquarters complex and barracks.

Before long, little was left standing except for the reactor plant itself, the prison complex, and Popov's underground bunker. Popov realized his small force was becoming annihilated, and knew he had to come up with something fast.

He radioed his submarine commander. "Sergei, our position is being bombarded by the paratroops. We need to respond in a big way to their attack, or our position here will soon be hopeless."

Sergei knew what he had to do. "Sit tight, Comrade Admiral. We will give them something to keep them busy. Can your troops mount a counter-strike once we soften them up?"

"We have no other choice, Sergei. Do what you can, and we will follow up."

Shevchenko contacted his two *Sierra*-class cruise missile subs, used mainly for short- to mid-range ship-to-surface bombardment. He fed them the coordinates of the airstrip, and gave them their orders. Each sub could fire three missiles. No more could be spared except as a last resort.

The first SLCM (sea-launched cruise missile) struck the concrete airfield just as a second group of paratroopers was dropped to back up the advance troops. A gaping crater was left where two dozen men had just landed. Two more SLCMs blasted away at the shocked paratroopers, who were told there would be little, if any, resistance to their drive. They began to scatter for better cover, even as more of their colleagues parachuted from transport jets overhead.

Popov ordered his forces to attack the airstrip. Now, sensing victory, the defenders mounted a counteroffensive that turned the paratroopers' assault into a rout. Those few who survived the counterattack were scattered in the ice- and snow-covered hills beyond the airfield. Three remaining *Hind* attack choppers were taxied out from the protective confines of the power plant and fired their machine guns and rockets at the fleeing invaders. The enemy forces had been virtually decimated. Popov had reestablished his control over the island.

Sergei was sitting at the command console in the control room, drinking a glass of strong tea, when he was interrupted by his radio operator. "Bridge, I have a message from the *Riga*."

"Bring it."

The radioman came into the attack center bearing a two-part form letter, which Sergei signed for and read. There were two targets entering the harbor, one of whose engines were making severe straining sounds. Ah, the destroyer and troop carrier. Sergei ordered his *Alfa* skippers into action.

The *Kuga* and *Luza* attacked the destroyer escort. *Riga* went for the disabled transport. It didn't take much to sink the troop carrier. It was already listing heavily to starboard. The *Riga* sent a well-placed torpedo into the already damaged starboard quarter, and the giant ship began to settle quickly at the stern.

Anticipating another attack, the five hundred soldiers aboard fastened their life jackets and systematically boarded inflatable life rafts.

*Riga's* skipper watched the orderly escape from the sinking ship and cursed himself. He was ordered not to allow the troops ashore. He quickly had two more torpedoes loaded and blasted out a cavernous hole below the stern. The troop carrier took on water too fast. The almost square bow broached, and the ship was sucked under the sea. Perhaps a hundred men were rescued.

The *Riga* surfaced, and with the decks awash, a gunnery crew took its place at the forward heavy machine gun. Their orders were clear: fire on the survivors. No one was to be left alive.

The destroyer escort came streaming to the rescue. Heavy guns trained on the *Riga* tried to hit the sub without endangering the troops bobbing about in life rafts. The *Riga* made a sudden dive to avoid the barrage, leaving the four-man gunnery crew to fend for itself, or drown. The survival of the sub and remaining crew was at stake, and the four men would have to be sacrificed to save them.

The skippers of the *Luza* and *Kuga* took advantage of the destroyer concentrating on *Riga*. They attacked the stern

185

quarters, one from each flank. *Kuga's* torpedo ran true and ripped a chunk out of the bow. The destroyer immediately answered with an ASROC barrage that chased the *Kuga* along the bottom of the harbor. The sub could not escape the sixty-knot rockets and exploded from at least two impacts.

Two sub-chaser choppers went after the *Luza*. They played a deadly game of leapfrog with the sub, dipping sonobuoys, hammering with the sonar, cutting off the escape, and keeping the captain and crew of the *Luza* working with a frenzy to break free. The choppers herded the sub like a steer at a roundup, showing no mercy on the undersea killer.

One chopper dropped a torpedo and guided it to the *Luza* using data transmitted by the sister helicopter, which was following the fleeing sub on its sensitive sonar. It detected an explosion, followed by a gusher erupting from the sea in the vicinity of the sub. The unmistakable sound of dying men confirmed the kill.

Thus heartened, the captain of the destroyer slowly churned toward the bobbing life rafts, hoping to rescue the survivors. *Riga's* skipper had followed the destruction of the *Kuga* and *Luza* and swore vengeance against the destroyer. He waited until the destroyer was in the midst of the survivors before loosing two torpedoes at the already chewed-up bow. The explosions triggered off the munitions magazine, which in turn ignited the forward fuel reserves. A flaming, oily film soon covered the water, incinerating the helpless soldiers trapped in the rubber life rafts, and sealing the crew of the destroyer in their tomb as it sank to the bottom. The invasion had been stopped, but at terrible cost. In all, the invading forces lost two submarines, two destroyers, and two troop carriers loaded with a thousand soldiers to the sea, and over a hundred men and dozens of jets on land. The defenders fared little better, with the loss of five of their six hunter-killer subs, their two largest surface ships, most of the strategic buildings on the island, and countless men. What price victory?

"They must be taught a lesson they'll never forget, Sergei. We showed them we can't be taken by the likes of them. Now we're going on the offensive to give them the message, Don't come back."

"Offensive, Comrade Admiral?" Sergei was just thankful to see the invading fleet turn tail and leave with the remnants of their flotilla. "Remember, they still have an aircraft carrier with at least half of their fighters intact, and two heavy cruisers. Isn't it enough that we've beaten off their assault and sent them home in disgrace?"

"Enough? I'll tell you when they've had enough. When I have the bastard in command of that fleet hanging by his neck from my flagpole. If we let them off too easy, next time Gorshkov will send up an even larger force against us."

The old man is really losing it, Sergei thought. He realized that his career in the Navy was finished—unless, by some quirk of fate, this warmonger that he'd put in with wound up at the top. The very top, at that. Otherwise, it meant certain arrest, and the thought left a queasy feeling in his bowels, just as certain execution by firing squad or torture, or both. He was quickly running out of options. He said over the ship-to-shore radio, "What would you like, Comrade?"

"That's better, Sergei. Sometimes it seems like you doubt me, that you don't really think I'm going to replace Gorshkov as Commander of the Fleet."

"No, Comrade, I . . ."

"I will, Sergei, as soon as I force the fools on the Politburo to resign . . . all except Defense Minister Charkov. I will make sure he becomes the next general secretary. Then, you'll see real Soviet power, Sergei. No more sellout treaties. No more paralyzing our military might for the sake of a little wheat that our lazy-ass farmers can't produce themselves because they're afraid of hard work."

The old admiral rambled on until Sergei Shevchenko could hardly stand it anymore.

"Then you'll see, Sergei. We will cover the Arctic with military bases. And we'll go back and show those aborigines in Afghanistan who their superiors are. And then, it's on to Iran, shut those religious fanatics up once and for all. Our first real warm-water port. Just think, Sergei, with me in command of our navy, and Minister Charkov as head of the Politburo, the world will be ours to take as we wish."

Captain Shevchenko let Popov run out of steam. There was no sense arguing with him. Even trying to reason with the admiral seemed beyond hope. Sergei rubbed his weary eyes. Let's just hope that if and when the old man does become the power behind the Motherland, I'm close behind to take it from him, he thought, the warmonger has gone mad. Sergei shook his head. What a shame.

The *Hind* helicopter came in low, barely skimming the waves, in order to keep below the fleet's radar umbrella. Captain Shevchenko had demanded extremely precise coordinates of the carrier and the two cruisers. Then, it was back along a reciprocal course just four meters above the water, and hope to hell the Badgers' radar can't get a fix on them. Stefan Batenko, the chopper's pilot, noted the exact location of the big carrier and radioed the information back to base.

The chopper attracted a lot of attention from the aircraft carrier's flight crew when Batenko pulled up close and buzzed the ship by flying around it in a circle, below the level of the deck. The sailors considered it friendly, and waved and cheered it on. The pilot turned to his gunnery mate. "Must think we're the chopper from that destroyer that didn't make it back. That ought to buy us some time, eh?"

The gunner was sullen. He knew this was a suicide run. Those bastards in charge didn't give a damn who they sacrificed to their causes. "Maybe we'll get to live ten minutes longer, comrade. Wouldn't that be nice?"

"Cut out that kind of talk, Yuri. It will get you nowhere."

"It won't get me any more dead than is already inevitable, Lieutenant."

Batenko headed the chopper toward the closer of the two cruisers, the *Lubovich*. "Navigator, mark the coordinates, and get them back to the base immediately."

"Yes, comrade."

The copilot had been watching the carrier out of the corner of his eyes, and spotted company coming. "Stefan, there's a chopper following us at five o'clock. It looks like one of the Gorkis that the destroyers deploy."

Batenko turned his head. "I see him. Yuri, he's yours as soon as I give the word. Meanwhile, I want to get closer to the *Ashkenatze*."

Two Badgers catapulted off the *Leningrad's* deck and went into a giant loop, remaining in a holding pattern above the ship.

"More company, Stefan." The copilot was pointing almost directly overhead. Then the chopper's radio began to squawk. "Pilot of the *Hind* helicopter HI-4, please identify yourself immediately."

The copilot ran his forefinger across his throat. "Uh-oh . . . they're onto us."

"See? I told you so."

"Shut up, Yuri. You're not helping things. Besides, it took them long enough. Navigator, did you radio back the last set of coordinates?"

"Yes, Comrade Lieutenant."

"Good. Then we've completed our mission. Now let's see if we can get out of this alive. Leo, raise them on the radio. Tell them we are the missing chopper crew from the destroyer. Tell them . . . tell them that we were shot down and stole this *Hind* from the traitors. Yes, that's good. Tell them that. Maybe it will buy us some time."

The radio operator sent the message. "They want our names and ID numbers."

The copilot asked, "Do you think they really have that information available?"

"Who knows? Let's try to bluff them. Give them our IDs. What do we have to lose?"

"Our lives."

"Yuri, stop being a defeatist. We still have a chance. Use your head, man."

The gunnery mate swallowed hard. They didn't have a chance in hell. What was the matter with these fools? Didn't they care that they were going to die?

"Comrade Lieutenant, we have been ordered to hold our present position while they check out our identification."

*"Damn."* Batenko removed his headset and turned to face his crew, while his copilot kept them hovering in place. "Well, men, we have several choices. One, we can just stay here like this and die when they find out we've been lying to them. Two, we can make a run for it."

The copilot interjected, "Stefan, we have that Gorki chopper above us to worry about, to say nothing of those two Badgers flying cover for it."

"Yes, that's something we have to take care of. That brings me to our third option. We can inflict as much damage on the fleet as we can before they shoot us down."

"You're crazy, all of you. I say, we do nothing. They can't possibly ID that missing chopper crew."

"Of course they can, Yuri. Now, take hold of yourself. At least we can still die like men."

The gunner began to breathe fast and deep. A crewman put a hand on his shoulder to calm him down. Finally, Yuri

190

let out a long, deep breath and settled down. "Okay, I'm sorry. Let us die like men."

"Good. Now, we can't outrun those jets, but the chopper should be easy, especially if we take them by surprise. Then, we attack the admiral's bridge on the *Leningrad*. And, if we get hit, I'll try to crash into whatever we can do the most damage to. Are we agreed?"

All except the gunnery mate raised their voice in accord as one man. "Agreed," they chanted.

Yuri looked at his comrades a little sheepishly when they stared at him. "Agreed," he smiled, and they all cheered, slapping him on the shoulders and messing his hair.

Batenko said, "Okay, then, I'm going to circle around the carrier and come up from under the flight deck, straight up at that chopper. Yuri, take it out as fast as you can. Ready?"

"Ready."

The *Hind* went in low and made a pass around the *Leningrad*. The chopper followed at a distance, to see what was going on. From under the cover of the overhanging deck, Batenko swooped out and aimed directly at the unsuspecting smaller chopper. "Now, Yuri. Shoot."

The gunnery mate lined up the target in his sights and fired off a volley into the cockpit. Several rounds found their marks, smashing into the glass windshield and hitting the pilot and his crewmen. More rounds cut into the overhead rotors, and the chopper jerked and hopped overhead before leaning on its side and crashing onto the *Leningrad's* deck.

Cheers went up aboard the *Hind*. "Good work, Yuri. Now, let's show the admiral what we're made of."

Lieutenant Stefan Batenko darted up to the superstructure of the carrier and located the quarters of the admiral of the task force. He leveled his craft in a direct line and rested his right thumb on the red trigger button. "Now," he shouted. Rockets slammed into the steel structure, exploding and toppling the starboard flying bridge. Batenko watched an officer plunge to the deck. Then, all hell erupted below.

Sailors began running out on deck with hand weapons, machine guns, AK-47 assault rifles, anything that would fire. Batenko circled around and made another pass at deck level. He fired off two more rockets and shouted, "Shoot, Yuri, shoot."

The two rockets carved out craters in the deck. But Yuri didn't fire his weapon. Stefan looked down at the gunner below him. He was slumped in his seat, the victim of a stray round. Then a burst of fire tore into the chopper's fuselage.

"We're hit, Stefan. They got Leo."

"Yuri's dead, too. I guess this is it."

The rear rotor began to sputter and miss. "Yes. I guess so. Let's get out of here, maybe try to take one of the cruisers with us."

With that, the *Hind* swept along the wave tops toward the *Lubovich*, which was streaming beyond a tanker. One of the Badgers dived and fired at the fleeing chopper, kicking up the surf behind it with six hundred rounds in four seconds. The chopper sputtered again, and Batenko began to lose control. "We're not going to make it. I'm going for the tanker. Farewell, comrade."

The copilot stared at the fuel tanker looming closer and closer. He closed his eyes and mouthed a silent prayer. Stefan Batenko placed his thumb on the red trigger, waited until the last moment, and opened fire with all his remaining rockets, then followed the shells into the side of the fuel ship. The brave crew of the chopper died instantly. The tanker exploded and burned for hours before the last charred remnants settled into the sea.

# Chapter 19

*"Sierra-one, Sierra-two,* this is *Hornet.* Come in, please."

"Reading you, Comrade Captain. This is *Sierra-one."*

*"Sierra-two* here, Captain."

Sergei was directing his submarine fleet from the deeper water to the north of the sub base. "You received the coordinates, comrades. *One,* you fire on the *Leningrad. Two,* the cruisers. Any questions?"

The two sub commanders, like Sergei Shevchenko, would follow their orders, even though disagreeing with them. That was what they were trained to do, after all . . . follow orders. They dialed in the coordinates that the *Hind* chopper crew had died getting for them. "Ready, Captain."

"We are also ready, Comrade Captain."

"Fire at will," Sergei ordered, and the bombardment commenced.

Aboard the *Leningrad,* Admiral Kasimov was awakened by an aide after dozing off for a two-hour nap, his only sleep in nearly a day. "Comrade Admiral, our radar has spotted some incoming about seventy kilometers out. The captain thought you should know."

"Are we ready . . . ?"

"As much as possible. We're all thankful you weren't hurt in the attack earlier."

"That chopper? He was here reconnoitering for these incoming missiles. Well, you know what to expect. They've got to have a good fix on our position. After all, that chopper was right on top of us."

The radio room rang up next. "Multiple ASCMs incoming, bearing two six five . . . range five zero meters . . . speed two four zero knots."

Kasimov keyed the ship's captain. "Vadim, begin evasive course at once. Are your ACM rocket launchers prepared to intercept the cruise missiles?"

"Yes, of course, Comrade Admiral. And I have a squad of interceptors out right now to stop them from the air."

The *Leningrad* began running a zigzag course, while Admiral Kasimov radioed the two cruisers to make sure they were doing the same.

At thirty kilometers out, the interceptor jets branched out, and each acquired multiple targets for the pair of rockets strapped under its wings. A dozen rockets were fired. Nine incoming missiles exploded prematurely and fizzled harmlessly to the sea. The interceptors had done their job, but it was not nearly adequate. Another array of submarine-launched cruise missiles was already on their way to the *Leningrad*, and six each were homing in on the *Lubovich* and the *Ashkenatze*. The normal procedure would be for the jets to return to the carrier, but their flight leader kept them in a holding pattern, about ten klics away. Never know, he figured, but there's no sense landing only to become a sitting duck for the missiles that might get through.

At five kilometers out, three projectiles arched downward toward the *Leningrad*. They were easily shot down by the SLOCUM antimissile rocket system. The second wave of missiles was still on the way. This time, the cruisers were also forced to fire their SLOCUMs to blast the incoming missiles, and they hammered the missiles with radar-jamming signals to throw them off course. And still the missiles came.

Admiral Kasimov was enraged. He keyed Captain Vadim,

the *Leningrad's* skipper. "We're pulling out. Order the ship about."

"But, Comrade Admiral . . ."

"No buts, damn it. I'm not going to sit here and be blasted out of the water. Now, turn the ship, and radio the cruisers to do the same."

"Aye, aye, comrade."

Kasimov was shaking his fist in anger. "I don't like this any more than you, Captain, but now is the time to pull out of missile range and regroup. I'm sending the two remaining subs back to the harbor. They'll be in position if any of Popov's ships try to break out. And when we attack next time, they will be there to clear the harbor for us. The next time, surprise will be on our side."

Captain Vadim nodded in agreement, but in his head he said, If there *is* a next time. He had gone below to give the orders when a well-aimed cruise missile came screaming in at wave-top height and slammed into the superstructure. Burning debris spewed from the wreckage, cutting down seamen, and setting off secondary fires on deck. Vadim's bridge was demolished, his executive officer slumped in the captain's seat, a bloody gash leaving his neck dangling flaccidly. Had Vadim not turned over the conn to his exec while he conferred with the admiral, it would have been him in that chair. Vadim wiped the sweat from his face with a handkerchief and went into the head to throw up.

An aide went to the bridge and found his captain rinsing his mouth in the sink. "Comrade Captain, are you all right?"

Vadim wiped his face with a towel and disgustedly threw the cloth into the sink. "I'll be okay. Have someone take care of EXO."

"They're coming for him now. He . . . he's dead."

Vadim kicked a filled wastebasket across the floor. "Tell me how the hell that missile got through our defenses?"

"I don't know, Captain."

"Of course you don't know. Nobody aboard seems to

know how to stop the missiles."

"Sorry, comrade. The *Ashkenatze* took a hit, too."

"What?" Vadim ran to the wall of windows and pulled back the blackout shades, revealing a panoramic view of his domain. He stared at the blazing hull of the heavy cruiser guarding his flanks a half mile out to starboard. Heavy black smoke rose from the foredeck. "Damn them. Damn that demon Popov."

He climbed down a steel ladder to the level below, where he wound his way through a series of hatch openings and staircases until he walked out on the flight deck. A winded aide struggled to keep up with his captain, who was clearly at least fifteen years his senior. Vadim grabbed a sailor rushing by wearing a yellow slicker with FIRE CONTROL stenciled on the back. "What's it like?" he asked.

The seaman saluted. "It's hell down here, Captain. Two of the Badgers were on deck when the superstructure fell down on them. One of the pilots was in the cockpit. I think he's dead. Right now, though, we've got to stop those fires before they get to the jet fuel. The pilot will have to wait."

The fireman went to join several others who were pumping seawater onto the burning deck, when suddenly one of the jets caught fire. With a mighty *whoosh,* the jet fuel ignited and spewed out fifty feet in each direction. The dead pilot, half the fire control crew, and the captain's aide were enveloped by the flaming liquid. Vadim's uniform caught fire and sent him screaming across the flight deck, flames raging from his entire back and head. He ran to the edge and kept on going.

A passing officer watched the fire extinguish when the man hit the water five stories below. "Who was that?" he asked a passing fireman.

The man in the yellow slicker was visibly shaking. "That was the captain," he whispered, closing his eyes.

A half mile across the sea, the *Ashkenatze* was setting off a magnificent fireworks display of its own. It was sinking fast

196

at the bows. Sailors in life rafts were already paddling toward the aircraft carrier. Only the *Lubovich* remained relatively unscathed, with only a gaping hole high above the waterline. Its crew was able to put out that fire quickly.

When the missile barrage stopped and the fires aboard the *Leningrad* were extinguished, the *Ashkenatze* survivors were taken aboard the carrier. Admiral Kasimov, himself now at the conn, and a sentry noticed a solitary orange survival raft bobbing on the surface a few hundred meters away. A figure seemed to be shouting to them through a bullhorn, and waving spastically.

A lifeboat was lowered and sent to check it out. The lone occupant of the raft was taken aboard and brought to the admiral, at the man's insistence. He said he was the deputy minister of defense, and he had a message from Admiral Popov to the highest ranking officer in the fleet.

Admiral Kasimov gave the orders for his ragged flotilla to return home. Then he invited the newcomer into his quarters and listened to what he had to say.

"He said what?"

"Please, Comrade General Secretary." The deputy minister of defense was quaking in his shoes. "I am merely repeating the demands of . . . what that traitor Popov has asked of you."

The general secretary pounded his fist on the long mahogany table, rattling the drinking glasses in front of the other ministers, and spilling water all over. "Disband the present Politburo? The traitor actually thinks we should resign under his threats and form a new government? What kind of fools does he take us for?"

What kind of a fool are you, comrade? Minister of Defense Yuri Charkov asked silently. He would have to get his deputy alone and pick his brain, see if he thought Popov was really serious.

"Even Comrade Charkov," the general secretary went on, "who has the most to gain from the traitor's little pipe dream, would consider this a blasphemy, eh, Yuri?"

Charkov shrugged and raised his palms up before him. "It seems our ex-admiral has become demented."

"So it seems. Well, comrades, what shall we do about this threat? Anyone?"

The stout interior minister rose. "Can we take him seriously? After all, he's got only a handful of ships and submarines left."

The KGB director said, "We can't let him get away with this. It's a slap in the face, and it can't go unpunished. I say, let's send another force up against the traitor, and this time, not a bunch of cowards. I hope I can assume that Admiral Kasimov has been executed for his failure?"

"Not yet. He has been arrested, and is being questioned by the GRU."

*"Nyet."* KGB director Plotnik almost spat the word out. "I demand that he be turned over to my people."

"In time, comrade . . . all in good time. But first, we want to gather any military information we can get from him and his officers. Next time, if there *is* a next time, we will be more prepared."

Yuri Charkov slapped his hands on the table. "If you ask me, Popov's a madman, a traitor not worthy of gracing with a reply. I say, just forget about him for now. Certainly don't give in to his mindless blubberings about restructuring the Politburo."

Interior got up. "But what about his threats to bomb Moscow and Leningrad and Polyarnyy? Surely . . . ?"

General Secretary Rimsky stood up at his place, smiling with outstretched arms. "Comrades, let's settle down. Perhaps Comrade Charkov is right. Let the issue calm down for now. We can always go up there and stamp out the arrogant bastard whenever we please, eh?"

All except KGB and Interior agreed.

"Fine. Now we can go on to something else." Rimsky noticed Charkov's hand rise. "Defense?"

"If you don't mind, comrades, I would like to debrief my deputy myself. In private, please. Would you be so kind as to release him to me?"

KGB growled, but nodded to his men guarding the deputy. He didn't trust Charkov to begin with, and now that he'd heard his name being mentioned as a future general secretary, he could never tell what he might do. Yes, he will bear watching from now on. The director of the KGB would see to that himself.

# Chapter 20

Boxer rubbed his eyes, unbuckled his seat belt, and reached into the overhead compartment for his only piece of luggage. He returned a pretty stewardess's smile and followed the stream of passengers into Washington National Airport. He grabbed a yellow Checker cab and instructed the driver to take him to the Pentagon. It was 0600 hours, and Boxer had been flying shortly after dinner, Alaska time. His stomach told him he should stop off for breakfast before meeting with the CNO, but he was impatient to receive his orders.

Mason's aide ushered Boxer into the chief's office. Mason was seated behind his desk. Seated on an adjoining sofa was CIA Director Cultrain. "Come in, Boxer. Have a seat." The CNO pointed to an upholstered chair across from his desk. Boxer saluted. "Morning, Admiral, Director."

Cultrain replied with a halfhearted wave. "Now that we're all here, Chi-Chi, we may as well get started."

"Yes." He looked up at Boxer. "We'll have our breakfast in here, so we don't have to waste any time."

A steward appeared almost immediately, bearing a tray with a coffee service and a platter of pastries, placed it on a cleared-off corner of the desk, and left the room without a word.

Mason poured coffee and motioned for the others to help

201

themselves. Then, between bites of an almond Danish, he said, "Boxer, we've gotten some very disturbing reports from out of the Soviet Union. You've been involved in that business in North Land, and it looks as if you're going to be our man to go up there and take care of the problem. The director here has come to me with these. Have a look." He passed a packet of $8 \times 10$ photos across to Boxer and finished his pastry. Then he reached for another and leaned back in his seat, munching a prune Danish and sipping coffee while Boxer perused the pictures.

"That's quite a little war party the Russkies have streaming toward North Land. What excuse did they give us?"

Cultrain chuckled. "Very astute of you, Jack. Ivan claims they were on war-game maneuvers. Now, check these out."

Boxer let out a long, low whistle.

"Those were taken a week later."

"Must have been some war games. The carrier and that cruiser are in bad shape. Where're the other ships?"

"You tell me," Mason interjected. "We wanted a closer look than these satellite photos give us, so we sent a weather forecast plane over North Land, under the umbrella of a Sentry. These are the pictures the pilot got before being shot down."

"Shot down? And we let them get away with it?"

Cultrain shook his head. "Officially, we weren't even up there. The Sentry was up too high for them to hit with their SAM batteries, and was able to monitor the recordings of the lower-flying weather plane. That's how we got these. The top one is a satellite shot, for reference."

Boxer placed the top two photos side by side in front of him, and the third and fourth alongside those. "The base here is in as bad shape as the remnants of the war-games fleet. Could it be that they were up against each other?"

"We think so," Cultrain answered, taking a sip from his coffee. "At least, that's what it looks like from those."

202

Boxer tapped his fingers on the second photo. "The only thing left standing is the nuclear plant. This headquarters building here is almost totaled." On the third picture he pointed to a circular field. "The prison compound is still intact. They were supposed to dismantle that. And it looks like the barracks took a beating."

Cultrain said, "The last picture has the airfield."

Boxer studied the pockmarked surface of the airstrip. "It would be difficult to land anything very large on that. It's almost demolished, along with the rest of the place. Except the plant."

"Exactly," Mason added. "We figure the Russkies don't want to take a chance on destroying it before it's safely turned off. That's where you come in."

"What do you mean, where *I* come in? So far, except for the lost plane, we have nothing to do with this."

Cultrain cleared his throat. "We believe—that is, the President and the Joint Chiefs believe that the people in charge at the base in North Land are out of control. That fleet was sent up there to take over, and it looks like they got their asses kicked, but good. If Ivan can't force its own subjects to carry out the directives of the wheat-deal accord, then we have to go in there and do it for them."

Boxer put down his coffee cup. "Now wait just a minute . . . not so damn fast. This is still an internal Soviet problem. Let them send someone else in to mop up the place."

"Just wait a damn minute, Boxer." Mason was out of his chair. "I'm giving you a direct order to take a sub in there and put that reactor out of business. And the damn submarine base they've got protecting it, too. Don't give me any of this crap about whose responsibility it is. I'm telling you to do it."

"You're asking me to wage war on Soviet soil. If we're caught up there, it'll mean another world war, for sure. I won't do it."

Mason was livid. He pounded his fist on his desk. "That's

it, Boxer. That does it. A direct act of insubordination in front of a witness. Your ass is mine, Boxer. I'll have you court-martialed in . . ."

"Sit down, Chi-Chi," Cultrain told him. "You're making a fool of yourself."

Mason glared at the director, his face bright red. He started to sputter something, but Cultrain ignored him.

"See here, Jack. We think that Ivan would like very much to put this facility out of commission, but that they're being held hostage by this . . . this warmonger, what's his name?"

"Popov," Boxer told him. "Admiral Boris Popov. Met him during the initial inspection last year. Arrogant son-of-a-bitch."

"Listen, Jack." Cultrain was trying his best to sound conciliatory. "We've been getting reports from our people inside the Soviet Union that several military installations, especially along the Arctic coast, have been bombed very recently. And we know it wasn't us. We think it was Popov. He is either getting his revenge or giving the bosses the message that he wants something from them that they aren't likely to provide him with otherwise.

"That's why we think it best that you go up there and put a stop to this business right now, while we still have a chance. Believe me, Ivan won't mind us doing his dirty work for him on this one."

Boxer rubbed his beard and pondered the director's remarks. "Maybe you're right, Cultrain. I'd still be putting a lot of good men in jeopardy for something I'm still not convinced is our problem. Give me some time to think this through."

Cultrain shrugged, and looked across at Mason. The CNO glared at both of them, but said nothing. Finally, the director said, "Okay, Jack, take twenty-four hours to make up your mind. Be back here tomorrow at 0700 with your decision."

204

Boxer took a deep breath, held it, and let it out slowly. "Fine. Now, if you'll excuse me, I've got some soul-searching to do."

"Just a minute." Mason's sharp voice cut right through Boxer. "There's someone here we've sent for to add to your crew." He pressed a buzzer on his desk and spoke into an intercom. "Send him in, now."

A young naval lieutenant stepped into the office in his winter dress blues. Mason said, "You remember Lieutenant Murphy?"

Boxer smiled. "Surf? Good to see you."

Murphy saluted and shook Boxer's extended hand. "I signed on aboard the *Manta*, Admiral Boxer. I thought you could use a good chopper jockey."

"You thought right, son. It'll be a unique experience for you, too. Our chopper is launched underwater from a forward compartment. Then, the rotor unfolds as you break the surface, and you're airborne. It carries rockets, a machine gun, and very sophisticated listening equipment. Feel up to it?"

"You bet. When do we get started?"

Cultrain answered that. "Admiral Boxer has a twenty-four hour layover here in DC before returning to Alaska. Why don't you join him for the day and fly back together tomorrow?"

Murphy nodded. Boxer said for both of them, "We'd like that fine, sir. Now, if you'll excuse us, I know a tavern in town that serves up delicious steaks for lunch. It'll give the lieutenant and me a chance to get better acquainted."

"Dismissed," Mason barked. "Be back at 0700 tomorrow."

Boxer and Murphy saluted and left the office. Mason watched them leave, then asked Cultrain, "What the hell did you go and do that for? I finally had Boxer by the short hairs. I could have had him stripped of rank, and maybe given him a dishonorable."

"What purpose would that serve us? We want him up there

in North Land. We need that nuclear reactor plant put out of action, and he's the man to do it for us. Besides, when he finds out what you and I already are privy to, I think he'll come around. And if he dies up there doing his duty . . . he dies."

Mason smiled for the first time that morning. "If he dies, he dies. I like that. I like that very much."


Boxer gave the cab driver directions to a location on NE New York Avenue. "Harry's Bar is my favorite lunch spot in town. I try to wind up here at least once whenever I'm in DC. You've got to try one of their Delmonicos. I'm treating."

"Sounds great."

They got to Harry's just ahead of the business lunchtime crowd, and were seated at a table to the side of the bar. Three televisions were on behind the bar, each showing Georgetown beating Villanova at basketball.

"DC's a big sports town," Boxer told Murphy. "And Harry gives 'em what they want. This place gets packed whenever a local team makes the playoffs."

Boxer ordered a Stoli on the rocks, and Surf, a cold draft beer from a pretty cocktail waitress in a short, sexy black outfit. Murphy followed her with his eyes until she was out of his sight. "A loaf of bread, a jug of wine, and her," he pointed with his thumb. "What more could a man want?"

Boxer smiled, trying to remember when life was ever that simple for him. It seemed like he'd been forty years old all his life.

When their steaks came, surrounded by fries and onion rings, each of them ordered a cold draft to wash it down. From time to time, they'd break off their conversation to catch a glimpse of an especially exciting play on the TV screen closest to them. Now Georgetown was leading by two, with only minutes to play, when a Villanova player went in for a lay-up, missed, and came down hard on the boards. When he pointed to the Georgetown center, claiming foul, he was instead hit with a charging violation.

The Georgetown fans went wild. The chubby Villanova coach was off the bench and onto the court, arguing with the referee, stamping his foot, cursing, and egging on his constituents in the crowd. Pandemonium broke out. Both benches cleared of players. Both teams converged on the court, pressing toward their opponents, pushed back by the few security guards.

The referee gestured to the Villanova coach that he was out of the game, the chubby coach gestured what he thought of that . . . and the screen suddenly went blank.

In a moment, a well-known anchorman was on the screen in front of a newsroom background. "This is a Channel Six newsbreak. This just in from Washington."

The lunchroom crowd at Harry's was pissed, and booed its dissatisfaction. They yelled, "Bring back the game," and "Get the jerk out of there."

"Sources within the Soviet Union have leaked word to Associated Press this morning of a ballistic missile attack on several major cities, including Murmansk, Leningrad, and Kiev. Just how extensive the damage is is unknown to us at this time. Indeed, it may be some time yet before even the Soviets can ascertain what has actually happened. And no one has yet claimed responsibility.

"Is this the start of World War III? Our correspondent Peter Fields has this report for us from the White House. Peter?"

The camera cut to a tall man in a tan raincoat standing before the front gate of the White House. Boxer downed his beer and blotted his lips on a napkin. "We'd better go back to the Pentagon. Looks like my mind's just been made up for me."

"Huh?"

Boxer reached for his wallet and signaled for the waiter. He told Murphy, "Looks like I've got to try and head off a third world war."

The guard opened the door to Igor Borodine's tiny cell and stood aside. "The commandant has sent for you, Comrade Admiral. Please come with me."

Borodine got up from his bunk, found his uniform jacket, put it on, buttoned it, and stood straight, with as much dignity as he could muster. He asked his young jailer, "Do I look okay?"

"You look fine," he lied. Borodine's complexion was sallow, his clothes ill-fitting, due to the loss of about fifteen pounds; and he had the sagging posture of a man who knew he was about to die.

Borodine combed his hair with his fingers, adjusted his cap, and polished the metal buttons of his jacket with a sleeve. He was forty-two years old, but today he looked ten years older. "You're lying, of course, Nicolai, but I appreciate your kindness. It's too bad they didn't allow you to speak to me all these weeks. I'm sure we could have been friends."

The guard merely said, "Right this way, please." He led him off down the long corridor, and onto an elevator leading to the main level and daylight. Nicolai walked beside him all the way to the office of the prison commander and knocked on the door.

So this is it, Borodine thought. They're finally tired of playing games with me, and it's time for my execution. Too bad, though. I'd rather die fighting for the Motherland, in spite of everything. His thoughts were broken with the opening of the door. He was beckoned inside.

He had to blink his eyes to adjust to the bright daylight flooding into the room from the window behind the prison director's desk. Standing behind the commandant was the

Chief Deputy of the Second Directorate, Feodor Doneck. Borodine pulled himself to attention and saluted the two officers.

As they returned his salute, Doneck said to the prison director, "Thank you for the use of your office, Comrade. You may leave us now."

The commandant got up and walked out past Borodine without saying anything. When the door closed behind him, Doneck reached behind the desk and came up with a bottle of vodka and two glasses. "Sit, Igor. We will have a little talk, and something to drink."

Borodine took the glass. "A condemned man's final drink, eh, Pasha?" He held it up in a toast. "To the Motherland."

"Yes, to the Rodina. And to the future as well, comrade." Both men drained their glasses, and Doneck refilled them. "What shall we drink to next?" Doneck asked, looking at his glass. "Oh, yes . . . here's to your new command."

"My *what?*" Borodine almost knocked over his drink.

Doneck was smiling. "Let me be the first to congratulate you on your reappointment as skipper of the *Sea Demon*. The repairs have been completed, and it's out of drydock."

Borodine drained off his glass and passed it back for a refill. "And my new assignment?" He lifted the fresh drink to his lips.

"You are familiar with the nuclear plant and submarine bastion in North Land."

"Somewhat. It was not yet completed when . . . before I found myself here in prison. So I am being assigned to command the submarine bastion on Severnaya Zemlya . . . it's very cold there, but at least it's far better than being in prison."

"No, Igor. The entire operation on North Land is under the control of Boris Popov."

Borodine almost choked on his vodka. "Popov? The madman? The Politburo ministers must be losing their minds. Popov should be the one in jail."

"Tsk, tsk, Igor. Lucky for you that it is only an old friend like me that has overheard what you said about the Politburo. An overzealous political officer would have you shot for treason."

Borodine downed his drink and put the glass down loudly. "That's not treason. Putting a butcher like Popov in charge of a nuclear plant could only spell disaster for the Motherland. They should have him removed before he starts real trouble."

"Comrade Igor, this is why I have fought so hard to have you spared. I'm afraid the damage is already done. Had they your foresight, we would not be on the verge of another great war."

"What?"

Doneck filled him in on what had taken place during the last few months. When he was through, Borodine was shaking his head. "What did they expect, that the leopard would change its spots? How do you propose to get rid of this monster, now that he's so entrenched? A dozen of our fighting ships have failed, even under the command of one as good as Comrade Admiral Kasimov. What could we possibly do to stop this . . . this warmonger, now?"

A smile broadened across the KGB man's face.

"Ah, I get it now." Borodine rubbed his beard. "You want me to lead another task force against Popov, from the *Sea Demon*. It might work."

"Igor, you underestimate yourself. The plan is to send up the *Sea Demon*, with you in command, and a strike force of storm troopers. The hope is that a small, elite force might succeed where a larger flotilla might not."

Borodine shrugged. "And if I fail, all you lose is a small band of fighters, and a skipper who was about to be executed anyway."

Doneck smiled. "If you want to look at it that way, comrade, go ahead. Personally, I think you have the advantage. COMSUBFLT for North Land is Sergei Shev-chenko."

"I taught Sergei most of what he knows. He's very good."

"But not as good as his mentor. At least, for your sake, Igor, I hope not." The KGB man reached across the desk and shook hands with Borodine. "Good luck. You leave in twenty-four hours. Very few people even know about this little venture of ours, and we'd like to keep it this way. The future of our government, even the entire Motherland, rides with you. Get that bastard, Igor."

"I'll do my best, Pasha. And thank you for the opportunity." The two of them stood up facing each other, taking in each other's features, each trying to read what was in the other's head. Then, Borodine turned and walked away a free man.

# Chapter 21

"Dive." Boxer gave the command, and the *Manta* settled into the sea off Barrow, Alaska. They were headed due north, under the polar ice cap. Boxer called his key officers and squad leaders around him in the galley, and, over steaming cups of coffee, he laid out his plan for them.

He unrolled a chart of the coast of Komsomolets Island, in North Land, together with several of the photos taken by satellite and the reconnaissance plane that was shot down. With a red marker, he drew a circle on the chart just inside the harbor. "That's our objective, men. We've got to get in there and shut down the nuclear reactor. Once that's achieved, we can send in missiles, or bomb the base without fear of a nuclear holocaust."

"What are we up against, Skipper?"

"We're not really sure, Rolly. Popov, the mastermind behind all the trouble up there, is an admiral in charge of a fleet of submarines, several support ships, and a few hundred ground troops, which controls a prisoner population of about five hundred."

"Doesn't seem like so much."

"Don't let the numbers fool you. Popov is heavily dug in. Look what he's done so far." Boxer spread the photos out in front of them. Rolly, Turk, Mean Gene, and Billy Lone

Eagle passed the shots of the land-based compound back and forth. Clemens was more interested in the ill-fated flotilla that Popov had practically destroyed. And he asked Boxer the big question.

"Skipper, if the Russkies couldn't take out their own man with a carrier, two cruisers, destroyers, and a few subs, how are we supposed to do it with only ourselves and the *Manta*?"

"Here's my plan."

All present gave Boxer their complete attention.

"First of all, each time the Russkies have tried an assault on North Land, it's been from out of their Kola bastion, here to the west. We'll be coming in under the ice cap from the north. I don't think they'll be expecting any opposition from the north."

Clemens scratched his head. "They'll at least have to take the trouble to set mine fields or nets to keep their backs covered."

"Right. Billy, you and your SEALs will have the responsibility of clearing the way for us to enter the bastion."

Billy Lone Eagle nodded.

"Rolly, you, Gene, and Turk will be dropped off up here, inland of the base, and work your way to the harbor. Your job will be to hit them from the rear, and try to get to the control room that keeps the reactor going, and shut it down. Billy, your men will try to get to the control room from the harbor, if you can slip in. We'll have several days for you all to learn how to work the computers that control the reactor. They've laid everything out for us in this packet." Boxer tossed a sheaf of papers onto the chart table, and Rolly picked it up.

Clemens smiled. "That gives us the easy job, Skipper. We have to fight our way into the harbor, pick up the men, and hightail it out of there. Then, we get to fight our way home." He took a sip of coffee. "What's our plan for that?"

Boxer looked at each of the men before him very somberly. "I hate to have to tell you this. Getting in will be

214

difficult. We don't know quite what opposition we'll face, and they'll be looking for another assault on them. But at least, we'll have some element of surprise. But getting out is another thing. I don't think we have a chance in hell of getting out alive."

Rolly Jones broke the silence that followed. "Well, I'd like to say that it'll be an honor to die fighting alongside as fine a bunch of men as this."

"I'll second that," Boxer added.

Turk raised his beefy fist and held it aloft. The others did likewise, then brought them together in a fighting man's toast. Not another word was spoken. None was necessary.


On the fifth day, the *Manta* emerged from under the polar ice, miles northeast of Komsomolets Island. There didn't appear to be any resistance from this bearing, but Boxer took the precaution of cutting his speed to seven knots to avoid detection. He took the *Manta* to within two nautical miles of the coast, and assembled Rolly Jones and his commandos. "Well, this is it, Major. You and your men will be let off here as soon as we surface. Good luck be with you, and remember, no matter what happens to us or the *Manta*, your objective is still to shut down that reactor, and destroy the control room so no one can start it back up again. There are already plans in Washington for a missile strike on this place the moment they get confirmation that the reactor is cold."

Turk asked, "How they gonna know that if we're not around to tell 'em?"

"Satellite photos," Boxer told him. "Using infrared computer-enhanced images, the power plant appears red, like this, when it's active. And blue, or blue-green, when it's cold." He showed them some sample pictures taken years before, after the Chernobyl power-plant disaster.

"You mean our own country is going to drop missiles on

us if we're not out of here?"

"We have one week to do what we came for, and clear out. At that time, if the images show blue, they strike."

The squad leaders looked to Boxer and Rolly, then among each other. You could feel the tension in the commando quarters. Boxer returned to the bridge and keyed the MC mike. "DO, take us up to periscope depth."

The *Manta* rose to within a few feet of the surface. "Search scope up," Boxer ordered. He stopped the scope just short of the surface, and angled the lens to check the skies for enemy aircraft. Seeing nothing, he raised the periscope all the way up and checked the surroundings on a three-sixty-degree azimuth. So far, so good.

Boxer signaled to surface. The *Manta* came to rest with decks awash. In moments, the first of the rubber rafts was positioned across the bow, held in place by the deck crew, while a squad of commandos with their gear and new Colt Commando assault rifles fitted with grenade launchers got aboard. Two more inflatables were soon filled with compressed air from the *Manta*, and the three squads prepared to get under way.

When the *Manta* settled back down to periscope depth, the three rafts were left bobbing in its wake. Rolly Jones gave the command, and his men started paddling toward shore, well aware that the sounds of their outboards would give them away to the enemy. After two hours of toil against a fierce chop, the thirty exhausted commandos dragged their crafts up onto the rocky shore. Rolly said, "Okay, men . . . you know what to do."

One man from each squad had the job of slashing their raft and burying the remains aong the rocks, leaving them no means of escape the way they came in. Their mission depended upon surprise. If the inflatables were discovered prematurely, the error could mean death. Rolly checked his maps and looked up at the sloping, snow-covered terrain ahead of them. With his squad leaders gathered around, he pointed out their position, and their objective on the far side of the hill, unaware of the eyes trained on them from above. "That's it, men. Remember everything we were taught, and let's do it. We've got a date with the skipper in seventy-two hours. And that's one date we don't want to be late for."

Boxer moved the *Manta* back into deep water and ordered a dive. "Whitey, take us down to six hundred. Steady as she goes."

The diving officer inclined the planes five degrees and gradually glided the *Manta* into the deep. "Coming to six zero zero feet. Diving planes are at null."

Boxer directed the sub around the northernmost tip of the island, and crept slowly up on the submarine bastion to the south. The squawk of his intercom broke the silence. "Conn, sonar. Target bearing one seven zero . . . range just under twenty miles . . . speed zero five. Twin screws, Skipper. I think we've got a boomer just inside sonar range."

"Good work, Hi Fi." Boxer adjusted the UWIS to take in a fifty-mile range. While this cut down on the details that could be seen on the console, it took in a greater area, and more possible targets. "Look here, Clem."

The exec came over to share the view with Boxer. *"Damn.* Two targets blocking our way into the bastion."

Boxer tapped a finger against the screen. "That's not all." He pointed out several blips beyond the closer pair. "Let's mark those positions on the chart. We'll probably have to deal with them when we get past these two."

"Roger that." Clemens went to work plotting the defending submarines on the chart. "The logical course seems to be coming in here from the west."

"Just like they want us to think. I'll bet it's heavily mined. No . . . these two babies are guarding the rear door. Everything else seems to be geared to defending against an attack from the west. We'll have to figure out some way to

217

slip past these two subs here."

Boxer cut speed to five knots. After two hours, he and Clemens reviewed the UWIS screen, hoping to get a better image of the harbor's defenses. And with the distance cut in half, they were again able to utilize the more detailed projection. "Hi Fi, do you read the newcomers to the west?"

Hi Fi Freedman had three UWIS screens as part of his console, one each at ten-, twenty-five-, and fifty-mile scales. "Roger that, Skipper. I make them to be *Alfas*, bearing zero four three and zero three nine degrees. Range about twenty miles. They seem to be guarding the mouth of the harbor, from just beyond the bastion."

Boxer rubbed his beard. "That seems a bit strange, sitting out there when they could stay within the protection of the bastion. We'll have to be especially wary of them."

"Conn, sonar. Looks like one of the targets is coming out here to take a look."

Boxer grabbed the intercom mike. "All hands, we will now rig for silence." He said to Clemens, "Lower the decoy prop, and have everything aboard that is unique to an American submarine turned off. Use only the noisemakers with sounds of Russkie subs when we need them. From here on in, all any other sub out there will know is that we're a Soviet boomer. Hopefully, that will keep us alive long enough to get in, nail that reactor, and get the hell out."

Clemens began to sweat when the air conditioners were lowered to disguise their identity. The waste disposal systems and the soda machine were turned off, cooking utensils were stowed, and half the crew got into their bunks, so as not to make extraneous sounds.

"Conn, sonar. This one is a monster. It's a boomer, maybe a *Typhoon* class. It's big enough. Making turns for one five knots on a bearing of one eight five."

Boxer said quietly, "We'll just sit this out. They probably picked up some noise out here and are just being careful. Unless they start hammering us with sonar, Clem, we'll just

218

keep quiet and hope they pass us by."

Clemens took his seat at the fire control module, trying to relax enough to quiet down his fast-beating heart. He knew he had to subdue the excitement of an impending fight, and began taking in slow, deep breaths. Boxer watched his exec's white-knuckled grip on the control handle relax, and he smiled to himself. Clem was a good exec . . . the best. Boxer was pleased that he could always count on him when they got into the thick of it.

He looked around the control room. His men were well trained for this. All eyes were glued to their instruments, ready to take action at a moment's notice. The *Manta* was ready for fight or flight in an instant. And all Boxer could hear was the sound of men breathing.

And then it came. At first, a single ping reverberated through the sub. Then a series of four more. The *Typhoon* was onto something, and wanted to make sure what.

Boxer said softly into the mike, "EO, cut speed to three knots. Whitey, negative five on the planes. Just let it drift downward. Mahoney, right rudder zero five. Come to two four zero."

Just as quietly, they repeated their orders, and the *Manta* slid deeper to starboard. For a few precious minutes, there was silence once again. And then the *Typhoon* reacquired its target. This time, the Soviet sub hammered the *Manta* with its sonar, blasting a staccato message throughout the hull. We've got you now, it seemed to say. And Boxer knew he had to answer the challenge.

"FTO, load and arm one and two, EO, all ahead two-thirds. Whitey, take us down fast to eight zero zero."

"Aye, aye, Skipper. Both officers and Chief White repeated and carried out their orders simultaneously. The *Manta* plunged to eight hundred feet.

The *Typhoon* was massive, 557 feet in length, and compared to the sleek, spearhead shape of the *Manta*, this bulbous, overblown cigar-shaped behemoth was slow and cumbersome. As the *Manta* picked up speed, the *Typhoon* was left awkwardly trying to make up the distance.

Boxer stood behind Clemens and said, "Be ready to fire when I give the word, Clem." He gave the helmsman orders, and the super sub did a smart turnaround, reversing its course. Now, the *Manta* faced its adversary head on.

"DO, planes negative zero five degrees." The *Manta* dived forward a quarter of a mile, coming up on the *Typhoon* a hundred feet beneath the larger sub. "Now, Whitey, planes up zero five. Mahoney, left rudder zero five degrees. Come to two six zero."

While his men repeated and complied with their orders, Boxer said, "I want a firing solution now, Clem."

"You got it, Skipper. Ready when you are."

"Fire one."

"One away."

Boxer watched the image of the Mark 48 torpedo swim toward the huge Soviet submarine lurking up ahead. The sound of an explosion told everyone aboard of their success. "Score that as a kill, Skipper," Hi Fi told him. "I can make out hull-popping sounds from that Russkie."

The torpedo ripped a gaping chunk from the outer hull of the *Typhoon*, letting the sea rush into the network of baffles between hulls. The hapless submarine was pulled to the bottom by the extra weight.

"Conn, sonar. Torp in the water . . . bearing one nine seven . . . range ten thousand yards . . . speed six zero and closing."

Boxer reacted instantaneously. "Mahoney, hard right rudder. Come to zero one seven."

Mahoney wheeled the *Manta* sharply to the right, coming up on a reciprocal bearing to the torpedo.

Boxer said, "Clem, fire two."

"Two fired."

"Whitey, dive . . . dive."

Minutes passed in silence. Boxer watched the image of a

submarine slip out of range of the UWIS. "He got away, Clem. That Russkie skipper knows his stuff, I'll give him that much. There was hardly time for him to evade our torp. He had to shoot and run."

"They know we're out here, Skipper. They'll be gunning for us now."

"We'll give them something to worry about." He keyed his MC. "Mahoney, return to prior course. DO, bring us up to three zero zero feet."

"Aye, aye, Skipper."

The *Manta* was soon headed for the northern approach to the harbor doing five knots. In a half hour, their steady progress came to an abrupt halt. It was as if a giant hand caught the sub and threw it backward. Men were thrown to the deck and crashed into bulkheads. Boxer grabbed a handhold on the COMCOMP computer, breaking his fall.

"What the . . . ?"

"Antisubmarine nets," Boxer answered Clemens's unspoken question. He keyed the engineer. "EO, reverse engines one-third."

The *Manta* backed out of the steel cable nets and came to rest a thousand yards back. Boxer summoned Billy Lone Eagle. "Sergeant, I'm going to need your squad to cut those nets so we can get through. And we don't have any time to lose. They know we're out here, now, and the more time we take, the better defense they can set up to stop us."

"This would be a good time for me and the boys to get off, Skipper. If we had the mini-sub to ferry us in to shore after we cut the nets, you could take the *Manta* right on in without stopping to pick us up."

"I'm not about to abandon anyone in these waters," Boxer told him.

"All respect, Skipper. This is what we're trained to do. We'll be okay, and you said yourself that you were up against time."

Boxer hesitated for a second, realized his options were

limited. What the SEAL squad leader had said made sense. "Right. How much time do you need to get ready?"

Lone Eagle straightened and puffed out his barrel chest. "Give us ten minutes."

"You got it."

While the SEALs donned their scuba suits and gathered their weapons and explosives into waterproof duffels, Boxer went back to the bridge to confer with his exec. "Clem, we'll have to get someone to launch the mini-sub."

Clemens didn't hesitate. "I volunteer, Skipper."

Boxer shook his head. "I need you here, Clem. Besides, I have you recommended for skipper of the next super sub built, and you could use the experience."

Clemens stood up and faced his mentor. "Skipper, I haven't run from a fight yet. I can pilot the *Guppy* better than anyone aboard, with the possible exception of yourself. I'm your man."

Boxer pondered his exec's request. Clemens was right, of course. He was the best man to take out the mini-sub, but he might be needed aboard the *Manta* when things got rough. Clem settled it for him.

"Skipper, you need me to run this tub like my girl back home needs a third tit," Clemens smiled, his cupped hands in front of his chest. "And, believe me, Jeannie doesn't need . . ."

"All right, Clem, I get the picture. Get suited up. I'll have the *Guppy* ready for you in ten minutes."

Several minutes later, Clemens was at the controls of the mini-sub, with Billy Lone Eagle's squad of SEALs in the rear launch bay. Lone Eagle gave a thumbs-up to Clemens, who signaled their preparedness to the bridge. "Ready to flood bay, Skipper."

Boxer keyed DO. "Whitey, flood launch bay."

The bay flooded and the hatch opened, letting man and machine drop out below, appearing, in a way, like a great female whale giving birth. The SEALs clung to cables attached to the sides of the mini-sub, and hitched a ride to the antisubmarine nets. A floodlight from the *Guppy* illuminated the work area, and the SEALs went about the job of cutting and blasting through the barrier.

"Stand by, Skipper. We're ready to set off the charges."

"Standing by, Clem. Go ahead."

With a signal from Clemens, Billy Lone Eagle ignited the small explosive packages his men attached to the steel cables and swam back to the mini-sub. Then, all at once, a dozen minor explosions opened a gaping hole in the net large enough for the *Manta* to fit inside, with the retractable sail in the lowered position.

Boxer maneuvered his sub through the opening, realizing that this was the point of no return. From here on out, there was no turning back.

# Chapter 22

Sergei Shevchenko didn't wait around to see if the torpedo he'd fired connected with the intruding submarine. He dived immediately upon firing, cornered hard, and monitored the progress of his fish from a safe distance. He was shocked to find an enemy torpedo racing after the *Hornet* on the reciprocal bearing, passing directly through the exact location he'd just vacated before running out of fuel and falling harmlessly to the bottom. "Not many who could do that," he told his exec. "That is a Yankee trick that not many Soviet skippers have mastered. Mark it well. It may prove useful to you when you have your own command."

His EXO nodded, not quite sure how the target sub pulled that reverse shot off so quickly. Sergei told him, "Order the helmsman to head for shore. Comrade Admiral Popov should know of this new threat."

En route, he notified the captains of the other four boomers under his command, two *Sierras* and two *Yankee*-class, as well as the remaining *Alfa*, that they had unwanted company. Closer to shore, he radioed the command bunker, "Comrade Admiral, we have intercepted a Soviet SSBN at the northern approach to the harbor. I think Gorshkov and his lackeys have mounted another offensive against us."

"Copy. Did you sink it, Sergei?"

Shevchenko didn't answer right away. He didn't quite know how Popov would react. Finally, he decided, well, what can I do but tell him? "Unfortunately, no, Comrade. They sneaked in and got a lucky shot off at the *Typhoon*, through no fault of ours. The enemy skipper is very good."

"You'd better hope he's not good enough, Sergei. See that the intruder is stopped. And it seems as if we have to teach the weaklings at home another lesson. Launch a ballistic missile at Kiev, to let them know we don't appreciate this at all. I shall send a message to the fools via satellite that unless this offensive is called off immediately, and a new Politburo installed within twenty-four hours, the next targets will be Beijing and Berlin. And I will be sure to notify the Chinese and the Germans that the destruction of their cities is in the hands of the present Politburo. Can you see it now, Sergei? Yellow hordes massed at the eastern borders, ready to overrun the Motherland, and NATO forces in the west preparing for war. Hah. The fools will have no choice but to meet my demands."

"Yes, Comrade Admiral. I shall work out a firing solution for Kiev. It may take some time if we want to have the maximum impact." Sergei was playing for time. He realized that Popov was quite mad, now, and would stop at nothing, not even the destruction of the Motherland, to achieve his impossible objective to command the Soviet Navy. Perhaps he could still become a hero of the people by taking over control of the bastion from the old man and bring him in to justice. Or perhaps they would find him guilty of treason, anyway. For the time being, at least, it was just a matter of staying alive through this.

"Yes, yes, Sergei. Just do it. I'll beam my demands to Moscow now. I just wish I could see their faces when they get the message."

"Comrade, perhaps it would be safer for you aboard the *Hornet*, in the event of another attack?"

"Nonsense. I'm perfectly safe right here."

"Very well, but, if you change your mind, I will be standing by, close at hand, to take you aboard."

Boxer gingerly picked his way into the harbor, keeping the *Manta's* speed down to five knots or less, hoping to evade the defenders long enough to sneak into firing position before he was noticed. And if he did get picked up on sonar, Boxer had a few more tricks up his sleeve. He hoped the twin props and the recording of Soviet submarine sounds which could be played out through a speaker system in the *Manta's* bows would fool the Russkies long enough for him to get in a first strike.

"Conn, sonar. I've got twin targets bearing zero six five and zero five nine . . . range five five zero zero and five thousand yards . . . speed on both is less than ten knots."

"Thanks, Hi Fi." Boxer took over Clemens's seat at the fire control console in the CIC. Checking the UWIS for precise coordinates, he calculated firing positions on both submarines. "FTO, load and arm tubes one, two, three and four." He figured, no sense being caught short.

There were two *Sierras* trying to figure out if the *Yankee*-class sub in their sonar was the enemy, or one of their own. The captain of *Sierra-one* decided to find out. He sent a sonar signal of five precisely spaced pings at the *Manta*. If it was the *Hornet*, or one of the other two *Yankees* in their bastion, the skipper aboard would respond with six pings, to which he in turn would reply with seven, and so on. Any other response would mean sudden death for the interloper.

Boxer realized he was being tested. At least he could turn the situation to his advantage. He had no way of knowing at which point the enemy would know he wasn't one of them, but at least he could use the sonar pings to home in on the two subs. "Hi Fi, start probing one ping at a time. Time them to match the pace of the incoming readings."

"Aye, aye, Skipper."

227

"Mahoney, swing from left to right from zero five eight to zero six nine."

"Right, Skipper."

"Ready, now."

Ping, . . .

Nothing.

Ping. . . .

Contact. Zero six zero . . . range four nine five zero. Boxer set the firing solution on the first target.

Ping. . . .

Confirmation on first target.

Ping. . . .

Nothing.

Ping. . . .

Nothing.

Ping. . . .

Contact. Zero six five . . . range not confirmed.

Ping. . . .

Range five three five five. Solution set. Ready to fire one.

"Conn, sonar. Torp in the water. Bearing . . . ."

"Damn." Boxer cursed his mistake and fired off tube one. He grabbed the MC mike and ordered, "Helmsman, hard right rudder one zero degrees." As the *Manta* hooked sharply to the right, Boxer discharged a noisemaker from a stern tube, hoping the turbulence in the water he just vacated, along with the noisemaker, would fool the torpedo into thinking that was its intended target.

A small explosion behind him told him his trick had worked. A much larger blast shook the *Manta*. Boxer knew then that his torpedo had scored a kill. But he'd lost his second target.

"Conn, sonar. I read another target behind us . . . bearing one nine zero . . . range four thousand . . . making turns for one five knots. Sounds like a boomer, Skipper. *Yankee*-class, like the one that fired on us outside the harbor."

"Roger that, Hi Fi."

"Skipper, torp in the water. Heading right up our tail at six zero."

"Whitey, dive . . . dive. Take us down to four five zero."

"Aye, aye, sir. That's mighty close to the bottom."

"I know where the bottom is," Boxer snapped, though more to himself than at his DO. "That damn torp is too close for comfort."

"Conn, sonar. That torp is still following us, Skipper."

"Helmsman, left rudder ten degrees. Come to two seven zero."

"Aye, aye Skipper." The *Manta* lunged to the left. Hi Fi reported the torpedo following and closing fast.

"Aft torpedo room . . . prepare to fire the blaster."

"Conn, sonar. That fish is close, Skipper. Range seven zero zero and right behind us."

"Fire blaster."

With a whoosh of compressed air, six mini-torpedoes sped aft of the *Manta* in search of the Soviet torpedo. An enormous blast propelled the *Manta* ahead. The blaster had done its work.

Boxer removed his cap and wiped sweat from his brow with a sleeve. Close. Now to give some back. "Mahoney, reverse course. EO, ahead two-thirds. All hands, hang on."

The *Manta* went through a one-eighty turn, leaving a huge knuckle of turbulence behind. "Sonar, conn. Hi Fi, find that damn sub that fired on us."

"Aye, aye, Skipper." Hi Fi Freedman set the sonar in the bows to active and hammered away in the vicinity they'd been picked up by the Yankee. After a long moment, "Got 'em."

"Give me that fix, sonar."

Hi Fi read off the coordinates. Boxer set up a firing solution on tube number two. "Now, sonar. Hammer the bastard hard."

The *Manta's* sonar rang through the Soviet boomer, and back to its source. A perfect fix. There would be no miss this time. Boxer called, "Firing two." His thumb triggered the red release button on the console. "Two fired." The diving officer immediately balanced the loss of forward weight by taking in more ballast.

Boxer followed the course of the torpedo on his UWIS screen. It ran true, following the sonar signal to the target. "Helmsman, left rudder ten degrees."

"Aye, aye, Skipper." Mahoney turned the wheel hard left, and the *Manta* vacated the premises just in time to avoid the major thrust of the exploding Soviet boomer.

Boxer let out a deep breath. Two down. At least one more out there that knows we're here. The *Sierra* that got away. I hope Clem got the SEALs off safely and keeps out of the line of fire. That would be one thing less to worry about.


Captain Mark Clemens worked his way through the inky darkness of the harbor until the water grew too shallow to allow concealment of the mini-sub. He was about two hundred yards offshore when the ten SEALs who had hitched a ride released their grips and tapped a farewell to him, letting him know that they were about to swim the remaining distance to the rocky shoreline. The last to leave, Billy Lone Eagle swam inches in front of the thick plexiglas cockpit window, flipping Clemens a thumbs-up thank-you before joining his men. In their black wetsuits, they looked and moved through the water more like seals than like men.

Well, at least he had saved them from a few hours of heavy underwater swimming to bring them this far. They would need to conserve their strength for the tough job that lay ahead. He turned the wheel, and the *Guppy* responded like a sportscar, whooshing through the water with incredible agility. Clemens felt quite secure in knowing that his craft was equipped with an excellent sonar system and two scaled-down models of the heftier Mark 48 torpedo. He also had an advantage over his sub's mightier cousins: with his high-intensity headlight, he could actually see where he was heading.

The shock wave of the exploding Soviet boomer had jolted Clemens out of his reverie. His first thought was that the *Manta* had been sunk. It wasn't until he tuned the sonar to a predetermined homing frequency that he picked up the familiar hum of the mother ship. The *Manta* was positioned to his north.

The towed passive sonar array trailing in his wake picked up the engine noises of another large submarine to the southwest. That would make it an enemy sub, and therefore, he could consider it a viable target. Clemens cut his electric engine to ten knots and stalked the newly acquired quarry. He checked his instrumentation console, a faint red glow of LED figures visible to his eyes, but shielded from the outside. The signal came in very strong. Bearing three one zero . . . range four thousand . . . speed one five on a course of zero one five. Heading in the direction of the *Manta*, Clemens figured to get a torpedo off first.

He slowed to five knots and aligned the *Guppy* with the enemy sub. Once he fed the coordinates into the torpedo's guidance system, all he had to do was get the hell out of there. The sound activated sonar system in the fish would do the rest. He set the bearings and turned the dial that armed the torpedo. He rechecked his instruments. Bearing three one five . . . range three five zero . . . speed and course the same. Clemens tripped through the checklist in his brain. Tube one hatch opened . . . torpedo armed . . . ready . . . fire one.

The tiny submarine bucked upward from the thrust of the spent torpedo. Clemens continued on the roll and veered away from the target. His sonar idicated the fish swam true. Suddenly, a pinging staccato rang through the *Guppy*, a dreaded sound that immediately caused a wrenching in his gut. Damn. Who . . . ?

The thunderous roar of his target exploding less than two

nautical miles away was deafening. The blood pounded in Clemens's ears and in his brain, pounding, throbbing, his head spinning. The roar and then the pinging and then the sphincters letting loose. And then the torpedo collided with the tiny submarine with such force that both boat and captain were blown into a million pieces of flotsam and jetsam that drifted lifelessly to the bottom.

Boxer had the *Sierra's* coordinates fed into the fire control console and sat there with his thumb on the red button, about to trigger the Mark 48 torpedo. The first explosion surprised him. There was no one up against the Russkie except him . . . and Clem in the *Guppy*. And then the second blast came, and surprise turned to shock. He tuned into the preset frequency and broke radio silence. "*Guppy*, this is *Manta*. Come in, Clem."

Silence.

Boxer tried frantically to raise the mini-sub. He adjusted the frequency modulator. He tried to home in on the *Guppy's* sonar signal. There was nothing at all. Boxer slammed his fist on the computer table. "Oh, no. Damn it. *Damn it to hell. Not Clem.*"

Boxer, normally a stoic who kept his feelings bottled up no matter what, felt a flood of sorrow, grief, and then anger well up inside. His mission had been to mount a strike at the nuclear plant and get the hell out. Now he didn't care if he got out alive or not. His mission became a vendetta. He would destroy every enemy sub within the bastion, or die trying.

He began by coolly calling out commands to the helm. The *Manta* swept the harbor from east to west, moving ever southward, trying to trap a Russkie sub with his passive sonar, careful not to give away his own position. Then came Hi Fi Freedman's tense call. "Conn, sonar. Target approaching. Bearing two zero nine . . . range five thousand yards . . .

speed one eight, and heading our way. Boomer. Twin screws."

Boxer had three torpedo tubes loaded and armed. From the CIC module he calculated a firing solution, and slaved it into tube two. Relentlessly he followed the Soviet sub toward the mouth of the harbor. Apparently its captain was trying to escape to the comparative safety of open water. Boxer rechecked his instruments, and in his head, he said, Fire two. His thumb pressed down on the red trigger . . . a hiss of compressed air, and the sudden rise of the bow announced the firing of the torpedo.

He monitored the progress of the fish, adjusting its progress via the wire guidance system which trailed from the rear of the torpedo. This is one that won't get away, he thought.

Seconds before the collision, Boxer picked out the rapid movement of an incoming torpedo on the large-scale UWIS. By the time Freedman picked it up on sonar and called out his warning, Boxer was already giving orders to his DO. "Whitey, dive . . . dive."

In less than a minute, a torpedo passed overhead, detonating against the noisemaker that Boxer had released at the start of the dive. That was followed by an explosion as his torpedo ripped into the escaping boomer. And then still another blast rocked his sub from behind. Someone had sunk the sub that fired at the *Manta*. There was another submarine out there with him, fighting a common enemy. Boxer tried to shake the ringing out of his ears, with little success. His head still woozy from the percussions, he wondered aloud, if not Clem, then who?

# Chapter 23

Major Rolly Jones led his white-clad troop up the slope of what they now referred to as hill 101 in two columns of fourteen. The men wore snowshoes, and bent low to avoid detection as they approached the ridge just above them. Rolly and Turk each led a column, with Mean Gene scouting ahead at point.

At that moment Gene was lying prone in the snow overlooking the compound below. Its rear perimeter was about three miles away, an easy ski from his present position. He reached into a pocket and came up with a freehand chart that they'd prepared from the reconnaissance photos aboard the *Manta*. Using a red pencil, Gene enhanced the diagram, circling the prison grounds, the troop barracks, and the relationship of the control room to the remainder of the nuclear power plant complex. He especially noted the way the slope fell away to the right past the barracks and around to the control room, which was really a cement block structure that appeared to be two stories high, with no access apparent from the rear.

As he penciled in the best approach to the control complex, his eye caught a flash of reflected light off to the left. He immediately flattened against the snow, his white clothing making him all but invisible against the background. Inch by inch, he backed off the ridge until he was behind it, out of sight of the crescent-shaped ridge on the far side of the compound. So, they had company. Had Popov posted sentries up at this point to protect their rear? He thought not. There was not likely to be any need for that.

Gene had made a note of the lay of the land behind the fortress below. The compound seemed to be in a hollow carved out of the rocky hills above it, a semicircle of mountain protecting it from Arctic blasts from the north and west. The crescent ridge was broken roughly in the center by a deep chasm that flared out into the valley below that rolled toward the harbor. Mean Gene had basically made up his mind that the best approach would be the path of least resistance, down the slope and to the right to the control complex. That would afford them some protection from whoever was on the far ridge to the south.

He removed his two-way radio, about to signal Rolly that it was safe to proceed, when the silence was punctuated by gunfire coming from where he'd seen the reflected flash. He scrambled to the vantage point atop the ridge and chanced to stick his head up for a look. A flurry of activity was taking place on the opposite slope. He put his field glasses to his eyes. About forty or fifty armed men dressed in blue were fighting their way down the slope toward the compound. Above them, a platoon-strength troop dressed similarly to himself was firing automatic weapons down at them.

Gene saw a dozen blue-clad men cut down before he rolled out of sight and notified his commander. "Rolly, Gene . . . we've got a whole lot of company having a little war of their own on the far slope. The diversion might give us the chance we need to sneak in unnoticed."

"Roger that, Mean Gene. We're on our way."

Rolly stopped his men long enough to put on skis and to watch the white-camouflaged forces overlooking the far side of the fortress lobbing mortar shells into the compound. Through his glasses, he watched a small group of five or six figures rushing from the devastated headquarters bunker into a waiting speedboat and skim across the surface of the harbor. From the harbor, he swept across the panorama before him. On the mountain slope opposite them, the blue uniformed fighters were down to about thirty men now, their attackers in hot pursuit.

"Russkie Arctic Wolves," Rolly Jones noted, pointing to the white-clad figures.

Gene and Turk nodded their heads. They had very recent memories of these fierce cold-weather fighters and would just as soon forget them. Rolly said, "Okay, men. Ready to move out."

Each of them checked his Colt Commando assault rifle and fitted an M-203 grenade into the launch, a corrugated tube which was affixed to the weapon below the rifle barrel.

"We'll give them a few more minutes, to see if the guard troops go to the aid of their men who are getting wiped out below that ridge. That would give us a great advantage. If not, well, we'll just have to make things happen ourselves."

They waited another ten minutes, long enough to watch the speedboat suddenly pull up near the northern approach to the harbor, where a monstrous submarine emerged to take six men aboard. Well, that was in Boxer's hands now. He had his own job to do.

Below them, it seemed that the troops entrenched within the compound were content to allow their comrades to be sacrificed, just as long as they themselves didn't have to leave the relative safety of the stronghold. Rolly said, "Turk and I will each take a squad along the edge of this hill, just where it falls off to this low ground. Gene, you take the others down here and go directly to the control complex. We'll try to hold them off for you."

Mean Gene realized there might be several hundred troops below in the barracks, and that Rolly's group were virtually sacrificing themselves so that he stood some chance of shutting down the reactor. The uncommon valor of his

237

colleagues never ceased to amaze him, and made him proud to be considered one of them. He saluted his major, and then shook hands with Rolly and Turk.

Rolly smiled at the tough, wiry squad leader and said, "Go on, get the hell out of here."

Gene led his men down the hill, keeping as low as possible, just barely visible from the compound below.

"Now," Rolly barked, and his group of twenty men raced down the slope. When they got within range, they began firing their grenades into the troop barracks.

Some of the guards began returning fire from the wreckage of their quarters. At the same time, the mortar fire was walking its way closer to their flank, and so they found themselves fighting a two-front battle.

Rolly realized that the Arctic Wolves would not stop with the crushing of the guards' resistance, that he and his men would become their next targets. He hoped that Mean Gene could get his mission accomplished before the Rangers were completely overrun.

Turk skied up beside him. "Major, I'd like to try something. Might buy us some more time." And he explained his plan to Rolly.

Jones nodded. "Might just work. Go ahead. We'll cover you."

The Rangers laid down a volley of automatic fire and loosed another barrage of grenades into the troop quarters. Turk fought his way to the gate of the prison compound and shot off the locks keeping the convicts inside. It didn't take them long to realize that they were now free men, and they stormed out of the open gate.

Two uniformed guards came running out of the prisoners' quarters and spotted the huge soldier dressed in white, urging their charges to make a run for freedom. They fired at Turk. A shot caught him in the left side of his chest, and his white uniform became stained with red.

The prisoners who had witnessed the shooting of their

238

liberator began shouting to one another. Two dozen of them turned and charged the two guards with a vengeance pent up from months of suffering and hardship under their heels. The guards tried to fire at them, realized it was futile, wheeled and began to flee. They were overrun by the prisoners, and beaten and stomped to death.

Turk began to sag onto his right ski pole. About ten of the newly freed men came to his aid, propping him up, carrying his weapon, and forming a living shield between him and the guards until they had him safely outside the compound. Bewildered, Turk lay there until some of his own men came to get him. He looked up and asked one of his men, "Any word from Gene yet?"

The answer was written on the man's face even before he spoke. "The word ain't good, Sarge. Mean Gene is gettin' his ass kicked down there. The place was heavily guarded."

"Damn," Turk swore. Unless Gene got through to shut down the reactor, all this killing and dying was for nothing.


Billy Lone Eagle led his squad of SEALs onto the rocky beach at the wrong time. A squad of Soviet storm troopers was mopping up a platoon of Popov's ground troops on the southeast slope of the ridge below him. They were also launching mortar shells onto the beach, blasting away at the remnants of the command bunker, the mooring facilities, the dry dock, and coming perilously close to his position to the north of the power plant.

He looked up at the gargantuan concrete and steel structure to his right and realized that it was do-or-die, whether they stayed there at their beachhead or rushed the control complex. This was no time for indecision. "Let's go, men. Follow me."

Lone Eagle led the charge up the beach to the power plant, using what little cover the boulder-strewn shore provided them. A series of mortar rounds chased them inland, finally finding their range before the last three of his men got to safety. Billy examined himself and his men. Their wetsuits were cut and torn from the coarse stone below them, leaving their exposed flesh raw and frostbitten. They would never make it if they didn't do something decisive, and fast.

He yelled back to his men, "Grenades. Two rounds apiece, then we go in. Let's go."

There were at least a dozen guards defending from the ground floor of the control complex, several firing from an opening on the second level, and a half dozen more outside.

"First things first," Lone Eagle yelled, and emptied a clip into the defenders massed outside the ground level entrance. His men followed his cue and cut down the last of them. Then the seven remaining SEALs pumped a round of grenades into the concrete building, demolishing the steel-clad door, and blasting through into the ground level of the complex.

From the second level, the two or three guards firing from a slit in the concrete wall shot and killed one of the SEALs.

Then, from seemingly out of nowhere, a small, wiry fighter dressed in white rounded the front of the building and burst into the room through the blown-out doorway. He emptied a clip from his Colt Commando, fired his grenade, and bolted out the door. The figure dived to the ground and rolled to his left just ahead of the blast from the grenade, which sent bloody debris flying after him.

A guard on the level above leaned out and fired at the prone man. One of Billy's SEALs cut the guard down with a quick burst from his Colt. "Now, rush 'em," Lone Eagle shouted, and led his men in a scramble to the building that housed the reactor's controls.

They found little resistance among the survivors in the ground level, and several SEALs started up the steel stairway. Billy Lone Eagle stopped just outside the complex to check on the fallen warrior. Carefully, Billy nudged the man with his foot. Getting no response, he used his boot to roll him onto his back. It was Mean Gene Greene, with a nasty blood-smeared gash on his forehead. Billy kneeled down to check for a pulse. It was very weak.

"You okay, Gene? Speak to me, man . . . don't die out here like this. You saved our lives."

Gene moaned and opened one eye. He took a look at Billy Lone Eagle, then at his bleak surroundings. "Oooh," he groaned, touching the wound on his head. He looked at his bloody fingertips, then at Billy. "I know this ain't heaven with you here, so it must be that other place."

The Indian laughed and gently helped Gene sit up. There was a bloody rock the size of a football where Mean Gene's head had hit. "Next time, watch where you're going."

This time both of them shared a laugh while the shooting died down inside the building. "I'm going in to the control room. You up to it?"

Gene rubbed his head, brushed himself off, and got up on shaky legs. "You kidding? I'm the guy who knows how to turn the damn thing off. Let's go, before they send reinforcements out here."

Billy Lone Eagle felt the hairs on the nape of his neck prickle. He wheeled and let his eyes sweep the area completely before turning around and following Gene inside.

Boxer took a few minutes to reassess his situation. There was a submarine somewhere in the harbor that was not particularly fond of the other subs he found there. The others being Soviet, there was no sense any more in pretending that the *Manta* was a Russkie boomer. But what really puzzled Boxer was, there weren't any other American subs operating up here, and only a handful of skippers capable of getting safely into the harbor and sinking an *Alfa* without being detected. One of them was Mark Clemens, now dead. The other that came to mind was a Russian, but

Igor Borodine was supposed to be imprisoned in Siberia. Maybe not.

Boxer withdrew his auxiliary propeller into its casing, releasing the *Manta* from the security of Soviet identity. Then he keyed his sonar technician. "Hi Fi, I want another sweep of the harbor. There's at least one more sub out there, and if my guess is right, it may be more dangerous than all the others put together."

Boxer commanded the helm to begin the search along the shoreline, and to work in a north-south sweep toward the mouth of the harbor. Whatever was out there would, sooner or later, show up on the UWIS. Or find the *Manta* first. Near the mouth of the harbor, almost at the farthest extent of the warm-water area heated by the reactor plant, a faint image appeared on the screen. "Hi Fi, do you copy the target?"

"Roger, but I can't make it out clearly. I'm having trouble with the thermal."

The meeting of the heated effluent from the power plant with the frigid waters of the Arctic caused an obscure layering effect at this point. Instead of a normal temperature gradient at a specific level in the sea, this condition wasn't as precise. Boxer realized this, a submariner's nightmare if you're the hunter, a blessing if you're the prey being hunted. In this situation, though, it could become a double-edged sword. He would have to play it cautiously for now. "Mahoney, come to zero seven one. EO, all ahead one-third. Keep it below eight knots until I tell you otherwise."

The helmsman repeated the command, as did the chief engineer, and the *Manta* turned northwest and very slowly followed the target Then several nautical miles ahead, the image of another submarine came into view at the edge of the screen. Freedman picked it up at the same time as Boxer. "Conn, sonar. Second target bearing zero three five . . . I can't make out the exact range or speed, Skipper, but she's at least ten miles ahead, and, Skipper, I have a feeling that our first target is following the new one."

"I reckon you might be right, Hi Fi. Keep up the good work."

Aboard the *Hornet*, it was a different matter. From the moment that Popov had been taken aboard, the old man began giving orders to the crew that had been used to only one master, Sergei Shevchenko. Sergei had taken his mentor aside, to try to get him to calm down, now that the bastion was almost surely lost. This second invasion had been better thought out than the first. Somehow, the assault force had gotten behind their defenses unnoticed, and had mounted an offensive on the compound. Add to that the unknown number of submarines that infiltrated the bastion and wiped out his already weakened forces, and there was no longer any reason to continue the struggle. Their only trump card was the Politburo's fear of setting off a nuclear accident in the reactor plant, and now it wasn't certain if they still held that.

No, Sergei couldn't tell all that to the white-haired old man who once commanded more respect than any other man in the entire Soviet submarine fleet, with the possible exception of Igor Borodine. And Sergei's only hope of survival was to successfully bring in his mentor for punishment, something he wasn't sure he could do. He would try reasoning with Popov.

"Sergei, why aren't we headed back into the harbor? I gave the helmsman a direct order."

Shevchenko shrugged. "Perhaps he was confused with all the orders we have been giving him lately, Comrade Admiral. Why don't you just leave the command of the *Hornet* to me, so you can concentrate on more important things?"

Popov thought it over for a few minutes, then walked smartly back into the control room, Sergei following in his footsteps. "Of course. Why didn't I think of that? Now, Sergei, order your men to return to the base, while I direct the launching of our remaining ballistic missiles."

Shevchenko's face turned pasty white. "What?"

Popov slapped him on the shoulder. "Go on now, Sergei. You are an excellent captain, so order your crew to return to base. And I . . . you'll have to admit, Sergei, that I'm a master tactician. I'll direct the bombing of the fools and cowards that attacked us. I'll teach those bastards a lesson they'll never forget. I . . . I'll wipe Moscow off the face of the map. Likewise Leningrad and Kiev, Warsaw and Prague. There are enough SLBMs to bomb London, Paris, New York and Washington . . . Beijing, Tokyo . . . ."

Sergei Shevchenko came to the sad realization that his onetime mentor was no longer rational—in fact, he was quite obviously mad. Sergei had known this time would come. He had to place the admiral under arrest, for the sake of mankind. He reached out and laid a gentle hand on the old man's shoulder. "Forgive me, Comrade Admiral. We can no longer go on with this charade. My crew has been instructed to return us to Polyarnyy, or perhaps Leningrad would be better. I can no longer allow you to remain in command."

"What? What the hell are you talking about, you young upstart? Take your damn hand off me."

Most of the officers and noncoms, as well as the guards that had come aboard with Popov, had crowded into the control room to see what all the commotion was about. The admiral turned to the lieutenant in charge of his guard unit. "Arrest this traitor," he yelled. "If he resists, shoot him." To puncutate his demands, Popov unholstered and brandished the automatic that he wore at his side, and waved it at the crew. Everyone jumped back out of the way, except their captain.

Two of the guards stepped forward to arrest Shevchenko. They were immediately restrained by the crew. The other guards wisely remained where they were.

Sergei shook his head. "I'm very sorry, comrade. You were like an uncle to me. Now, for your own good, for the good of everyone, I have to place you under arrest. Please give me that gun."

Popov was livid. He began to shout unspeakable invectives at Sergei. "You want my gun? I'll give it to you, you cowardly traitor." The old man pointed his automatic pistol at Sergei, who managed to deflect it just as it went off. A round careened off the bulkhead and struck one of the crew.

Sergei snatched the pistol from Popov and turned it on the admiral. "I'm sorry, comrade, but you leave me no choice. You're under arrest."

Popov lunged forward in a range. "Why, you . . ."

The gun went off at point-blank range. A round entered Popov's abdomen directly below the sternum, tore through the heart, and lodged in the spine. He died instantly, his body doubling over and toppling to the deck at Sergei's feet.

Shevchenko stood there looking down at the body of the old man, the smoking gun still in his hand at his side. His exec looked at his captain's grim face, the beginning of a tear starting to well up in his eyes. "Comrade Captain, it couldn't be helped. You did all that you could."

Sergei didn't acknowledge him. He just kept staring down at his former mentor, at the pool of blood now forming beneath the body. "Somebody get him out of here. Be gentle."

The mood was broken by the cackling of the intercom. "Comrade Captain, this is the sonar officer. I have acquired two different targets converging on us."

The call instantly brought Sergei back to full alertness. "Show me." He raced to the sonar screen and took a spare headset from the officer.

The SO said, "Target number one, right here." He was tapping the pale green screen. "An *Alfa*, by the cavitation noises. Maybe one of ours?"

Sergei shook his head. "No. They're all gone. What of the other?"

"Target number two," he paused, and looked directly at his captain. "Indeterminate. I can't quite make it out, Captain. I don't think it's an *Alfa*."

Sergei Shevchenko made a quick decision. The *Alfa* was the fastest submarine at sea except for a few experimental models around the world. What were the odds of one of them being up here at this particular time? "We go for the *Alfa*. That's our most immediate danger."

Sergei gave the commands to dive to within twenty meters of the bottom and to remain silent, engines cut to absolute minimal thrust. They would wait out the *Alfa*, and at the right moment, strike, with surprise on their side. No chance of outrunning the faster sub. Gently, the *Hornet* settled into a dive while the crew rigged for silence.

# Chapter 24

This was the moment Igor Borodine had been waiting for. From the amount of radio chatter that had been coming from her, he was sure that this was the command sub. At very least, COMSUBFLT was aboard, and with any luck, Popov himself. He had been stalking this vessel for thirty-six hours, and now the boomer was within torpedo range. Borodine ordered a dive.

Borodine followed the progress of the SSBN sub, aware that his target was being stalked by the *Alfa* that had nosed onto his experimental image screen. He was not surprised that the boomer's skipper had chosen the *Alfa* as his primary target. For all Shevchenko knew, Borodine was still rotting away in a Siberian *gulag*. At any rate, Igor Borodine sat strapped into the chair, his hand resting inches from the trigger mechanism that would send either the boomer, or the *Alfa*—or both, if need be—to their doom.

Borodine's exec, Viktor Illyavich, stood by at the screen, studying the cat-and-mouse game being played out before them. "The *Alfa* seems to have lost our friend, comrade."

"Wait, there it is." Borodine was pointing to an almost imperceptible movement on the screen from the image representing the *Hornet*. "The *Alfa* must have reacquired her."

"You're right. Look: two torpedoes. Shevchenko isn't taking any chances."

Borodine spoke into the intercom. "Torpedo room, load and arm one and two."

"Yes, Comrade Admiral. One and two tubes loaded and armed."

Borodine watched his image screen with fascination, observing the *Alfa* turn and run with two torpedoes chasing it. The *Alfa* blip altered course, then again, keeping Viktor busy recalculating a firing solution. And then, before their eyes, the white image of the hunter-killer sub stopped suddenly, then dissipated into nothingness. "Viktor, quickly, prepare a firing solution on the *Hornet*. Our work here is almost over."

"Firing solution prepared." The exec turned to look at his commander. "Fire when ready."


Boxer watched one target, then another, dissolve from the UWIS screen. "Got 'em. Good shooting, Igor. Saved me the trouble." He was sure by now, from the sound signature, that he had been stalking the Soviet rival to his own super sub, the *Sea Demon*. And nobody was capable of driving her but Igor Borodine, a skipper so much like himself that if their two nations were not always on the brink of war, he and Igor would be best of friends. As it was, they'd saved each other's neck on several occasions, though they were enemies.

Friendship aside, Boxer knew that he'd never get his strike force safely out of there with Borodine and the *Sea Demon* around. Boxer would hunt down and destroy the *Sea Demon* with Borodine in it because it was his duty, and the mission called for it. Too bad, he reflected . . . I'd rather have a drink with him than kill him.

Boxer quickly figured the firing solution on the Soviet super sub when a second image appeared on the UWIS.

Another *Alfa*. Damn. The Russkie hunter-killer sub was after his prey. He watched the image of the *Sea Demon* flit around the screen trying to avert an attack. It was too late . . . the *Alfa* had pulled up on Igor while he was concentrating on his own targets. The explosion that followed reinforced what he suspected.

"Hi Fi, lock in on that target." Boxer punched his calculations into the fire-control console and ordered his two loaded tubes armed. To himself, he muttered, "I'll get 'em for you, Igor."

The image of the *Sea Demon* began to stir, and the *Alfa* went in to deliver the coup de grace. Boxer realigned a torpedo to run into the *Alfa's* sonar field, rather than for a clean kill. He knew that even if he sank the killer sub, Borodine would be a goner. There was no way to stop the *Alfa's* torpedo, once fired. Boxer could only hope to scare the *Alfa* away from the damaged super sub. It was the least he could do for a friend.

Boxer had read the enemy skipper correctly. At the last moment, the *Alfa* veered away from the *Manta's* torpedo and fired along the reciprocal path.

"Mahoney, right rudder ten degrees. Come to one five zero." As the *Manta* lurched out of the line of fire, Boxer fired off a noisemaker into the turbulence left behind. The torpedo exploded harmlessly to the rear, and Boxer figured his luck was stretching thin. It was time to attack.

"Hi Fi, I want a fix on that *Alfa* now."

"Aye, aye, Skipper. Target bearing three four six . . . range four thousand . . . speed three eight knots on a course of zero three zero."

Boxer keyed the MC. "EO, all ahead full. Helmsman, right ten degrees . . . come to zero one five." As the *Manta* changed course, Boxer prepared a firing solution on his target.

"Conn, sonar. Target's heading out into deep water."

Boxer said, "Mahoney, stay with her. Adjust to zero zero five degrees. EO, get us up to four five knots."

"Aye, aye, Skipper," they chorused, and the *Manta* closed the gap.

Boxer watched the *Alfa* suddenly stop and turn to face him. Her skipper realized he couldn't outrun the strange submarine on its tail, and decided to fight it out. Boxer was ready. "Ready to fire four," he warned his crew. The killer sub drew closer. Boxer's thumb rested on the trigger. "Four launched."

The *Alfa* reacted by getting off a torpedo of its own. It should have turned and run. Boxer waited until the last possible moment to dart to safety. Meanwhile, he remained at the CIC console, making minor adjustments to ensure a hit.

The *Alfa's* torpedo sailed barely overhead while the *Manta* dived to avoid the exploding Soviet sub. Boxer ordered a new course to take them back to pick up his strike force.

"Conn, sonar. I have a fix on that scuttled Russkie sub. Do you want to go in for the kill?"

Boxer thought about Igor Borodine in a crippled submarine at the bottom of the harbor. Maybe Igor could extricate himself from this one, he thought . . . maybe not. But if he dies up here, it won't be by my hand. "Negative, Hi Fi. Not enough time. We're overdue picking up the Rangers as it is."

The *Manta* ran swiftly now, its sonar actively seeking any remaining targets. When it appeared there were no other submarines in the vicinity, Boxer ordered his DO to surface. At periscope depth, the antenna was raised. The calls for assistance from Rolly Jones were immediate and constant. Boxer walked over to the radio and took the microphone from the technician. "Rolly, this is Boxer. Do you read me?"

"Roger that, Skipper. We're in pretty deep shit here.

While Gene and his men have been working on those control computers, we're being overrun by a platoon of Russkie storm troopers firing down on us from high ground. We're getting ripped apart."

"Copy. Can you make it down to the harbor? Any kind of boat you can commandeer to get you out to deeper water?"

"I can see some kind of tug that hasn't been sunk yet, Skipper, but we're not going anywhere without Gene. We all leave here together, or not at all."

"There isn't time, Major. Now get as many men as possible and get into that tug. We have to blow that control room before the Russkies stop us."

Rolly cursed at Boxer for being right, and at Gene for being so slow. Gene had memorized the commands to shut down the reactor, but the computer keyboards were in Russian letters. Jones glared at his two-way radio, pressed the switch, and said, "Can't hear a thing, Skipper. Must have a bad connection. Do what you have to do. We'll catch up to you as soon as the rest of my men get here. Out." He turned off the radio and stuffed it in his pack. Some of his men had heard the conversation, and none made a move toward the tugboat. They were with him to a man.

Boxer tried vainly to regain radio contact, but his orders went unheeded. He shrugged, put down the mike, and returned to the bridge. Rolly had deliberately disobeyed his orders, but Boxer knew that, under similar circumstances, he'd do the same thing for his men. As a last resort, he called in the chopper pilot. "Surf, the guys are dying out there on the beach. Do you think you can give them a hand?"

"You bet, Skipper. Give me ten minutes."

Surf suited up and made his way forward to the chopper's launch silo in the bow. He strapped into the strange craft whose rotors were folded downward. He thought the whole thing resembled a telephone booth with a propeller. The chopper sat inside a watertight chamber that was catapulted from the sub with compressed air. And, if all went well, once out of the water the lid popped off and the sides fell away, the rotors rotated, straightened out, and picked up enough speed to keep him airborne on his own. If it didn't work out precisely as planned, he'd be the Navy's first official human cannonball. He keyed his radio. "Ready when you are, Skipper."

"Roger that, Surf. Ten seconds to launch and counting . . . nine . . . eight . . ."

In the chopper, Surf braced himself and picked up the count. ". . . Three . . . two . . . one . . . launch."

The G-force of the ejection was more than Surf had figured on, and it surprised him that he was actually flying the damn chopper twenty feet over the harbor. He pulled back on the all-purpose yoke, and the helicopter soared high above the water. In a second, he regained his orientation and headed inland, checking the controls for the rack of rockets attached to the underside of his craft, and the machine gun which protruded from just beneath the cockpit. He was ready.

He headed high over the power plant to assess the situation. It looked grim from his vantage point. Rolly and a small group of his men were holding onto a position behind the control complex. A force of white-clad Soviet storm troopers were attacking from the south and southwest. Pandemonium broke loose in between, with hundreds of prisoners running amuck, and sixty or so soldiers dressed in blue firing on anyone in sight.

Surf came in over the nearest squad of storm troopers and fired a rocket into their position. He buzzed off before they realized what had happened. Then he hovered over the control complex and raised the Rangers on his radio. This time Rolly's handset worked. "Ahoy, Rangers. Here comes the calvary to your rescue. Can you make it to that old tugboat in the harbor if I cover you?"

Before Rolly could answer, Gene and a half dozen others burst out of the blown-out doorway, yelling for everybody to run for it.

Rolly stopped him. "What's the status of the reactor?"

Gene smiled. "We did it. We shut it down. It's set to blow in five minutes. We gotta get out of here *fast*."

Rolly turned to his men behind him. "You heard him, men. Move out."

The Rangers and the surviving SEALs ran crouched low to the ground for the harbor. Rolly said to Mean Gene, "Give me a hand with Turk."

The big man was propped up against a boulder. He was bleeding profusely from the wound in his chest. Rolly said, "Okay, Sergeant, we're ready to go home."

Turk shook them off. "Won't make it. Hurt too bad." Even as he spoke, blood trickled from the corner of his mouth.

Gene said, "We're not leaving without you."

"No use. Leave me your weapons, and all your grenades. I'll hold them off for you."

Rolly and Gene looked at each other, reluctant to leave their friend.

Turk looked each of them in the eye. "It's all over for me. Prop me up behind that boulder over there on that rise. Hurry up, you guys, you're wasting time."

They knew he was right, and half-dragged, half-carried Turk to the defensive position he pointed out. Rolly looked down at the compound and knew the big man could hold off a small army from there. They unslung their Colt Commandos and handed them over to Turk, along with their M-203 grenades. Then Rolly unpinned his major's stripes and affixed them to Turk's parka. He saluted, and said, "I'll never forget you, man. Thanks."

Turk looked up, reached for the farewell handshake, and said, "You better get movin'. You're runnin' out of time. Oh,

253

and Major, one last request."

Rolly turned back.

"Your forty-five. I'm not going to let them take me alive."

Rolly Jones unholstered his .45 automatic and handed it to Turk. Then he caught up with Gene and never looked back.

Surf kept the Soviets at bay while most of Rolly's men made it safely to the tugboat, one of the few vessels or structures still intact on the waterfront. He strafed any troops brave or foolish enough to come after the Americans. He watched Turk fire off round after round of grenades at the approaching enemy forces. Then the control building alongside the power plant exploded, sending boulder-size chunks of concrete flying. He saw a mortar round land a few feet from Turk's position, and the big man was cut down by shrapnel. He was a big man in more ways than one, Surf reflected as he veered off over the harbor. There was little more to do now but make sure nobody followed the Rangers by boat.

From above, he saw the *Manta* surface, and hovered overhead to show the commandos the way, then covered them while they cut engines and climbed hand-over-hand across a line secured between the tug and the sub's bridge. When the last man was aboard, Boxer radioed the chopper. "You have to ditch, Surf. I'll put a raft out for you."

Surf watched three SEALs manhandle a life raft over the deck and into the water. He was circling the boat looking for a good place to put down when a SAM missile homed in on the heat of the chopper's engine and blew them into a fiery cascade. The rescue crew watched him die, there one moment, gone the next.

Boxer climbed up onto the deck, followed by Rolly Jones. There wasn't a chance that Surf had survived the crash, but the two of them watched the debris settle into the sea until there was nothing left. Rolly stared at the carnage still taking place ashore. "Looks like all hell broke loose, Skipper."

Boxer studied the flaming buildings and bursts of mortar and rocket fire as the storm troopers fought the guards, who also battled with the escaped prisoners, who fought furiously for their freedom. He did a quick reckoning, and by his count, the Pentagon was due to call in a missile strike on this frozen hell in twenty-four hours. He put a hand on Rolly's shoulder, and said, "Nothing more we can do here, Major. Let's go home."